'*You* give the commands,' Anne said bitterly. 'You have persuaded him to imprison his own mother! He's no more than your puppet.'

'He's a man who has never been loved, Madame,' Richelieu said quietly. 'Such people are very cruel when they're roused. Don't rouse him now. Don't play at politics this time.'

'I shall do as I think fit,' she blazed at him. 'I'm not afraid of him, or you. I've nothing to fear!'

'No,' he agreed. 'Because I've suppressed your foolish correspondence with Gaston. You turn pale, Madame,' the thin lips smiled at her, 'and well you might. Madame de Fargis was a fool; her folly nearly ruined you. I warned you before and you wouldn't listen. Don't join this particular cabal against me.'

'I'll work against you as long as I live,' Anne said. 'I'm not a liar, Monsieur Cardinal, nor am I a coward. You've tormented me, insulted me, persecuted those I loved for a reason too shameful to admit! I shan't forgive it. I won't forgive it!'

'It is *you* who are ashamed, not I,' Richelieu reminded her. 'My love for you has been your only shield for twenty years. It will go on protecting you whether you wish it or not.' He bowed very low to her, and left the room as quietly as he had come into it.

About the Author

Anne of Austria

Evelyn Anthony

CORONET BOOKS
Hodder and Stoughton

Copyright © 1968 by Anthony Enterprises Ltd

First published in Great Britain in 1968 by Hurst & Blackett.
Published by Hutchinson Library Services 1974.
First published in 1994 as a paperback by
Hodder and Stoughton, a division of Hodder Headline PLC.

The right of Evelyn Anthony to be identified as the author of
the Work has been asserted by her in accordance with the
Copyright, Designs and Patents Act 1988.

10 9 8 7 6 5 4 3 2

A CIP catalogue record for this title is available from the
British Library

ISBN 0 340 57555 7

Typeset by Phoenix Typesetting, Ilkley, West Yorkshire.
Printed and bound in Great Britain by
Cox & Wyman Ltd, Reading, Berkshire

Hodder and Stoughton Ltd
A Division of Hodder Headline PLC
338 Euston Road
London NW1 3BH

Author's Note

This is a novel, but the characters and principal situations have been faithfully interpreted according to historical fact. I have condensed Chateauneuf's intrigue into the final denouement at the Convent of the Val de Grace to spare the reader the repetition of almost identical intrigues over a period of years.

The paternity of Louis XIV was openly ascribed to Richelieu at the time of his birth, and the King's brother Gaston d'Orleans was exiled for publicly saying that the baby Dauphin was a bastard. It has never been proved conclusively that the Sun King was illegitimate but I have taken the view of contemporaries that Richelieu was in fact his father. It was also rumoured at the time that Buckingham's murder was the work of Richelieu's agents, and I have incorporated that view into the book. Wherever possible I have quoted from letters and diaries and State documents of the period, but the sender of the copy of Cinq-Mars Treaty with Spain to the dying Cardinal remains a mystery. Again contemporary opinion and much circumstantial evidence points to Anne. Richelieu's gratitude and affection for her right to the end encourages this belief.

EVELYN ANTHONY

London 1967

Prologue

One fine April morning, in 1617 the sun shone down over the ancient city of Paris, sparkling along the length of the river Seine, and the Queen of France sat in her apartments in the Louvre embroidering an altar cloth for her private chapel. It was a peaceful occupation, and the ladies of her household were grouped round her, sewing or talking in low voices. In one corner, the Queen's Spanish lady-in-waiting, Madame de Las Torres sat a little apart, reading aloud from a book of spiritual maxims. Anne bent over her embroidery frame; she wasn't listening to the boring advice of the Spanish mystic, which Madame de Las Torres thought would do her soul so much good. She was trying to decide, with all the vanity and concentration of her sixteen years, which of her three hundred dresses and which set of jewels she would wear for the Court Ball that evening. Her vanity was only too excusable, and it was harmless enough. When she came to France two years earlier, even the French Court where so many beauties shone, admitted that the new girl Queen was likely to eclipse them all.

Anne was tall, and her figure was slender but voluptuous; her hair was a fiery copper gold, a colour of such rarity that she was often described as fair or red. In an age when women painted heavily, Anne's skin was remarkable for its natural whiteness, and without the disfiguring freckles that usually spoilt women of her colouring. Her eyes were the piercing Hapsburg blue; the slightly full lower lip, a family characteristic which made so many of her ancestors ugly, only enhanced her loveliness by the hint of sensuality. She loved being Queen of France; she was even prepared to try and love the King, which was a difficult duty to perform, but worth the glory and the excitement of her new life. He was the same age as herself, a moody, dark-eyed boy who seemed uneasy in her company; whenever they met he was always with his friend M. de Luynes, whom Anne had been told she must despise because he was low born and poor. In Spain such people weren't allowed to approach the sovereign. Madame de Las Torres and all the other stiff duennas who watched over Anne, disapproved of the laxity of the French Court, and tried to hedge their young mistress in behind a wall of protocol which was intensely annoying to the King, and even more so to M. de Luynes. But favourites were the thing in France. Anne had learnt that in her two years, and come to such terms with it that she could be pleasant to de Luynes, who was her husband's shadow, and agreeable to the adventurer Concini, who was the equal shadow of her mother-in-law, Marie de Medici. Her mother-in-law was Italian; she came from Florence, which was a great trading centre, and Anne could understand how she preferred the company of one of her own people, even though Concini was no more a gentleman than de Luynes. What was inexplicable to the girl, still in her teens, was how a formidable, fierce and vulgar tyrant like Marie de Medici could let herself be ruled by her favourite. It was the monarch's right to bestow, if he pleased to do so; it was the subject's privilege to receive, or more properly to give, whatever his sovereign exacted. This was very much the Spanish view of Royalty, and Anne was too deeply imbued with it to see both her husband, who surprisingly hadn't yet consummated the marriage, and her mother-in-law, who had been Regent of France since 1610, dominated by their inferiors. It was odd, but she accepted it, making a little mental shrug at the stupidity of it all. It didn't matter. Her husband Louis would come to her one day, and she would receive him dutifully, as a Hapsburg should, and give him heirs to his throne. And she would continue to enjoy her life in France, so much freer and gayer than in Madrid, now that she could see it in perspective and wasn't homesick any longer. She had been born the daughter of a King, and now she was the sister of the King of Spain; her birthright was a throne, and that of France was a sufficient compensation for marrying a young man she had never seen, and discovering when she did so, that he wasn't at all what she had hoped. She was not romantic; her whole life had been a preparation for the position she now occupied. Duty, virtue, and authority were taught to her at the same time as a rigid religious code, a version of the Catholic faith which was peculiarly Spanish. Anne didn't think of love or being loved; such things were never mentioned in any context but those involving abstracts, like the love of God, or the duty of a wife to her husband and children to their parents.

At sixteen, already mature physically, endowed with health, beauty and an appetite for life, Anne had never been touched by a man. She was unaware of it, but Louis' reluctance was causing the Spanish Ambassador a lot of anxiety. Even her ladies speculated on what ailed the King, that he delayed so long.

She turned to the Duchess de Montpensier, who was near her, and whispered, 'I think I'll wear red tonight; I haven't worn my rubies for almost a week now.'

'Madame de Las Torres won't approve,' the French lady-in-waiting murmured. 'She prefers dark colours.'

'She's dowdy,' Anne said, and they both giggled. 'I've made up my mind, and nothing will change me. Red it shall be.'

If Anne had learnt a good deal about the French Court, then those near her had also learnt something about her. Her will was formidable for such a young girl. Once determined, Anne never retracted or compromised. Her servants and attendants knew by now that to contradict or forbid her anything was the one way of making her immovable.

She was gay, and amiable, but she had a cutting tongue and those blue eyes could freeze anyone who tried to take a liberty with her. Madame de Las Torres had heard the Queen talking, and then laughing during the reading, and she looked up, her lips pursed with disapproval. At that moment the door to Anne's room burst open. The Marshal de Bassompierre, one of the greatest nobles in France, rushed into the room, followed by half a dozen men, some of them armed. The ladies sprang up, there were shrieks of fear, and the oldest of the duennas actually fainted. Only Anne made no sound. She got up from her chair, moved her embroidery aside and waited. With a movement she kept her Spanish ladies from crowding round her.

'Your Majesty,' Bassompierre gasped out, 'forgive me, but the King sent me to you. You're to come with me, and join him immediately. For your own safety!'

'What's happened?' Anne said. 'I shan't move from here, Marshal, until you tell me what has happened!'

'Concini is dead,' the Marshal said. 'He was shot ten minutes ago on his way out of the Louvre. There's been a Palace revolution, Madame, in the King's favour! That's why he wants you with him. Soldiers are on their way to arrest the Queen Mother, but there may be fighting. Ladies, I insist that you obey the King and bring Madame to his apartments!'

'I'll come at once,' the Queen said. 'Will somebody please help Madame de Villequieras to her feet? Else she'll be left behind.' And with Bassompierre and his men escorting her, Anne made her way to the King's private apartments. There was so much excitement, that she couldn't get near him at first. His salon privé was crowded with people, all shouting and pushing; there was a sudden movement towards the windows, and Anne found herself gathered into the crowd and passed among them so that she too could see what everyone was looking at. 'There Madame, look down below! See what my dear de Luynes has done for me!' It was Louis beside her; his black eyes were burning with excitement and there was a flush in his sallow face; he looked almost feverish. 'Sire, what is it, what's happened – is Concini dead?'

'Dead?' It was the first time in two years that Anne had heard her husband laugh. 'Look below. That's how dead he is!'

Out of the window, Anne saw the main courtyard was full of people. Armed guards were posted round the entrance gates, and a group of men were dragging something slowly across the cobbles. It was the body of Concini, whom Marie de Medici had loved, pulled by his feet out of the Palace where he had ruled so long and with such foolish ostentation. A trail of blood followed after him, staining the cobble-stones bright red; his magnificent clothes were dark with it, and mired with filth. The corpse was flung into the middle of the court, its head lolling, the ashen face turned up to the sky. Anne shrank back, covering her face from the sight.

'The dog is dead indeed,' another voice said in her ear, and opening her eyes, averted from the horror below, Anne saw de Luynes beside her. The King's arm was round his neck.

'So perish all the King's enemies,' the favourite said. It had taken him six months of constant intrigue to bring this murder about, and rid the King of his mother's influence. With Concini dead, they could safely confine the terrible Regent, and without her influence he, de Luynes, would soon be as rich and powerful as the man he had just had assassinated. Anne looked at him and froze in horror. He had seemed a pleasant, subservient man, old enough to be Louis' father. Now he looked her up and down with eyes she had never seen before. Arrogant, contemptuous, totally triumphant. But why at her expense? What had she done, that he should suddenly reveal himself an enemy – it was Louis who gave the answer, and he gave it before the whole excited crowd around them.

'De Luynes, de Luynes,' he said, 'I love you for what you've done today. Now I can be free of my mother, free of Concini – free to be happy with you!' Putting both arms around his favourite's neck the King kissed him.

1

One week later a strange procession left Paris, crossing the Pont Neuf. The route out of the city was
lined with hostile, silent crowds. In the first coach
Marie de Medici, Queen Mother of France, sat with
a handkerchief pressed to her swollen eyes, weeping loudly and pausing between her sobs to curse
and swear in her native Italian. She was going into
exile. The most powerful, the most feared woman in
the kingdom, Regent for her son Louis XIII, since
1610, Marie de Medici was leaving Paris in disgrace,
dismissed by her son and his favourite de Luynes.
She cried for herself, but also for Concini. They had
never been lovers, but the bond of blood was strong
between them. Concini had made her laugh; he had
understood when she raved or threw things because
their temperaments were the same. There had been a
mutual understanding and indulgence between them
which had finally made him the most powerful man
in France. And with his power had come wealth and
honours and a voice in the Government so loud that
no one else was heard. The young King had disliked
him, but then his mother had always treated Louis as
a nonentity and he was too shy and feeble-willed to
show his feelings in a positive way. What a fool she'd

been, she lamented, so blind to her son's weakness and duplicity! The very people who watched her coach roll by were the same savages who had invaded the Palace, found the favourite's body and dragged it out to wreak a horrible vengeance in the streets. What was left of his corpse had been finally dismembered and displayed on the very bridge where she was crossing. She lowered her handkerchief to glare out of the window, and giving way to her feelings, she spat. Her son had refused to see her for a week; when he did so, de Luynes the murderer was with him, and Louis' attitude had made her long to revert to old habits and send the brat sprawling with a box on the ear. At sixteen he considered himself a King. A King when he couldn't play the man! She had married him to Anne, one of the most beautiful Princesses in Europe, and the miserable clown hadn't been able to consummate the marriage. His mother's hot Italian blood boiled with contempt for him. She had always despised him and preferred his brother, Gaston Duc d'Orleans. Now real hatred was added to a natural antipathy between mother and son. He had turned against her. He thought to be free, with his unnatural craving for de Luynes, but he was a fool, as she often told him to his face. He had sent the cleverest man in France into exile with her. She would be back.

In the last coach in the procession, the man who had served Marie de Medici as Secretary of State for the past two years, leant back and closed his eyes as if he were asleep. He wore the simple dark dress of a cavalier, but there was a Bishop's ring on his finger. Armand de Richelieu was thirty-two. Besides being the fallen Secretary of State, he was also Bishop of Luçon and almoner to the young Queen Anne. He had lost everything except the Bishopric, and he followed the turbulent Queen Mother into exile in spite of all his attempts to change sides at the last moment and stay on in the King's service. He had done this for two reasons. The first was his insatiable ambition; he thirsted for power as some of the saints were said to do for God. Power and politics were his passion; they had absorbed him from the beginning of his adult life; they had beckoned and tempted him away from his episcopal duties and undermined his vow to serve God and his flock by the siren call to service with the King. He knew what he wanted; he was no priest by nature nor by inclination. As a second son of a poor noble family, he had entered the Church by tradition and because his family had a right to the Bishopric. He had tried to absorb his energies and his intellect in the affairs of Luçon and its people, but Paris called him, and when he was in his twenties, he answered that call and went to see the givers of appointments and the fountain heads of power, the Queen Mother and her Italian favourite Concini.

He was a handsome young man, slightly built, with pale grey eyes and delicate hands that moved in flowing gestures. He knew how to flatter and how to serve. He had entered the Royal Service and in a few months transformed the humble office of Secretary of State from the role of a clerk who wrote down the decision of the Council, into a powerful political post. All these considerations had driven Richelieu to frantic attempts to placate de Luynes and take the King's side after Concini's murder. But the second consideration was equally strong. He didn't want to leave Paris because he was in love with the young Queen Anne; the post of almoner was as important to him as that of Secretary of State. Love and politics; politics and love. They didn't mix, of course. He had no illusions about the folly of his devotion to the Queen, but it was the first time in his life that he had felt emotion for a woman. Unlike the King he was no introvert, but of all the priestly vows, celibacy had been the easiest. He was too occupied to trouble with women or waste time in the tedious intrigue of love affairs. His cloth protected him, and his ambition forbade the risk. And then, when he came to Paris, he had seen Louis' young Queen and he was lost at once. He had been very humble, very discreet; no one watching him attend on her in his official capacity could say there was anything remarkable in the good-looking Bishop's words or attitude towards her. But desire for her burned in him. He knew the nature of the King and that de Luynes would be the first of many. She had always been gracious to him, but restrained and formal, because she was a Spaniard, and he was a priest in her eyes, and not a man. This hadn't troubled Richelieu. Time was his ally; the girl, still a married virgin, needed time to grow into a woman. Just as Richelieu needed time to become more than a Bishop and her humble almoner. The King was a boy; he had exchanged his mother's domination for that of a man who would very soon be hated to the same extent as Concini. The Court was a snakepit of jealousy and intrigue. Louis had abandoned his mother, but this was only temporary. De Luynes would fall, and Marie de Medici would return in triumph. And so would her good friend and protégé, Armand de Richelieu.

*   *   *

'Madame? May I disturb you?'

Anne looked up in surprise. She had gone into the Chapel at Tours to pray, not because she felt the need of it, but because there was nothing to do but sew with her ladies, walk in the gardens or listen to the angry monologues of her reinstated mother-in-law Marie de Medici. The King spent no time with her now; two years of de Luynes' domination had driven him further from her than ever. She was still a virgin, and at nearly nineteen, Anne understood only too clearly the disgrace and danger inherent in this fact. The Chapel at Tours Castle was very old and dimly lit. She had gone there to make her devotions because it allowed her the luxury of being alone for a while. She turned and saw a man standing behind her, half in shadow.

'Who are you? Come into the light!'

The man moved nearer until the light of the devotional candles fell on his face. He was dressed as a cavalier, his brown hair worn long and smooth, with a small, neat beard emphasising the fine breeding of his face.

'My Lord Bishop!' Anne exclaimed. 'Why, you moved so silently you startled me. What do you want?'

Richelieu bowed low. His eyes were gentle; she had noticed since he had come back as the right hand of Marie de Medici, that he was very assiduous in paying attention to her, who was generally neglected these days. He had very large eyes, of a peculiar clear green, and they were always warm when he looked at her. She liked him, and she appreciated his courtesy to her. She came to him and smiled. She was more beautiful because she was a little older, and the lovely face had fined down in the past two years.

'I beg your forgiveness,' he said. 'I didn't mean to frighten you. I saw you come here, and I felt this was the opportunity I've waited for – the chance to speak to you alone. Will you permit me?'

'Of course,' Anne said. 'Won't you pray first, my Lord Bishop?'

'No,' Richelieu said gravely. 'I've made my devotions for today. I want to talk to you, Madame. My difficulty' – he paused and smiled a little, in irony at the situation and himself, 'my difficulty is to know where to begin. That must sound ridiculous from someone who's renowned for talking, like myself. But alas, Madame, you'll have to bear with me. If I'm clumsy, will you forgive me?'

'I can try,' Anne said. She was confused by the odd way in which the Bishop spoke and the intense gaze of those disturbing eyes.

'I was your almoner,' he began in a low voice, 'when you first came to France. You were a child, Madame, but still so lovely that you took the breath away from all who saw you. I remember it well, indeed the day I first saw you has never left my mind! I served you, didn't I, Madame, even in those days when you were often homesick for your own country, and all was strange about you?'

'How did you know,' Anne said. 'For the first few months yes, I was very sad. I often wept. But no one noticed.'

'I noticed,' Richelieu answered. 'I knew by your beautiful eyes when you cried, just as I knew when you were happy too. I watched you and tried to watch over you at the same time.'

'Why are you saying this to me,' Anne said. She

put a hand behind her and held on to the prie-dieu; she needed support, some kind of strength because she had begun to feel strangely weak while the soft voice went on and the tenor of his words became more intimate.

'Because I want to serve you now,' Richelieu said. 'Now, when I'm in a position to be really useful to you. And only at the beginning of influence, Madame. I have a seat on the Council now; that is the Queen Mother's stipulation, and the King and de Luynes have given way.'

'They've given way to everything they're so afraid of her and you too,' Anne said. 'She made her civil war and she won; the King and that creature of his capitulated at once. I congratulate you, my Lord. A seat on the Council is a great honour.'

'I shall have more honours, more power.' He stepped close to her then, and there was nowhere she could move to get away from him. 'I shall be the first man in France, Madame. And your humble and devoted servant always. Will you believe that? Will you accept my devotion and let me guide you?'

'I don't need guidance,' Anne broke in on him; she was trembling with a sense of danger, and every moment the nature of that danger threatened to reveal itself. This was no priest standing before her, no Bishop offering her wisdom and support. This was a young man, his eyes ablaze with terrible illicit passion, moving inch by inch towards her in the Presence of the God he had vowed to serve in chastity and faith. 'I don't need help. Stand aside from me and let me leave this place!'

'Not till you've heard me out,' he said. 'You need

all the help in the world – now and in the future. The King is a pederast! You know that now – everyone knows it. What will your future be, with such a man? How have you fared under de Luynes? Well, wait and think what monsters may rise up from that perverted depth to humble and torment you – to counsel your divorce, even your death! Ah, Madame, Madame,' he cried out, 'don't shrink from me, don't spurn what I am trying to offer! I love you. There' – he reached out and caught her hands in his; he had an iron grip which she couldn't break. 'I've said the most important thing of all. I love you, Madame, with my whole heart. I know my star is rising. I want yours to rise with it. I want to lay myself and all my powers at your feet today and for the rest of my life. Accept them. I beg of you, accept me for what I am, your devoted admirer, your passionate slave!'

The next moment he had brought her cold hands to his mouth and was burning them with kisses. A second more, and Anne knew she would be in the grasp of arms equally strong and that what he was doing to her hands would be done to her mouth. She made a violent movement, wrenched herself free and struck him across the face with the back of her hand. The sound of the blow echoed dully in the old stone chapel vault. Richelieu had stepped back from her; for a moment Anne stood speechless, trembling, and then her anger and outrage rescued her from an assault as frightening as it was unexpected. Her own senses had turned traitor. The sensation of faintness was due to a terrifying desire to let him take her in his arms, to melt and succumb before something that was as glittering as fire in its intensity and just as lethal in its consequences. She took refuge from herself and him in one factor, more dreadful than his attempt to make love to her or her wish to give way and let him do it. He was a priest. This had made her shrink from him first, before he had gone too far. He was a celibate, bound under pain of blasphemy, never to touch a woman or indulge in earthly love. This saved Anne at that moment.

'How dare you! How dare you speak to me like that – how dare you touch me! You're a blasphemer – a renegade to your vows!'

He did something unexpected then; with a hand to his marked face he dropped on one knee before her.

'Forgive that too,' he pleaded. 'Forgive the weakness that's greater than any vow on earth. I'm no true priest – I hadn't any choice. My love for you may be a blasphemy, but before God I'm not ashamed of it! I stand condemned by you, and I kneel to your virtue, your perfection. Only say that you pardon me! Say that you'll let me stand close to you, however humbly, so that I may serve you.'

She had fully recovered herself now; the sight of him kneeling brought him into perspective. A profaned priest, and also an upstart, a nobody from some French province with a petty title. Her pride and her Royal blood were insulted beyond bearing by the advance he had made to her. It was intolerable, unforgivable.

'You've often been called an upstart, sir,' Anne said. Her voice was cold and level; she prepared her deadly shafts with care and loosed them at him. 'An adventurer, hiding behind the cloth of the Church. A fawning, flattering schemer, dedicated to his own advancement. I see how right your enemies are when they describe you so. I see also that you are low born, and have no place among gentlemen. Stand aside, and be certain of one thing. I shall never speak a word to you in public if I can help it, and I shall devote myself to making the King and the whole Court see you for the evil upstart that you are!'

She walked past him, the skirts of her brocade dress brushing against him where he knelt. She left the Chapel and prevented herself from running all the distance down the gloomy castle corridors to her own rooms; her page and two ladies were behind her now. They had been waiting while she prayed alone inside the Chapel. They mustn't see that she was agitated. No one must ever know what had happened to her there, no one must share her humiliation and above all her growing sense of horror and self-disgust. That night Anne went to bed, pleading a headache, and in the shelter of her bed with all the curtains drawn, she lay and remembered him and shivered. In the morning, she received in audience, and because Marie de Medici was reconciled with the King after the civil war, and de Luynes in hourly fear of dismissal, most of the courtiers neglected Anne to pay their respects to her mother-in-law. There were few people in her ante-chamber, but when she came into the room, correctly dressed in a velvet gown, stiff lace collar framing her face, ready to enact the travesty of her position, she saw him standing there among the meagre crowd, his purple Bishop's robe glowing in the morning sunshine. And without a word Anne turned her back and went into her room. He hadn't given up. He had accepted her blow in the face and the pitiless insults of the day before, and come again to try and see her. To try and win her over. It made her so uncomfortable, so anxious, even to think of him, that she felt the first real hatred of her life for this man, this nobody de Richelieu. Hatred was her defence. Not only against him but also her own nature. She tended it carefully until it grew and strengthened and became a part of her. By the time he had fulfilled his prophecy, made in the Chapel at Tours, de Luynes had died, just in time to avoid being murdered at the behest of Louis who had grown jealous of him, Gaston d'Orleans was grown up into a handsome, spoilt young rival for the throne of France and Anne was twenty-four. That was when Richelieu became a Cardinal and the King's First Minister. He had kept his word. There was no higher he could climb in power.

*   *   *

'It is a dull morning,' the King remarked. He had hoped to spend the afternoon hunting, and the torrents of rain would make the going soft and muddy. He was in a bad temper, and it showed in the sallow, discontented face and the dark eyes half closed in boredom. He was always bored these days and always melancholy. Life had so little that attracted him and even the things he loved, like hunting and shooting birds, could be spoiled by a caprice of the weather. He had not replaced de Luynes after he died, simply because his mother had dominated him yet again to such an extent that he was quite emasculated. She kept everyone at a distance from him, and forced him, to his misery and disgust, into an attempt at consummating his marriage. It had been a wretched failure, proving only that he could father a child because by some miracle Anne's womb was filled as a result of his inept unwilling action. Then she had lost it, leaving him still at the mercy of his younger brother Gaston, who presumed more and more because he was the heir. Louis retreated into isolation; he whittled wood into toys, painted crude pictures, and when he wasn't on horseback or out with a gun, abandoned himself to utter boredom and despair. 'It would rain today,' he repeated. 'I've been looking forward to going out this afternoon.' He glanced out of the window at the lowering skies as if even the elements conspired against him.

'The weather will clear, Sire.' When the Cardinal said something he had a way of making it come true. Louis found this a comfort, and immediately he brightened.

'Do you really think so?'

'I am sure of it.' Again that marvellous confidence, that soft command of the situation. He didn't miss de Luynes so much since he had Richelieu close to him.

'Then I shall be able to hunt after all. Who did you see in the ante-room?'

The King's ante-chambers were crowded with people for his morning levee. He had sent for Cardinal Richelieu before them all, partly to irritate his nobles, of whom he was afraid, and also because he was depressed and needed comfort.

'The Princes, Sire, M. de Rohan, M. de Soubise; a great many important people. I despaired of seeing Your Majesty today there were so many waiting.'

'Let them wait,' Louis said. 'They all bore me, except you. They'll grow to hate you, you know. They hated de Luynes before the end. Everyone I like is taken from me.' He had conveniently forgotten how much he had resented the wealth and power de Luynes had taken for himself. But most of all he hated him because he proved the falsity of his devotion by marrying, and this was the beginning of his downfall with the King.

Richelieu shrugged. 'I have Your Majesty's protection and the favour of the Queen Mother. I can afford a few enemies.'

'Perhaps,' the King said, lapsing into fresh gloom. 'You're clever enough, Richelieu. You may be able to protect yourself. Be sure I can't promise to do it for you.'

'Sire,' the Cardinal had a habit of moving close to the person he addressed when emphasising something. It was a habit that made the King a little nervous. For such an elegant, slim man, the Minister gave an impression of height and strength which was an optical illusion. 'Sire,' he repeated, 'you must realise something. You are the King. You have the power to raise up or level to the ground; people and things belong to you, not you to them. You are the first man in the kingdom. The King. Everyone owes you loyalty first and last, no matter who they are.'

'Rohan – the Princes – my brother? My friend, you dream, you dream when you talk of loyalty from my nobles and from Gaston!'

'If it's a dream,' Richelieu said quietly, 'then I shall make it a reality. I shall make them all bow the knee to you, Sire. If you trust me completely.'

'I do,' Louis said, who had never been able to trust anyone. 'Of course I trust you.'

'You are the King,' Richelieu repeated. Then he took the slack hand and bowing low he kissed it. He glanced out of the window and smiled. 'See, the clouds are breaking. There will be sunshine by mid-day.'

'Then I shall hunt,' Louis exclaimed. 'How clever you are, Richelieu. You said it would turn fine. You may hunt with me!' Again the Cardinal bowed. 'You do me too much honour, Sire.'

The King hesitated. He had heard something which had made him angry and suspicious, and he didn't know how to introduce it without spoiling the pleasant afternoon he'd planned.

'I hear you went to see the Queen yesterday,' he said. The cold grey eyes averted from him for a second, normally they were fixed on his face until he felt slightly mesmerised by their unblinking scrutiny. 'Yes Sire, I did.'

'I was told,' Louis muttered, 'that the Queen received you badly.'

'Alas,' the Cardinal said. News travelled fast indeed, and it seemed that the story of his final attempt to reconcile himself to Anne had reached the ears of Louis. It had been foolish; Richelieu was quite capable of judging his own mistakes, and he could finally admit that his long and unsuccessful attempt to repair the damage done in the Chapel at Tours was the greatest mistake he had ever made. She hated him. He knew it now, because the wound she had just inflicted on him was still raw and bled inside if it were touched. Again and again she had rebuffed him, ignored him, sent his advocates away with stinging contempt. But yesterday she had surpassed herself. And he had had enough. He hated too, he told himself, and at that moment it was true.

'What happened?' Louis asked him. 'Gossip is so unreliable. Tell me about it.' Richelieu could feel the gloomy sullen gaze upon him, watchful for a word too much in favour of his wife, anything to betray the unlawful affection for her of which his Minister had been accused. He hadn't really believed it, but the accusation hung in his mind, unanswered, and it gnawed at his peace.

The Cardinal smiled, and it was a bitter smile, truly reflecting the pain and anger in his heart. She had gone too far, struck too deeply to be forgiven this time. She might not love him, or allow him to forget that he had abased himself at her feet like any impassioned fool. Now she would learn to fear what she so publicly despised.

'I went to Her Majesty to pay her my respects. After my appointment as your Minister, Sire, I hoped to find her favour. As you know she's never hidden her dislike of me. I hoped to win her over so that I might therefore serve you better. I waited in her ante-chambers, just as I had done with Her Majesty your mother, who received me very kindly, and when the Queen saw me, I knelt at her feet and offered her my devotion and desired her favour. Must I tell you her reply, Sire! It pains me still to think about it, to remember my humiliation.'

'Go on, go on,' the King commanded. He could never resist stories of how others were hurt or be-littled in a world where he felt permanently at a disadvantage. It all bore out the spiteful scandal whispered to him yesterday, but the slant was different. Entirely different, and fascinating.

' "I thank you, M. Cardinal Minister. As Queen of France I cannot accept your patronage or the opinion of those who've seen fit to elevate you to such high position. I only trust you'll serve the King's interests as fervently as I am sure you serve your own." Those were her words, Sire, and they were listened to by half your Court. M. de Chalais thought them very funny. He laughed in my face as I retired.'

The King didn't say anything for a moment. He repeated the words to himself; there was an authentic ring of cutting arrogance about them which he recognised. One phrase in particular, 'nor can I share the opinion of those who've seen fit to elevate you.' That shaft was aimed at him, making him look a fool, criticising him. Half your Court, Richelieu had said. De Chalais laughing. His face began to flush, slowly under the dark skin. Suddenly he jumped up, and banged his fist on the table. He made these sudden movements when he lost his temper; he often smashed ornaments or overturned furniture when he lost his self-control.

'How dare she insult you! How dare she criticise my choice!'

Richelieu shrugged slightly. 'Don't be too hard on her, Sire. She's young and wilful, and perhaps you've indulged her temper too often. I'm only your Majesty's servant. Insults to me don't matter, but she was wrong to call my appointment into question. That reflected upon you.'

'Of course it did,' Louis said furiously. 'By God, I won't tolerate it, I won't be defied by her. You told me I was the King, Richelieu. Well, she had better be one of the first you teach to recognise that!'

'I can only advise you how to do it, Sire,' the Cardinal said. 'I don't think I can endure the mockery of her friends and her hostility until my feelings heal a little. I think I must keep in the background, where I won't offend her.'

'You will stay beside me,' the King said. 'Close beside me. I value you, my dear Richelieu, you know that. So does Madame my mother. She's often said you were the cleverest man in France.' Richelieu bowed, but said nothing. 'Come,' Louis patted his shoulder, 'we shall go hunting. The sun is really coming up. And be comforted! I shall punish the Queen.'

*   *   *

In the Royal apartments at the Louvre, Anne was dressing for a Ball Marie de Medici was holding in the Luxembourg that evening.

Her bedroom was luxuriously furnished with a dressing chest of inlaid Spanish walnut, and a Moorish chair, exquisitely worked in ivory and mother of pearl. The walls were hung with tapestries, and a rare Florentine mirror, the gift of her mother-in-law, hung down one side of the room, reflecting the state bed on its dais; the crimson velvet hangings embroidered with gold and worked with the Queen's cypher, were looped back, showing the wide expanse of coverlet which Anne had worked herself since she had come to France. She had chosen a dress of pale blue satin, with an underpetticoat of silver thread, and she was laced in tightly, to emphasise her small waist and hint at the full breasts concealed under the fashionable collar of silver lace. A single egret plume was fastened in her red hair by a brooch of sapphires from Ceylon, and she wore a necklace of the same pale blue stones as large as pebbles round her neck. As Infanta of Spain she had brought a fabulous chest of jewels as part of her dowry; her emeralds were the envy of every Queen

31

in Europe. At twenty-four she was a fully matured woman of astonishing beauty; voluptuous in body, with a dazzling white skin, smooth rounded arms ending in lovely hands that glittered with diamonds, and a classic face framed in a mass of gleaming, fiery hair. Inevitably there were men at Court who angled for the attention of this exquisite Consort, so shamefully neglected by her husband. It was three years since he had occupied that bed, and there were aspirants who sought Anne out, and sighed and gazed at her with obvious meaning. She encouraged them, not out of promiscuity, but because she was young and starved of love and admiration. There was no harm in being courted, especially since nothing attracted her less than the thought of repeating her experiences as a wife. Sex horrified her; flirtations innocent and mercifully safe, were all the substitute she had needed so far. She was gay in a Court where the reigning Monarch shunned society and spent his evenings listening to doleful music played on two guitars and a violin. She loved pageantry and state and adorned every occasion by her elegance and natural dignity. And she loved dancing, and theatricals, and card games, anything which provided amusement; inevitably she attracted the men and women of like tastes who sought escape from Louis' melancholy and Marie de Medici's obsession with herself and political intrigue. Anne's little circle was a merry one and very close, and her appeal to women was stronger even than her fascination for men. She didn't arouse jealousy; plain women and beauties adored her, women of the worst moral reputation pitied her chastity but saw it as a virtue, and she had learnt to accept the world as it was and her friends for what they were worth, rather than what they did in a private capacity. Her Spanish ladies had been sent away in one of Louis' jealous fits, and after missing them for a few months, Anne settled down to the lighter companions who were provided by the great ladies of France. The chief among them was the bold and beautiful woman whom de Luynes had married, now married to the Duc de Chevreuse.

'Madame, here is your fan.' Anne turned to the lady-in-waiting who had come up to her, and shook her head. 'Marie, that's lime green! How can I wear it with this colour? Don't play tricks or I'll be late and the King will be furious. Get me one that matches this blue.'

'Try it,' the Duchess de Chevreuse urged her. 'It will be magnificent, a perfect contrast! As for His Majesty – well, he's always furious anyway, so why trouble about him. Let him wait.'

She added this in a whisper, and Anne laughed. The colour did go rather well. She studied herself with the fan open and then closed, hanging by its silk cord from her left wrist. Marie was right; it looked very elegant. But then Marie herself was always elegant.

'You're right, as usual,' the Queen said. 'Do you approve of me otherwise?'

'Let me look closely, Madame.' The woman who came into the circle of candlelight was a blonde; she was handsome rather than beautiful, with a brilliant voluptuousness more enticing than her mistress's classic loveliness; her eyes were large and blue and seemed to dance with lights whenever she looked at men; her wit was famous, and she satisfied her sensual appetites without protest from her husband. He had found her a trial, and he said so. He was

33

glad to be free of her wilfulness, her extravagance and her restless demands. She was generous by nature, and she had formed a deep friendship with Queen Anne, for whom she was guide and confidante. And she made Anne laugh, and this was something the Queen could not do without. She enjoyed the high spirits and irreverence of her friend, and followed the course of Marie's numerous love affairs with indulgent amusement. The Duchess was a brilliant mimic, among her other gifts, and she made fun of everyone Anne hated. The King. She would pull a long face and lope up and down in a masterly impersonation of Louis. The Queen Mother – she satirised her table manners and her bad language until Anne cried with laughter. And of course, His Eminence the Cardinal Minister! Marie de Chevreuse had never liked Richelieu; the priesthood did not inhibit her in the least, but she found his indifference to her mortifying, and it was aggravated by the obvious obsession he had with the Queen. Marie loved Anne and was extremely jealous of their friendship; she saw the burning eyes of the Cardinal and divined in the same second that he was madly in love with her. Her suspicions and dislike were aroused immediately. She wanted no rivals for Anne's affection and confidence, and she set about mocking the Cardinal with a savagery that made Anne writhe with embarrassment. He was her slave, Marie pointed out, and then collapsed in shrieks of laughter. Her poor, celibate suitor, his heart thumping beneath his soutane for a word, a glance from his Royal goddess! And she would mince up to Anne, one hand held out in imitation of the Cardinal offering his Episcopal ring to be kissed, and mimic him unmercifully.

Anne had never told anyone of that scene in the Chapel at Tours. That secret was hidden from everyone, even her confessor. When Marie ridiculed Richelieu she turned a knife in Anne of which she was completely ignorant, but it drove deeper and deeper until it culminated in the brutal denouement between them which had been the talk of the Louvre ever since. Anne's pride was stung by the Duchess's innocent mockery, and her pride had suffered unbearably in her marriage to an introvert, who outraged her innocence after five years of waiting, and had avoided her ever since. She had lost his child, and this was a terrible misfortune, but she had become reconciled. At least she wasn't barren; Louis himself had proved that and this was her safeguard against the annulment she knew he would have liked to get. And she didn't intend to be repudiated, sent home to Spain to waste her life at the Escurial in the shadow of others, or worse still, retire to a convent because her presence in the world was an embarrassment. She was dead to love, indifferent to domesticity. Nothing remained but the ambition of her Hapsburg blood and now this was the strongest emotion of which she was capable. The French law forbidding women to ascend the throne hadn't hampered either Catherine de Medici or Marie, the Queen Mother, from enjoying as much power as any King, and therefore Anne bore her empty marriage with patience. Louis was very delicate; he often fell ill and several times in the last few years he had seemed likely to die. Marie de Medici was old; somehow, if only she waited and survived the hazards of her husband's hatred, her time would come.

She stood, while the Duchess spread her skirts wide, and shook out the stiff petticoat at the front.

She took as much trouble with every detail of the Queen's toilette as she did with her own. Ruthless, merciless to her enemies, Marie de Chevreuse was incapable of meanness or duplicity to a friend, and she had grown to love the young Queen as if they were the same flesh and blood

'There, Madame! Magnificent! I'll swear you break the good Cardinal's heart all over again!'

The Duchess laughed and got up. 'Oh, I'll never forget it,' she said, turning towards the older lady, Madame de Senlis. 'Her Majesty was superb. "I trust you'll serve the King's interests as fervently as I believe you serve your own . . ." I thought the miserable man was going to die!'

The story of Richelieu's humiliation had travelled fast. Madame de Senlis frowned.

'I think the Queen was ill-advised,' she said. 'The Cardinal is high in the King's favour.'

'He must be,' Anne retorted sharply, 'for the King spoke to me for the first time in three days to say "I recommend M. the Cardinal to you."'

Madame de Senlis shrugged. 'Your Majesty can insult whom she pleases, but I think it was a pity to make an enemy of him.'

Anne of Austria turned round.

'I am not interested in your opinion,' she said coldly. 'Leave me; wait in the ante-chamber.' She turned to Marie de Chevreuse; there was a spot of angry red on each cheek. 'I detest that creature. I'm sure she's a spy for the King.'

'Very likely,' Marie agreed. 'But then you can't win all hearts, Madame. One or two can be near you and continue base and jealous. Don't trouble about her. You were quite right to put our friend the Cardinal in his proper place. You've nothing to fear.'

'Why should I be afraid?' Anne demanded. 'Who is this creature but a nobody who started his climb with my mother-in-law? What right has he to dare come and try to patronise me! It was outrageous!'

'You struck him to the heart,' the Duchess said. 'I've kept telling you, Madame, you've made a conquest of the creature. From the first, he's been following you like a pet dog, all melting eyes and unspoken passion!' – she made a gesture of contempt. 'As if a nobody like that could hope to come near you. Of course,' she added, 'he might be useful to you if you were prepared to stoop to him a little. He could talk to the King, and persuade him to be kinder to you. But I don't think you'd want his advocacy, Madame. I think you'd feel sullied ever after if you spoke a pleasant word to that snake, knowing how he dares to think of you!'

'I'd sooner go into a convent,' Anne said. 'I'd die before I spoke a word to him! Of course I don't believe a word of what you say about the other thing; you're mischievous, Marie; you imagine everyone's in love with someone. That man is incapable of feeling. Think how cunning he's been; think how he mediated between the Queen Mother and Louis, so that in the end he became indispensable to both. Now he's First Minister, called to the King before the Princes of the Blood! Did you hear about that? I suppose he imagines himself another de Luynes!'

'He should remember what happened to my late husband then,' the Duchess said. 'If he hadn't died of St Anthony's Fire, he'd have been murdered like Concini; the time was surely coming for it. And the King was more than ready. He's never been true to anyone, Madame. If the Cardinal thinks he's in favour for long, then he's a fool. The King will abandon him.'

Anne looked at the little jewelled watch hanging from her waist. 'Come, Marie, it's nearly time. The last time I was late my dear mother-in-law rebuked me at the top of her voice!'

'Not in M. d'Orleans' hearing, I swear,' Marie retorted smiling. The attentions of the King's handsome young brother paid to Anne were a general joke; they pleased her, demanding nothing but sisterly indulgence in return. And they infuriated Louis.

She rose, and Marie hurried to open the door for her; the rest of her ladies, headed by Madame de Senlis, were waiting in the ante-room. They had just reached the entrance to the public corridor, when a page in the King's livery met them, and bowing low, handed the Duchess a note addressed to the Queen.

In silence Anne broke the seal, moving under the light of a flambeau set in the stone wall, and read the few lines scrawled in Louis' untidy writing. Slowly she folded the paper. For a moment she stood there in the circle of her women, her jewels glittering in the torchlight.

'The King has excused me from attending the Ball this evening,' she said. She turned and walked back to her rooms. One by one the ladies-in-waiting moved after her; the King's prohibition applied to them as well as their mistress. Madame de Senlis glanced at the Duchess de Chevreuse.

'As I said, my dear Duchess; the Queen was ill-advised.'

*   *   *

The Queen Mother's Palace at the Luxembourg held eight hundred guests that night. She entertained the King and her younger son Gaston d'Orleans at a Banquet, and then took her place on the dais near her son's throne, and the Ball began. She was a heavy woman with a large appetite; she had been pretty as a girl, animated and lively minded. In middle-age she had become bad tempered, suspicious and vulgar; she harboured resentments and old wrongs and harped on the time when she and Louis had been enemies. She had kept her promise and wreaked a frightful vengeance on her son and his country for that banishment to Blois. Civil war had brought her back to Court, established there as much by the skill of the Cardinal standing beside her that evening as by the arms of her supporters. She had a place on the Council; her views were consulted and her wishes deferred to on every point of government, but she still hated her eldest son and grudged him even the illusion of his power.

Her small green eyes scanned the dancers, while her fat fingers played with the ropes of perfect pearls she wore. She fidgeted constantly when she was still; she nibbled sweetmeats or chewed grapes, spitting the pips on the floor, and she talked and grumbled continuously. Her son Gaston passed in front of her, leading a niece of the Duc de La Valette by the hand. He was a good-looking youth, much pre-occupied with himself and his appearance; a foolish narcissist encouraged in every spoilt little tantrum and irresponsible excess by his besotted mother. He looked up and smiled at her, and her face softened in a tender smile. 'How well he dances,' Marie de Medici said over her shoulder. Richelieu had been standing beside her, one step down from the throne, listening to her interminable talk, watching the dancing in which he could not take part. He had seen Orleans and his mother displaying their affection. Nothing pleased them more than doing so in public; both were exhibitionists by nature, and they derived great pleasure from the discomfort these demonstrations caused the King. His mother never smiled or signalled when he passed. Whenever she saw him she scowled. Orleans turned and as he executed a graceful turn in the dance, he bowed low to his mother. She blew him a kiss.

'What skill,' she said. 'Such a graceful leg. He has so much of his father in him.'

'He has indeed, Madame,' Richelieu agreed. It was impossible to imagine anyone less like the courageous, roistering King Henri IV, with his cheerful, 'Paris is worth a Mass', acceptance of the Crown of France, than the petulant Gaston d'Orleans. Unless it was the melancholy, quasi-homosexual King. But Gaston was handsome and gay; he was therefore popular. He loved pretty women and didn't suffer from his brother's sexual inhibitions. His mother was always inferring what a splendid King he would make. As a result of this, the brothers hated each other, and Marie de Medici continued to dominate them both.

Richelieu saw the King moving near them; he was stiff and bored, his sallow face drawn with gloom. Richelieu had manœuvred her back into power, but privately he considered the Queen Mother a monster in her relations with her eldest son. Difficult and devious as he was, Richelieu sincerely pitied Louis.

'The Queen is in disgrace,' Marie de Medici said suddenly. 'The King is furious with her.'

'So I believe, Madame. I'm sorry to hear it.'

'You may also be sorry to hear that you are sup-posed to be responsible,' the old Queen countered. 'Let me advise you, my dear friend; don't make too many enemies too quickly. And don't trust my son, he turns on everyone in time. Now it's the Queen, before that, he turned on me. It's the mark of a weakling. He hates character in other people, my dear Richelieu; if you want to advance, never let him see you have any.'

The Cardinal listened to this maternal appraisal in silence.

'There's no need to make trouble between Anne and my son,' Marie went on. 'He hates her enough as it is. He's only looking for an excuse to make her life a misery!' She leant over the side of her chair and spat a mouthful of pips on to the floor. When she looked up at Richelieu her eyes were narrowed, wondering. Suddenly she nudged him in the side, and laughed.

'What's she done to you, my friend? What's she done to raise the devil in you, eh? She's a fool if she has, I'll say that for her. I know you, my dear Armand, and I'd as soon tease a rattlesnake!'

'Madame,' he said gently, 'I promise you all I have ever done for the Queen was try and serve her. I shall continue in the same way. I mean to intercede for her tomorrow with the King.'

The following day Anne received formal notice from her husband that she was not required to attend any reception at the Louvre or the Luxembourg with-out his express invitation, nor to hold any reception of her own. He would prefer, the icy letter said, that she didn't leave the Palace without first asking permission from him, the Queen Mother, or his trusted and loyal Minister, the Cardinal Richelieu.

2

Four months had passed since Anne had been turned back from the Ball at the Luxembourg, and in that time she had appeared in public only once. The King hadn't spoken more than a dozen words to her at a reception given for the two English emissaries, the Lords Carlisle and Holland, who had come to France to sign a peace treaty between the two countries and negotiate the marriage of Louis' little sister, Henrietta Maria with Prince Charles of England.

Anne had taken her place on the dais, her chair a little lower than Marie de Medici's, which was a humiliation she had grown used to now, and given the two Englishmen her hand to kiss. Otherwise she had played no part in anything. But even so it was a brief escape from her dismal confinement at the Louvre, where the days ran into each other in a routine of such intolerable boredom and inactivity that Anne felt she would go mad unless she saw the outside world. She never left her apartments without asking permission, and out of the three people empowered to give it, she chose her mother-in-law as the least embarrassing. Marie was not deliberately unkind. She usually said yes, when Anne asked if she might drive out of the city or ride for an hour or two with some of her ladies. But if her mood was irritable, the old Queen refused Anne's pathetic request, and she spent long hours mewed up in her apartments while the sun shone outside and all the world enjoyed themselves. It had been difficult to believe at first; she and Marie de Chevreuse and all her other ladies, de Senlis excepted, expected the King to lift the ban on her freedom after a week or so. Once, Anne had sent him a message, but she was so angry that the wording only made him more vindictive, and his reply repeated the restrictions.

Four months, and she had been firmly isolated from the Court, as effectively imprisoned as if she were in a fortress. And she knew who was responsible. She had seen him at the ambassadors' reception, conspicuous in his brilliant scarlet robes, a cross of large diamonds on his breast, and for a moment they had looked at each other.

'Now, Madame,' the piercing glance said, 'have you had enough?' Her answer was to return him such a glance of hatred, that he turned away. She would never give in, and if this miserable isolation was the price she had to pay for her defiance, then so be it.

All news of events at Court came through the Duchess de Chevreuse. Marie's affection for the Queen had become a fanatical devotion. High spirited, fiercely independent and with a long, vindictive memory, Marie elected herself Anne's champion, and her first act was to spread the most malicious and degrading stories about Richelieu. Employing all her arts as a mimic and leader of fashion at the most malicious of Courts, she made a pastime of ridiculing him and encouraging her friends to do the same. She had become the mistress of Lord

Holland, who was rich and charming, and quite a good lover for an Englishman, as she confided to the Queen. And this was part of her policy to help her beloved friend. England and France were going to be united by the marriage of the Prince of Wales and Princess Henrietta Maria. It wouldn't look well if the English discovered how the Queen of France was being treated and Marie made it her business to tell them. On one of her rare walks in the Louvre gardens, Anne and Marie went ahead of the other ladies, their arms around each other's waists like schoolgirls, which was a familiarity Madame de Senlis deplored. She was not in Louis' pay, as Anne had first supposed. She had been recruited by Richelieu to spy on her mistress, and daily reports of everything Anne said and did were sent to him. They always included references of a bitter and insulting nature to himself.

'Keep a good heart, Madame,' the Duchess said. 'When the Duke of Buckingham cames to Paris to take Henrietta back to England, you'll have to be brought out into the light! My dear Holland will make it so awkward for the King that he'll have no alternative.'

'I have already written to my brother,' Anne said, 'telling him how I'm being persecuted, and he'll protest to Louis. But it's not Louis who's responsible, you know that!'

'Ah, yes, I do indeed. Every time I see that thrice-damned priest I turn my back on him!'

'Oh don't, Marie, don't,' Anne begged her. 'See what he's been able to do to me! He'll only find a way to punish you!'

'He's not in love with me,' the Duchess retorted. 'He can bear my insults better than he can yours.

My God, how you must have wounded him that day. I thought he was stricken, but I'd no idea how deep it went. Never mind, banish the creature from your thoughts. I heard from my little Englishman that Buckingham is coming in May, after the proxy wedding. I just can't wait to see him!'

'Why?' Anne asked. 'From what I know, he's just another favourite, and the English are as silly about that as the French. He's just an adventurer, that's all.'

'Now, Madame,' Marie chided gently, 'forget the ways of Spain; favourites are the thing these days, especially one like this Englishman. Holland has a miniature of him – I've never seen such a god! He's so handsome it's impossible. I said so, to Holland, I said – my love, the artist flattered him – and he said not at all. He's better in the flesh. The English King adores him. But then, he adores men, you know, that's how this one began his climb. Holland says that women can't resist him either, and the Prince Charles worships him too. He must be most remarkable.'

'He must,' Anne said.

'Holland has written to him about you, at my suggestion,' Marie went on. 'He rules England through that stupid King James – Holland says he's a dreadful old creature, like a drunken Scots baggage man, and always filthy dirty. Never washes – not even his hands! Where was I – yes, this Buckingham is the real King. And I have an idea that he could be very useful to us.'

'But how?' Anne asked her. Marie's impetuous mind went almost too quickly; she was full of plots and intrigues so complicated that she hardly knew the key to them herself. 'How can an Englishman, even if he is so powerful, possibly be any use to me?'

'Madame, when it comes to politics, you are a child,' her friend said firmly. 'Listen. Our enemy is a certain Cardinal, isn't that so?'

'Yes,' Anne said bitterly. 'Oh yes, it is!'

'Good. Then the more people work against him, oppose his policies and undermine him with the King, the sooner he'll be out of office! He is negotiating with the English; once turn the greatest man in England into his enemy, and how long will he last? Come, don't trouble about it. We'll go through all your wardrobe tomorrow, Madame, and order some splendid new gowns for the festivities, and you leave the intriguing to me!'

Richelieu had proposed the alliance with England, and the marriage of Louis' sister to the future King Charles. It had appealed very strongly to the King when his Minister explained the strategy. He had taken office and promised to make the King strong. It was essential to weaken and then destroy the power of Louis' Huguenot subjects if this promise were to be kept, and the authority of the King established over all his people. Louis listened and approved. First, the Cardinal said in his gentle way, make friends with Protestant England, and alienate them from their co-religionists in France. Men like Rohan, de Soissons and Soubise had always relied upon English help when they rebelled against the Crown. This marriage and this alliance would cut off that friendship and leave them isolated. They would then be much more at the King's mercy.

And most important, Richelieu stressed, they must make the Duke of Buckingham the ally of France, because he directed the policies of his country, and

King James refused him nothing. With Buckingham's support, they could even do what he and Louis often talked about when they were alone and looking into the future. They could attack the Huguenots at La Rochelle and raze the great Protestant fortress to the ground. Then the King would truly be master of France.

And so, on 11 May 1625, the little Princess Henrietta Maria was married by proxy. Her bridegroom was now King Charles of England, for the old reprobate James had died suddenly, and her proxy husband was the Duc de Chevreuse. The wedding took place on a platform built outside the doors of Notre Dame Cathedral, and it was conducted with great splendour. The little Princess was pale and silent; many times during the ceremony she was seen wiping away tears. She had never seen this young man to whom she was being married and she dreaded leaving France for England, that gloomy, heretic isle of fogs. The charm and culture of the Lords Carlisle and Holland had done much to reassure her, but as she made the solemn vows of lifelong fidelity to a complete stranger, Henrietta Maria bent her head beneath its diamond crown and sobbed. Anne watched the ceremony beside Louis. She had indeed been brought into the light, as Marie had foretold, and after her long seclusion she dazzled the Court by her beauty and the richness of her dresses. The King sat in his chair of state upon the platform, with a scarlet and gold canopy over his head, and stole a look at his wife, brilliant in peacock blue and emerald green, the great emerald necklace which the Conquistadors had brought back from

Peru, glowing round her white neck. Her beauty didn't move him; on the contrary, he was jealous because everyone looked at her and the people of Paris cheered her when her coach appeared. But he had been forced to lift his restrictions on her.

During this period, when there were state receptions every evening and the Court was host to a large number of important English nobles and their wives, the Queen of France couldn't be excluded.

So Richelieu had said, assuring him that Anne was suitably subdued and would be more obedient henceforth. But he regretted it. He would have liked to shut her up completely, properly, in some place where she could never get out.

On 14 May the Great Hall of the Louvre was crowded with anyone who could claim or bribe a place to see the reception of the Duke by the Royal family. It was exceptionally warm that early summer day, and the sun poured in through the long windows on to the thick ranks of men and women lined up on each side of the Hall.

It was an excited, restless, brilliant gathering, dressed with all the splendour of colour and jewels of a flamboyant age, and a continuous fluttering ran through it from the movement of countless fans, fighting the stifling heat.

Soldiers of the newly formed King's Musqueteers lined the path leading to the dais at the end of the room, magnificent in their scarlet cloaks and shining breastplates, forming a guard of honour at the steps of the throne.

The Princes of the Blood and their wives waited near the Royal family in strict order of precedence, and the Cardinal Minister stood at the head of the King's Ministers.

Louis sat motionless, one hand resting on the golden pommel of his sword, watching his elegant brother Orleans out of the corner of his eye. His mother sat on his right hand, laced into a dress of heavy crimson velvet, with a wide fan of stiffened lace spreading behind her head; her cheeks were scarlet with the heat. On his left, in a chair set lower than the Queen Mother's, sat the Queen of France.

For days Marie de Chevreuse had been talking about this moment; she was so excited by her stories of the Duke of Buckingham, so full of anecdotes about his wealth, his personal beauty, his terrible moral reputation – she said this in tones of breathless admiration – that Anne herself was infected by it, and became excited by the idea of this man who was more than a man. She knew much more about him now, his humble origins, his shameless exploitation of the old King's passion for him, and when she baulked at this, Marie assured her laughing, that Buckingham was no mincing pederast, but a vital, ruthless man who kept his slobbering master at his feet by keeping him at bay.

The most handsome man of his age, the most dissolute Court favourite England had ever seen – the most profligate spender whose debts ran into millions, with a poor little heiress wife whom he neglected for the eager English beauties. Marie became so infatuated with the idea that she made Lord Holland very jealous. Sitting on the uncomfortable chair, a few feet away from her dour husband, Anne fanned herself with a long ostrich plume fan, its handles set with

49

pearls and diamonds, and waited for the arrival of the legend.

She had chosen to wear white; it was a brilliant choice because the snowy silk made her look cool by comparison with the hot faces everywhere in the over-crowded room, and her rich hair was dressed loosely round her head, with a thick strand curling over one smooth shoulder. A half coronet of diamonds and pearls shone above her forehead, and the same stones were in her necklace and a bracelet, set with a miniature of her brother, the King of Spain.

The murmuring of the crowds gathered outside the Palace suddenly became a roar, and every head turned towards the entrance. The sound of a procession grew more audible, the clattering of horses, and the shouts of the officers lining the route to present arms, and then the bright doorway into the Great Hall dark-ened, as the Duke of Buckingham, with his French and English escorts, entered the Palace.

There was no mistaking him, for he was half a head taller than anyone else, and he walked with the swaggering ease of a man well accustomed to Kings, with one hand laid carelessly on his sword hilt.

Anne watched him mount the steps of the dais, and kiss Louis' hand; it was the first time she had ever seen the act of homage performed with such arrogance.

Louis welcomed him with a set speech, stammering slightly as he always did whenever he spoke in public, and the Duke replied. He drawled; his French was mannered, with a strong accent, and as he spoke he glanced coolly away from the King at all the members of the Royal family in turn. His eyes rested on Anne for several seconds, and she saw the expression in them change to something like recognition. She also saw that they were a brilliant blue. He was certainly the best-looking man she had seen in her life.

Buckingham finished his speech. He kissed Marie de Medici's hand, and turned with an almost impatient air to greet the new Queen Henrietta Maria of England. He remembered her too, though far less clearly than the startling red-haired beauty who was Queen of France. He dismissed Henrietta Maria as far too small and undeveloped for her age, remembering the evening two years before when he and his friend Prince Charles had travelled to Paris incognito, and watched a Court Ball from the public gallery. They were on their way to arrange for Charles' marriage to a Spanish Princess, and the Prince had surprised him by admiring the delicate, dark little girl he saw dancing in the Hall below. The Duke had nudged him, pointing out a woman with red hair. There, he whispered, there was a beauty . . .

She was even lovelier close to; exquisite, with that colouring. His appetites, indulged to the point of satiation, sharpened suddenly at the sight of her slim neck, and the shadow between her breasts. He bent over her hand, and the contrast of her delicate, pale fingers between his own became a stab of pleasure when he kissed them.

He looked up quickly, with the confidence of a man whom success never eluded, and saw that Anne's face had flushed.

'Welcome to France, my Lord Duke.'

Her voice was fascinating; he was sick of the shrill tones of his native Englishwomen. He noticed that the gloomy King had turned his head, and that the dark eyes were watching with slow hostility. Buckingham smiled slightly. All Europe knew of Louis' preference for young men to his wife, and remembering the slobbering devotion of King James, the Duke sneered inwardly. But James was a kindly buffoon, and his wife had tactfully ignored the succession of page boys, and always been amiable to himself, when he became the King's favourite. James was different to that dour man who had turned his head away, and was staring at his shoe buckles again. It had been possible to feel a condescending affection for James, as he felt it for his weak and kindly son, King Charles.

His eyes were fixed on Anne; it was against all etiquette and his entourage were fidgeting, but he stood and stared at her as a man does who sees the thing he's searched for all his life. He'd sought it in wealth, in Royal favour, however degrading, in the satisfaction of his tremendous vanity, in the pursuit of power, in whore houses and the bedrooms of great ladies, without even knowing what it was he wanted, until he saw the Queen of France.

'Your Majesty's servant,' he answered her, and slowly backed away.

Soon after everyone had been received, the King and the two Queens came down and mingled with the crowds. Anne had hardly left the dais, before the Duke of Buckingham was at her side.

'Madame,' Marie de Chevreuse was able to fight her way through the crowds at last and reach the Queen. The King and his Cardinal Minister were at that moment talking to the Duke of Buckingham; at least the Cardinal was talking, while Louis stood by and watched the Englishman with eyes like stones. 'Madame, at last! May I present Lord Holland.'

Anne turned and gave her hand to a handsome dark-haired man with a slight beard cut to a point.

He wore a large drop pearl in his left ear and this gave him a romantic, piratical air. He bent very low and kissed her hand. 'My humble respects, your Majesty. May I say something?'

His French was perfect, even the accent was very good; though all the English nobles spoke the language they murdered it in the process.

'Of course, my Lord,' Anne said. She was very flushed, but not because she was hot. In fact she felt cold and her hands were trembling.

'You are even more beautiful, more of a goddess than my dear Duchess described you. And Madame, her descriptions have been lyrical indeed!'

'She is apt to exaggerate,' Anne murmured.

'Never,' Marie said. 'Did I exaggerate about the Duke? Isn't he from another world, another planet?'

'Yes,' Anne said slowly. 'Yes, one might think so.'

'Dear Holland,' Marie turned quickly to her lover. 'I've left my fan in that corner over there, by the window, see, where the tall woman in green is standing talking to one of your suite – be my deliverer and get it for me. I'm dying of this heat!'

As soon as he had gone she turned to Anne. 'My God, Madame, did you see how the Duke stared at you – it was as if he'd been struck dumb! I thought he would never let go of your hand. You've made a conquest of him – at first sight!'

'Don't be foolish,' Anne said desperately. 'Don't talk like that. Haven't you seen the King's face?'

'Yes, and I've seen yours too. Stop looking at him, if you can, just for a moment, and tell me what he said to you just now.'

'Nothing,' Anne shook her head, 'I can't remember.' The blue eyes had held hers in a long, eloquent stare. The deep voice, with its strong English accent, usually so ugly in others, was like a slow melody telling her how he had seen her once when he was in Paris incognito, and not known who she was. Her beauty, he said, had dazzled him then, from the distance of a public gallery. Now, face to face with her, he couldn't believe that nature was capable of such perfection. Anne had listened, helpless to stop the flow of compliments, caught by the force of that personality and the undisguised emotion until she found him taking her hand in his and pressing her fingers as he kissed them. One man once before had done that; she read the same shameless longing on Buckingham's face as she had done on Richelieu's all those years ago. The eyes of both had been fixed upon her lips, and the same sensation of excitement began to rise in her, draining the colour from her face, making her limbs tremble. One had been a priest, and she had fled from him and from herself in horror. That was long ago, long before Louis' clumsy violation. She was older now, more starved of love in its ultimate form than she had realised. Flirtations with Gaston, her brother-in-law, with gallants like D'Elboeuf had been more than enough before, but no woman would be allowed to dally with this man. Just by standing close, she felt as if he were overpowering her physically. And then they had been interrupted.

'Your Majesty . . .'

'My Lord Duke!' She had turned, hearing that hated voice, the tones lighter and smoother than the Englishman's but full of charm and friendliness. Richelieu made a very low bow; 'I beg your forgiveness, Madame, for interrupting what is so obviously a very pleasant conversation. May I conduct His Grace to Her Majesty the Queen Mother? She sends you her compliments, Madame, and hopes that you, too, will join her. Later.'

It was Buckingham who answered. 'How can I abandon the Queen of women, even for the mother of my Queen? Alas, Eminence,' he made the Cardinal a bow, 'you seek to separate us.'

'Go to Her Majesty,' Anne said quickly. 'I will follow; I must speak to the King.'

'Farewell for the moment, Madame.'

Under Richelieu's eye, he went on one knee to Anne, and taking her outstretched hand in his, he kissed it fervently. By custom the lips did not even make contact with the skin. 'Even a moment away from you will seem like eternity.'

'What did he say,' Marie was repeating. 'Everyone was watching you together! And the way he knelt and kissed your hand. My God, I thought your friend the Cardinal was going to die with jealousy!'

'He paid me compliments,' Anne said at last. 'Extravagant ridiculous compliments. How did the King look – Marie, did he see it?'

'He never took his eyes off both of you. Without seeming to watch, of course. But it was Richelieu who betrayed himself.' She laughed, and waved to Holland who was struggling to get back with her fan. 'He's still your slave, Madame, believe me.' For a moment she grew serious. 'But be careful with Buckingham from now on. There's only one thing worse than a rejected lover, and that's one who sees another man accepted. And my beloved Madame, innocent as you are, you accepted the Duke in front of everyone!'

When Louis led the procession out of the Great Hall, said farewell to his wife, his mother and brother, and to his guest of honour the Duke of Buckingham, he made a sign for Richelieu to follow him upstairs to his private apartments. With his pages and gentlemen in attendance, Richelieu a few paces behind him, the King walked the long corridor to his first ante-chamber without speaking a word. Inside, he said one word only to his suite, who were waiting to undress the King and prepare him for going hunting. 'Wait.' As Richelieu bowed low, preparing to withdraw, Louis beckoned him back. 'No,' he muttered. 'Don't leave me. Come, I want to talk to you a while.'

They passed through the second and third ante-chamber until they were in the King's own bedroom, and alone. He flung his plumed hat on a chair. 'What did you think of the Duke of Buckingham?' he asked suddenly. Richelieu was warned by the narrowed eyes and the mouth, pinched tight with anger.

'He's a very handsome man,' he said quietly.

'I thought him overdressed,' the King snapped. Richelieu remembered the purple velvet suit, covered with huge pearls, the enormous diamonds in Buckingham's hat and sword hilt; the tanned, arrogant face and the expression on it as he talked to the Queen.

'I also hear he's brought a suite of seven hundred with him,' Louis continued. He walked to the window and stood staring out, his hands twisting behind his back.

'Englishmen have no taste,' the Cardinal said softly. 'They cover themselves in jewels like buccaneers after a successful raid. Forgive the big pearls, Sire, and the retinue larger than the one you take with you when travelling. The Duke means no harm; I thought he went out of his way to be charming.'

He'd seen Louis watching Buckingham with the Queen; he'd been watching himself while the admiration played between them like lightning. And he had had time to fight his own agonies of jealousy for the sake of the English alliance. Buckingham must be protected, but Anne, gazing into those other eyes, surrendering visibly – and the spiteful, mischief-making Duchess de Chevreuse – that was another matter.

'He paid more attention to the Queen than he did to my mother,' the King said at last.

'The Queen is very beautiful, Sire,' Richelieu's voice was gentle. 'You shouldn't blame him for that.'

'I've never seen her beauty.'

'Ah, but others see it. The Queen is young, frivolous, perhaps; if she encouraged the Duke, you must forgive her. Unlike yourself, Sire, she bears few responsibilities.'

'Few responsibilities and no children,' Louis muttered. 'When I begot a child with her she miscarried. And do you know why? She fell and injured herself, running a race with that strumpet Chevreuse! Christ's Blood, do you wonder I don't seek her bed after that?'

'No, Sire, and since you've mentioned Mme de Chevreuse, I've often thought how unsuitable a companion she is for the Queen. The Queen needs the guidance of a much older woman; someone who'd impress on her her duties to you. Why not attach the Duchess to the new Queen of England's suite and send her away to London? I could doubtless find a more suitable lady to attend the Queen.'

Louis looked at him thoughtfully. 'The Queen hates you bitterly enough; if we send the Chevreuse away from her she will become implacable. And of course the Duchess hates you too. You knew that?'

'Your welfare, and the welfare of France, are more important to me than even the Queen's enmity, let alone a strumpet. Your description, Sire. Send Mme de Chevreuse to England.'

'I shall, my friend. But look to yourself! Don't underestimate my wife's ill-nature.'

The Cardinal smiled, 'I don't. Now, Sire, may I retire? I have a lot of work to do before the Banquet this evening.'

Louis waved his hand wearily; he was becoming heavy and depressed again. The prospect of the Banquet bored him as all official functions did. His aversion sprang from the secret knowledge that he, the King, would be overshadowed by those nearest to him; by his mother, by his handsome brother Orleans who was the heir presumptive, and lastly his beautiful wife, with whom he always felt uncomfortable.

Now another rival had appeared. Buckingham. The Court had been gossiping about him for weeks; his appearance in Paris that day had caused a sensation, and never had the ill-assured King felt less of a man than when he watched the Englishman with his wife.

'Richelieu!'

The Cardinal paused; he saw the hanging head and the King's hand flicking his gloves against his knee. It was the aimless gesture of an unhappy child.

'Yes, Sire?'

'I shall be glad when the Duke of Buckingham leaves.'

Richelieu bowed his head.

'So shall I, Sire. The sooner Queen Henrietta sails for England the better. I shall attend to it.'

*   *   *

Paris became the gayest capital in Europe in the weeks that followed Buckingham's arrival. Every day there were hunting parties, and fêtes, a play in the evening and a Ball, either at the Louvre or one of the great houses of the French nobility. There were brilliant firework displays, which delighted the people of Paris, who got drunk on the King's largesse and had their own festivities in the streets. And the ballad singers and pamphleteers did a fine trade in scandal sheets about the Duke of Buckingham's love for the Queen.

Wherever they appeared, they were the centre of attention, and etiquette demanded that they meet at every public function. At the Ball held by the Queen Mother two nights after his arrival, Buckingham had danced with Anne for most of the evening, and when he wasn't dancing, he stood by her chair, or followed her if she moved across the room. To a Court where subtlety was essential to the enjoyment of a love affair, Buckingham's conduct was considered insane. His declarations of passion were so loud and universal, that the wits hourly expected him to confide them to the King.

Some of the women sympathised a little because the desperate humility of the man made him suddenly touching; there was none of his old arrogance left when he approached the Queen. He was impervious to the warnings of his own entourage and to the growing fury of the King of France; he ignored the gentle orders from his own master Charles, to curtail his stay and bring the new Queen back to England.

His stability, strained so severely in the long climb to his fantastic fortune, broke down under the impact of real love. He had found the most beautiful woman in the world, the embodiment of high breeding, the antithesis of his own vulgarity. Acceptance by her, possession of her, would transform the sham of his nobility into a fact.

It meant nothing to Buckingham that she was a Queen. He had exploited the weaknesses of Royalty too successfully to have any respect for it, and the fact that she was married meant less still. He adored her; one night spent in her arms would wipe out the memory of the slobbering, pawing James of England, of his own parvenu beginnings, and the sickening debaucheries with which he passed his time at home. He cursed Louis, and sometimes threw himself on his bed and wept because a few hours had to pass before he saw the Queen again.

He wrote her impassioned love letters, and entrusted them to Marie de Chevreuse. He liked the Duchess, because she was his closest link with Anne. The story he heard from her of Anne's loneliness, her humiliation and the growing persecution by the Cardinal Richelieu drove Buckingham to frenzy.

'Tell her,' he exploded, 'that if any danger threatens her at any time, she has only to send me one word, and every soldier, ship and sword in England will be sent to her defence!'

Marie de Medici gave a Banquet in honour of the Duke, followed by a masque, in which the new Queen of England, Henrietta Maria, danced the leading part with Buckingham and the King, Anne and the whole Court watched in the splendid great Hall of the Luxembourg. It was one of the most stately and colourful occasions Anne could remember; her mother-in-law's Palace was full of treasures from her native Florence. The whole Hall was reflected in the rare looking-glasses, massively framed in gilt wood, and some of the finest early Italian masters hung upon the walls in place of tapestries. Marie had done much to enhance and widen French taste by her introduction of Italian furniture and decorative style. The King and Queen and Marie de Medici sat together on a raised dais, on their chairs of state. The Hall was lit by wax candles, because tallow smelt too strongly, a great extravagance, but typical of the Queen Mother's lavish gestures when she entertained. A band of musicians played in the gallery above the Hall, and down below the company of dancers, led by the little Queen Henrietta Maria, danced a long and stately mime of Venus and Apollo. Anne couldn't help but watch the figure of Buckingham in a suit of cloth of gold, embroidered with so many diamonds that he seemed to be on fire when he moved. He danced superbly, his masculine grace and sureness made the diminutive Queen of England seem like a child, and stole all the attention from her.

He was so handsome, so very splendid. When she was away from him, Anne despised herself as a weakling and a fool, giving encouragement to such a man. When he was near her she forgot everything but the sensation of being loved and wanted by a man who would dare anything.

That was what frightened her, his reckless disregard of elementary caution; his contemptuous attitude to her suspicious husband, and his violent dislike of the Cardinal. He feared nothing, but Anne feared with good reason. At the end of the masque, Louis rose, and turning gave his hand to lead Anne down. He hadn't spoken a word to her since the evening began. 'It was beautifully done, Sire,' Anne made an effort. 'Her Majesty, your sister, danced exquisitely.'

'With such competition from the Duke, I fear she came off badly, Madame,' Louis said. 'So many bright jewels and such a glittering costume. No wonder the English Treasury is almost empty. Ah, here comes the sun god himself! To pay homage to you, no doubt.'

She felt her colour rising. There was such a cold rage in Louis' eyes that they seemed to burn as they looked at her. Buckingham was coming towards them; he held his golden half mask in one hand, and carried a long ivory cane with a gold and diamond top. He swept the King a bow, and then he repeated his performance of the first night they met, and went on one knee to Anne.

'Congratulations, M. Buckingham,' the King said. 'A very pleasant entertainment. My wife enjoyed it even more than I did.' And turning, the King walked away and left them.

Buckingham got up and came to her; they were a little isolated in the throng which had overflowed onto the floor when the masque ended and it was possible to speak a few words without being overheard.

'Madame,' he said, 'I danced only for you. And your beautiful eyes were on me, I saw them, watching all the time!'

'I beg of you,' Anne whispered. 'Be careful what you say, don't stand so near and look at me like that. The King is watching, see, there is that scarlet fiend beside him – oh, Buckingham, please don't compromise me!'

Obediently he moved back from her a pace. 'I

wouldn't hurt you for the world,' he said. 'I love you, Madame.'

'You mustn't say that,' Anne besought him. 'It's insanity, there's nothing we can do!'

'A few moments alone with you, really alone, that's all I crave,' he murmured. 'Is that insanity, is that impossible?'

'It is for me,' Anne said. 'Please take me to the Queen Mother, we dare not go on talking here.'

He gave her his arm, and together they moved through the crowd which parted to make way for them, until she had reached Marie de Medici, who was talking to her son Gaston. Orleans was in a bad humour. He had sulked continuously since the Duke had arrived, because this dazzling personage had taken all the attention for himself, and Gaston found the pretty ladies more interested in Buckingham than in him.

He was very petulant because he hadn't been included in the masque, and equally cross because his lovely sister-in-law seemed so besotted by the man. He had paid her several visits and found that she was quite abstracted, and often didn't listen to what he was saying.

'My compliments, your Majesty. Monsieur.' Buckingham bowed to them, and excused himself. As he backed away, he made another bow, much lower than before. This was to Anne.

'You were wise not to linger,' Marie de Medici said sharply. 'My son is looking so jaundiced I doubt not he'll be ill with jealousy.'

'I couldn't help it, Madame,' Anne said. 'I was left with the Duke. The King walked away and left me there.'

'Eh, very likely,' the old Queen shrugged. 'But for

your own sake, my daughter, be careful. A lover in secret is one thing, but this public courtship is another matter. Gaston, go and fetch my little Henrietta to me.'

'Will you be with my mother when I return?' Orleans asked Anne. 'I've hardly seen you this past week. You're not so nice to me any more. I believe it's the fault of this damned Englishman!'

'I'll be here,' Anne promised. 'And it's not his fault, I promise you. Come to see me tomorrow; we'll take chocolate together.'

Gaston departed smiling; his vanity was appeased and because Anne had made him happy, the old Queen decided to give her some advice. She tapped Anne's arm with her fan; 'One word, my daughter, while we're alone. I'm sure you're innocent of any wrong with Buckingham, but if you value your life, don't let him compromise you any further. I've heard my son talking, and he'll make you suffer for what's passed already. For God's sake, don't become the Duke's mistress . . .'

'Madame,' Anne gasped, 'I wouldn't . . .'

'Bah, don't play the hypocrite with me,' Marie said. 'You'd like to. But resist. That's all I advise you. Resist, or you'll die for it.'

*　　*　　*

A large selection of the Court believed that Anne had become the Duke's mistress in spite of the precautions taken to watch her movements. Only Richelieu knew that this was not true.

That knowledge was the one thing which enabled him to bear Buckingham's insults, to stand by day after day and see the woman who had repulsed him so brutally, smile and soften to the advances of another. She had fallen in love with him: she blushed when the Duke spoke to her, there was an atmosphere of quivering tension between them and his spies told him that she spent hours over her toilet, and that she was receiving letters in secret. They also told him that she and the Duke had never spent five minutes alone together.

And with this assurance he pacified the King.

Louis sent for him several times a day to hear reports of his wife's movements. 'You tell me she went riding this morning with her ladies,' he said, throwing the Cardinal's report down on his writing table. 'Did Buckingham join them?'

'He intended to, but I had instructed Madame de Senlis to turn off at a certain point and lead the Queen back to Paris. The Duke rode out in vain, Sire.'

'She would have met him,' Louis muttered. 'Only she dare not disobey Madame de Senlis because she knows I'd hear of it. She would have met him and contrived to get separated in the forests . . . then she would have betrayed me.'

'The Queen is watched night and day, Sire,' Richelieu answered. 'But you warned me once not to underestimate her. Therefore I say that if she intended to become Buckingham's mistress, she'd find a way to do it, whatever we did. We can hardly imprison her because he pays her compliments!'

'Imprison!' Louis laughed fiercely and swung round. 'If she lies with that foreign upstart I'll send her to the Place de Grève!'

Anne's death was what he really wanted, because he had suffered through her; suffered because she offered no competition to those instincts of which he was so ashamed. If he could only get rid of her he might marry someone else, someone he could talk to easily, and if she were kind and patient, learn to love like other men. One word from Richelieu and he would have had her brought to trial. But the will of the Cardinal always interposed, disguised by humble words, and he was somehow unable to resist it.

'If the Queen dishonours you, Sire, I shall find out. And I'll see that she submits to your justice, rather than your mercy.' Louis scowled, biting his heavy lower lip, and looked away.

'She's made a mockery of me,' he said. 'As she once did of you. Why do you plead for her . . .'

'I plead for the reputation of Louis the Just,' the Cardinal retorted. He had invented the sobriquet himself and seen that it was circulated.

'The Queen has been thoughtless, and you must punish her for that in your own way, Sire. But not with death, for a crime she hasn't yet committed.'

Yet. The word brought the King's head up and his dark eyes fixed on the face of his Minister.

'You must trust me, Sire,' Richelieu continued. 'From the moment you mentioned your suspicion I've surrounded her with spies. I've kept nothing from you; my only concern is your honour. And when the Duke of Buckingham leaves France, and the Queen is still innocent, as I'm sure she will be, we must take measures to protect her from herself.'

'I trust you, Richelieu,' the King said slowly. 'In this, as in everything else. Write to the King of England and say my sister is impatient to join him in London.'

The Cardinal bowed low. 'I will, Sire. A most wise

suggestion.' He had already written to Charles two days before.

*　　*　　*

'Madame,' the Duchess de Chevreuse whispered. Anne of Austria looked up. She was playing faro with Marie in her rooms, and she was losing because her thoughts were anywhere but on the game. 'Go on playing,' Marie murmured. 'But get up and go into your closet in a few minutes. I have a letter for you.'

'That's fifty louis I've lost already,' Anne said loudly, for the benefit of her other ladies who were sewing in a window corner. 'I've no luck at this game today. After this hand, I shall give up.'

Ten minutes later she rose and went towards a small writing closet. When Mme de Senlis moved to follow, Anne stopped her with an imperious gesture; the closet led into her oratory, so there was no means of escaping her apartments. Therefore Richelieu's spy sat down again, while Mme de Chevreuse shut the door behind her mistress. The two women went into Anne's oratory; it was dimly lit by candles burning before the tiny altar, but it was guarded from eavesdroppers by the fact that the closet door creaked too loudly for anyone to slip in unheard.

'Give it to me.'

Marie drew a square of paper out of her dress and moved away from her mistress, while Anne read Buckingham's letter by the guttering candlelight. Like all the others, it expressed his love for her in the most extravagant terms, and ended in the usual plea for a meeting alone. She stood motionless for several moments, re-reading it, and then held it to the candle flame until it flared up and dropped to the floor. Deliberately, she trod the ashes into dust on the marble altar step. At last Marie spoke.

'Madame, what are you going to do?'

Anne turned to her. 'Nothing. There's nothing I can do. Have you seen the King's eyes? One indiscretion would mean my death. When did he give you this?'

'This afternoon, after we came back from riding. He went out with his gentlemen, hoping to meet you . . .'

'But de Senlis turned back,' Anne finished bitterly. 'She's well trained, that creature. God help her, if I ever get a chance to revenge myself for this!'

'He's like a man demented,' the Duchess said. In her long experience of lovers, she had never seen a suitor so besotted as the Duke.

'Madame, do you love him,' she whispered. 'Because if you don't, for the love of God end this insanity once and for all. You're risking so much, and for nothing! You talk about the King – but have you seen the Cardinal? Have you seen his eyes when you and Buckingham are together? I tell you, he's mad with jealousy!'

'I have forbidden you to mention that name,' Anne ordered sharply. 'All these strangers appointed to my household, your attachment to the Queen of England – who do you suppose suggested that to Louis, who's too stupid to think of anything so subtle for himself? That miserable fiend!'

'Do you love the Duke?' Marie persisted. 'He's begging for one word of hope.'

'I love him,' Anne said quietly. 'Tell him that. Tell him my love gives me the courage to go on without hope, as he must, if he values my life. And tell him that if he ever wants to see me free and more than Queen in name, he must destroy the Cardinal.'

'Madame,' Marie said, 'I'll give the first part of your message, but leave the Cardinal to me.'

The door to the closet creaked suddenly.

'Get back, kneel, for God's sake,' Anne whispered, and rushed to her prie-dieu. A moment later Mme. de Senlis entered; she saw nothing suspicious; only the Queen praying before her altar, and the Duchess kneeling behind her at a respectful distance.

She retreated with the excuse that it was nearly time for Her Majesty to dress for the play the King had ordered for that evening.

*　　*　　*

Richelieu had bought a house at Reuil, just outside the city. It was a week before the departure of the new Queen of England and her suite. Buckingham had been forced to set a date for leaving, and the whole Court was accompanying them to Calais. The Cardinal was tired that night when he came home, after a day spent with State business and a long, exhausting evening at the Louvre, where the King sat in silence, so visibly bad tempered that no one dared to come near him.

But there was still one more visitor to see, before he could retire to bed. His chamberlain met him in the hall, took off his heavy scarlet cloak and bowed. 'Father Joseph is waiting for you in the salon, Your Eminence.'

'Good. Send in some wine, then go to bed.'

The oak panelled salon was dimly lit by a few

candles, and a log fire burned in the grate. A man in the grey robes of Capuchin friar rose and came to kiss Richelieu's hand.

'I'm sorry you've had to wait so long,' Richelieu said. 'I couldn't leave earlier.'

The monk shook his head and smiled. 'Time is never wasted. I have been meditating.'

He pushed his cowl back, revealing a long face, thin to the point of emaciation, with heavy lidded eyes of a piercing blue. Seven years earlier the wealthy Count de Tremblay had renounced his title and his great possessions to enter one of the strictest orders of begging friars. The man who had become Father Joseph owned nothing but the patched habit on his back. He had first met Richelieu at Luçon, when he was attracted by the brilliance of the young Bishop and his grasp of politics. They had become friends, and remained so. Father Joseph was his confessor, adviser and confidant. There were no secrets between the Cardinal and the monk.

And to the Capuchin, Richelieu confided his plan to attack La Rochelle and destroy the Huguenots as a political force in the Kingdom.

And after them, he would direct French arms at Spain, because Spain was too powerful, and the hereditary enemy of France. But first La Rochelle, and he emphasised this, pointing his finger at a map which was spread out before them.

'La Rochelle?' Father Joseph questioned. 'It's impregnable; heavily fortified on land against attack, and impervious to siege because of its outlet to the sea.'

'Those points hadn't escaped me,' the Cardinal said

drily. 'We will come to them; especially this outlet to the sea.'

'And when do you propose attacking La Rochelle?'

'As soon as Buckingham leaves France.'

'And do you still count on the English to abandon the Huguenots?'

The Cardinal shook his head. 'No; thanks to the Queen, my plan has failed completely. Because of Anne of Austria; Buckingham hates me as bitterly as he hates the King. He'd welcome the chance to attack France. I even believe he's madman enough to think that he could claim the Queen as the price of victory over us! No, Father, Buckingham is our enemy, and Buckingham is England. They'll come to the aid of La Rochelle. We shall have to defeat both.'

The monk finished his half glass of wine. 'Is it the fear of precipitating war with England that's made you protect the Queen?' he asked suddenly.

Richelieu stopped abruptly and turned to face him.

'Why do you say I'm protecting her?'

'Because everyone knows someone is staying the King's hand in this affair, and I know it must be you.'

'He hates her,' Richelieu said slowly. 'She's injured his pride, but she hasn't hurt his honour; if she had, I'd have no mercy on her. Believe me, Father. If Louis harmed her, we'd have war with Spain and England! I have no sentiment towards her,' he said fiercely. 'If I've restrained the King, it's for the good of France!'

'Do not deceive yourself or me,' Father Joseph said calmly. 'I know what you feel for her, I also know it's wrong. No nation goes to war in defence of a Queen found guilty of adultery; not even Spain.'

The Cardinal sat down after a moment, and crossed one leg over the other. His shoe buckles were set with rubies, and they gleamed as his foot swung to and fro. 'She hasn't committed adultery,' he said. 'And there's another reason. France must have an heir, and the King's as likely to beget one with Anne as with any other woman. At least we're certain she can bear a child; her miscarriage proved that. The King knows his duty; sooner or later the thought of his brother Orleans succeeding him will make him return to the Queen.'

'But he's delicate,' Father Joseph objected. 'If he dies childless . . .'

'Then Gaston d'Orleans will be King of France. And Marie de Medici will be virtual ruler. We shall have the days of the favourites and the civil wars all over again. And since Orleans hates me, I and probably you, my dear Father, will find ourselves on the scaffold.'

'Orleans isn't your only enemy,' the monk said.

Richelieu smiled. 'The Queen Mother too. I know; her protégé has become a little too powerful; I appear devoted to the King rather than to her, and her beloved Gaston is always pouring poison into her ear, and she can't resist him. She would like to see me fall, and before long she'll try to bring that fall about.'

'You've risen too far and too quickly,' Father Joseph explained. 'And you deceived a great many people in the beginning into thinking they could use you. The disillusion has made you many enemies.'

Richelieu turned his pastoral ring round on his finger till the jewel was hidden.

'Which will strike at me first, and when?'

Father Joseph looked at him; he looked younger

than his forty years, deceptively frail, until one met those stone grey eyes.

'Those nearest to you will strike first. The blow will come from Paris, if my instinct is correct.'

'And the nature of that blow?' the Cardinal questioned.

Father Joseph shrugged. 'Who can tell? An intrigue, an ultimatum to the King to dismiss you. It might be anything.'

'I don't think so,' Richelieu turned the ring round again, so that the big stone caught the light.

'I think it will be assassination. That's what I would do in their place.'

* * *

The little Queen Henrietta Maria was leaving for England at last and the French Court followed her to Calais for the State embarkation. It was a fine opportunity for the people to see their King, and the route was lined with crowds all the way from Paris. It was a triumphal progress, even for the gloomy Louis, marred only by the size and splendour of the English escort, with Buckingham prancing ahead on a magnificent white horse. He looked pre-occupied and bad tempered; he often twisted round in his saddle to stare back along the road for a sight of the procession escorting the Queen. Henrietta Maria and her ladies, Marie de Chevreuse among them, travelled with the curtains of the royal litter drawn back, and the new Queen of England waved sadly to the crowds who had gathered to see her on the last part of her journey to an unknown country and a husband she had never seen.

She won the people's sympathy and they cheered her warmly, as they cheered their King, the son of their beloved Henri Quatre, and then pushed forward with a murmur as the Queen of France passed in her carriage. She was certainly beautiful, with her perfect features and that magnificent hair; the talk of her love for the English Duke had gone all through France. Public opinion resented it so much they even cheered Marie de Medici.

Anne leant back in the carriage and closed her eyes; the peering, pushing crowds got on her nerves. In Spain, the people were kept in their place; they would never have been allowed to get so close. In two more hours, they were to halt at Amiens, before the final leave-taking at Calais. Anne dreaded Calais.

Her courage wavered at the prospect of saying a formal farewell to the only two people in the world she loved, one of whom she knew she would never see again.

Vainglorious, splendid Charles Villiers, Duke of Buckingham. He had lit the dull twilight of her life like a comet, and the brilliance of his passion for her was about to fade over the seas to England, leaving loneliness and humiliation and the malice of the King. She thought of him, and bit her lips to quell her longing to give way, just once on this last journey and rest in his arms. One memory, her instincts tempted, one secret comfort against the life which stretched ahead. Life with Louis; boredom, loneliness . . . She knew the King, she thought bitterly, and she was beginning to know the implacable spite of his Cardinal. They'd sent Marie away from her; that was another miserable parting. She would never forgive Richelieu for that. Never.

'Leave the Cardinal to me,' Marie had said, and she'd asked no further question. Gay, affectionate Marie. How she would miss her. The Duchess had promised to get herself sent back to France; Henrietta Maria was something of a simpleton and Marie would wheedle permission out of her without much difficulty. And while she was in England, Anne wouldn't lack news of the Duke. It was dangerous, but she'd promised to do it, and knowing her resourcefulness, the Queen agreed. A letter from him at least; and a means of writing back . . .

The whole entourage stopped at Amiens; it was the last stage of the journey to Calais, and Buckingham's last chance of an informal meeting with Anne. The weeks in France had changed him; he was thinner, more quick tempered; he ate less and drank more and the thought of the Queen of France had become an uncontrollable obsession. He lay awake, repeating Marie de Chevreuse's message, 'Tell him I love him.' Without that assurance he felt he would have gone mad. He became desperate, as the time left to them shortened; King Charles had come to the end of his patience at last. He ordered the Duke to bring his Queen to England and not even Buckingham dared delay any longer. Anne and her suite were staying in a large house at Amiens, and the Duchess de Chevreuse gained permission to join her mistress for a last evening. It was she who arranged that the Duke and some of his gentlemen should pay their respects to the Queen. It was a warm and lovely night; the Duke's suggestion that they should walk in the gardens was accepted, and Anne led the way out into the cool avenue, flanked by trees and shrubs in bloom. She walked with Buckingham at her side, pointing out the different flowers in a voice that trembled on the edge of tears.

'I'll come back,' he whispered suddenly. 'No matter how, I shall return to Paris and see you again. I'll ask nothing from you, nothing; just that I may see you!'

'I beg you,' she pleaded. 'If I break down and weep, someone will report it. Don't talk of parting, don't talk of anything.'

He saw a pathway branching to the left, shielded by thick bushes; one glance assured him that the others had fallen back, and the next moment he caught her arm and turned her down the path. For the first time since he came to France they were alone, and the next moment Anne was in his arms. He gave her no time to cry out and his strength paralysed her; they stood locked. His passion enveloped her like a sheet of flame, under the stimulus of his experienced kisses she caught him round the neck, breathless and straining against him. For a second her eyes opened; they stared into a face, half hidden by the bushes, and a hand rustled the stiff leaves, parting them to see.

Blind instinct guided her. She wrenched her head back and shrieked for help. He released her, and she shrank back trembling, listening to running footsteps and the voices of her ladies calling. The spy behind the hedges had slipped back to join them. As the first of her women ran to her, Anne saw Mme. de Senlis among them, and thought in shame and terror that the Duke was compromised, but she had saved herself. She turned away from him, struggling against hysteria, trying not to hear his protests and see him led away.

In the privacy of her own room she fainted. Her condition was so distressed that her physician ordered her to be bled, and trembling for their own negligence in leaving her for a moment with the Duke, her entourage gave out that the Queen was ill with shock and outrage.

On the twenty-second of June, Henrietta Maria sailed for England. The Duke of Buckingham stood on deck, his eyes straining towards the shores of France until they blurred and vanished in the Channel mists.

Some months later Anne was at Fontainebleau when she received a letter. The letter came from Brussels and it was smuggled in to her by her valet La Porte. La Porte and most of her servants and attendants who remained loyal to her had been dismissed by the King when she returned from Amiens, but the letters from London, and finally from Brussels, still reached her at the risk of her friends' lives. Madame de Chevreuse was in Brussels; having secured her dismissal from England, she dared not come back to France to face Louis' fury over the incident at Amiens and the blame he attached to her for encouraging the Duke. Raging in self-imposed exile, Marie had no doubt who had directed the King's attention to her part in the affair. And Anne's letters, filled with complaints of the supervision and insults to which she was subjected, placed the responsibility in the same quarter. She was forbidden to write or receive letters, to step outside the Palace without the King's permission; to receive any man in audience; to approach her Royal husband without making a formal request like any humble courtier. Her rooms were deserted except for those who had to wait on her, for the Queen's friendship inevitably brought disgrace.

And the Cardinal's influence over the King was

only equalled by his power over France. All this she wrote to her confidante, adding that the only person who befriended her and relieved the tedium of her life by constant visits was the King's brother Orleans.

The letter she received that afternoon in late autumn was unusually short. It contained news of an admirer of her Majesty whose devotion had increased with his absence, and who was even then negotiating to return on an embassage to France. And it counselled patience in her misfortunes, for those who loved her, at Court and at a distance, were about to remove the author of them very soon.

3

'I met the Duc d'Orleans on my way to your Majesty, this afternoon,' Richelieu remarked.

He was sitting in the King's study at the Louvre, while Louis read and signed some documents. The King looked up; he was thinner and more sallow; he had been ill again, with one of the seizures which alarmed his doctors and which were rumoured to be epileptic. He had been bled into a state of exhaustion; only a fundamentally strong constitution enabled him to survive both the sickness and the cure.

'Is he coming here?' Louis frowned, his pen suspended. The Cardinal watched a drop of ink gathering on the end of the quill, when it dropped on to the paper, he raised his eyes and answered.

'No, Sire. He was going to visit the Queen.'

Louis threw the quill down. 'I have forbidden her to hold audiences,' he said. 'My brother knows that; he knows she's under my displeasure. He goes out of his way to defy my authority!'

'I know, but you can hardly forbid it without causing a serious scandal, and one which is quite unfounded,' Richelieu responded gently. 'They are brother and sister-in-law; if you forbade them to meet it would seem you suspected another relationship.'

Louis twisted like a man in physical pain at the insinuation. First Buckingham and that disgraceful scene at Amiens which his mind, warped with insane jealousy, could hardly distinguish from adultery, and now, when he was revenging himself on her and the scandal was dying down, his own brother. His eyes narrowed and darkened with suspicion. 'Why does he visit her?' he demanded. 'Why does he pay her so much attention when he knows how guilty she is!'

The Cardinal shrugged. 'No doubt he sees her beauty, Sire. Innocently of course; and he's spoilt. He's never been taught to respect your wishes.'

'Has the Queen?' Louis asked him bitterly.

'I think so, Sire.'

Richelieu had watched her, pitiless in the pursuit of his revenge; seen her pale face and reddened eyes, the result of the penalty he had inflicted for the common knowledge that Buckingham had held her in his arms. But a mild punishment compared to the cruel longings of the King. Only the meanness of the humiliations he had suggested, concealed the fact that he had saved her from actual imprisonment, he had thwarted the King with such skill that Louis believed his actions to be determined by his own wisdom. And that sense of justice his Minister was always praising.

However much he hated Anne, Richelieu admitted to himself that he had to protect as well as persecute. He wanted her alive and free as Father Joseph pointed out, because he meant one day to take the final masculine revenge upon her.

Now the same doubt that tortured Louis ravaged him. Buckingham was gone, her little Court had dispersed; she was alone except for the company of a few dull waiting women. Until the King's brother, his deadly enemy, started trying on Buckingham's shoes.

He thought of Gaston d'Orleans, already an experienced roué at eighteen; always in debt, idling and dissipating his time away with one insolent eye on the throne and the other on his delicate elder brother. What was he doing with Anne, who was friendless and had no amusements to offer? What was the intrigue; amorous or political, or both?

'I think those nearest to you will strike first.'

Father Joseph's quiet voice came back to him as he sat watching his unhappy King writhing with jealousy of his brother. Was this the beginning of that blow, this friendship between the helpless woman who hated him and the young Prince who resented his power?

And was he to watch another man replace the Duke in her affections, a man he couldn't send back to his own country, couldn't arrest or banish because he was the heir to the throne and too important to be touched?

'It's a pity Monsieur your brother isn't married,' he remarked at last. 'A wife would divert him from this foolishness with the Queen. Perhaps the subject might be mentioned again.'

'It shall be,' Louis promised. 'My mother and I have selected Mlle de Montpensier for him. She's the wealthiest heiress and one of the noblest born women in France. But my brother has practically refused to marry her! And my mother keeps telling me to wait, to have patience with him.'

'Ah, the Queen Mother's heart always softens towards him,' Richelieu sympathised, knowing that never since his wretched childhood, had Marie de Medici shown the least indulgence to her eldest son. 'And the Duc objects because his bride is a commoner. He wishes a foreign alliance; it would strengthen his position, give him political power. He would feel less dependent upon you.' Richelieu paused. 'All excellent reasons why he should not be allowed to do anything of the sort. Mlle de Montpensier is the perfect choice.'

'He wants to marry for ambition,' Louis muttered. 'He has no loyalty towards me.'

'He must content himself with being heir to the throne of France,' the Cardinal said. 'Take my advice, Sire. Order Monsieur the Duc to marry the lady, and proceed with the wedding arrangements.'

* * *

'I will not marry that creature!' Gaston d'Orleans' voice rang out in Anne of Austria's room. 'Her back's crooked!'

He had been walking up and down by the long windows, banging a gold topped stick on the floor with rage, and he swung round to face his sister-in-law. Anne sat in a window embrasure, looking up at him, the sun reflected like fire in her red hair. She was simply dressed in pale yellow satin, with a deep collar of delicate lace, caught at her breast by a brooch of magnificent opals and diamonds.

Orleans' doublet and breeches were velvet; a short cloak hung from his shoulder, and his dark hair was curling round his collar, in the love locks made so popular by the Duke of Buckingham. His handsome face was convulsed with peevish fury. He stopped before Anne, one hand flung out in a rather feminine gesture.

'My dearest sister, don't you support me?'

'I do,' Anne answered. 'I know what that devil's persecutions mean and I support you with all my heart!' She looked round and caught one of her ladies looking up from the piece of tapestry she was working. The remark would be whispered in Richelieu's ear before the evening. Orleans followed her look, and his eyes narrowed and his lips pursed until he bore a sudden resemblance to the King in a vindictive mood.

'Your needlework annoys me, Mademoiselle. Retire!' He knew Anne could not give the order because it wouldn't be obeyed, and he made her a triumphant little bow when the woman left the room.

'No doubt she's spying through the keyhole, but she can't hear anything,' he said. He sat beside her, resting both hands on the top of his stick.

'As I said before, I will not marry the creature,' he repeated quietly. 'It's easier to acquire a wife than to get rid of one once they're acquired, and I'm damned if I'm going to make Mademoiselle Crookback Montpensier Queen of France!'

'You speak as if the King were already dead,' Anne murmured. Orleans regarded his stick with attention.

'I heard they despaired of his life at one time during that seizure,' he remarked, his voice very low. 'He's certainly not strong, my good brother. And when I succeed him, as I certainly shall, I want a Queen of my own choosing.'

'I shall envy her,' Anne said bitterly. 'In God's name treat her better than the King has treated me.'

'I deplore that treatment.' The dark eyes glanced sideways at her. 'I can imagine how boring your life is, my dearest sister. In fact, some friends of mine, and M. de Chalais – so devoted to the dear Duchess de Chevreuse – they're always writing and he's been to Brussels to see her – as I was saying, some friends of mine were discussing the tedium of your life and we've agreed on an amusement for you.'

Anne smiled wryly. 'A new needlework design? That's what the Queen Mother suggested when I asked her to intercede for me.'

Orleans shook his head.

'Needlework? No. My dear mother has always occupied her tongue and her hands rather than her mind. . . . No, I suggest you read some history. French history, my dearest sister. Beginning with the life of Anne de Bretagne.'

She turned towards him so sharply that he lifted one hand in a gesture of warning.

'The keyhole, remember. It seems you know the story.'

'She was twice Queen of France,' Anne said; she was looking out of the window, her face hidden; her cheeks were blazing with excitement.

'She married one brother, he died, and she married the other one,' Orleans finished. 'Would the prospect appeal to you?'

'More than anything in the world.' It was a fierce, low whisper, and the Duc smiled.

'Now you see why I cannot possibly marry the Montpensier,' he said cheerfully. He was waiting for Anne to ask him if he loved her and make some declaration for her part, but she said nothing. For a moment his vanity was hurt; he was as close to being in love with his beautiful sister-in-law as it is possible at eighteen; however, the degree was limited by a passionate pre-occupation with himself.

After a pause Anne said suddenly, 'You say M. de Chalais has seen Marie?'

'Indeed he has. And I hear she made him a very happy man during his visit.'

'She sent me a letter,' Anne went on. 'It said that my friends were about to remove the author of my misfortunes; those were her words.'

Orleans smiled. 'She was quite right, my sister, they are. That's the other matter I wanted to discuss with you, since we've settled the first. The Court leaves for Fontainebleau in a few days, and the Cardinal is going to his house at Fleury. At Fleury a company of my gentlemen will call upon him, led by M. de Chalais. And a happy accident will occur.'

'And what will the King do?' she whispered.

'Nothing; without the Cardinal to support him. He will do what he did before that wretch schemed his way into his confidence; obey my mother. And my mother obeys me.'

Her thoughts were racing ahead; she looked into the cynical, cunning young face so close to her own, and knew that the murder of Richelieu was only the first step in a more terrible plan.

'If the King insists on punishing those responsible for this accident,' she said coldly. 'What then?'

Orleans' thin eyebrows raised. 'He may find it necessary to abdicate. And if you're not a widow, then the marriage can be annulled.'

He yawned, and raised himself on his stick. He bent over Anne's hand and kissed it lightly.

'You have an admirable spirit, dearest sister. Till Fontainebleau. And Fleury!'

*　　*　　*

It was nearly midnight, and the house at Fleury was very quiet; most of the servants had gone to bed on the Cardinal's orders, but lights were burning in his study. While his valet de chambre slept in the ante-room, Richelieu sat at his desk, working on despatches from abroad. He was reading an account of the friction Queen Henrietta Maria's Catholic priests and ladies were causing in London; egged on by Buckingham, the mild Charles was threatening to send them all back to France, and quarrelling bitterly with his young wife. It was a poor revenge, the Cardinal thought contemptuously, and if Buckingham hoped to get back to Paris to play the peacemaker, he was going to be disappointed.

The King would never allow him to set foot in France again ... Richelieu paused, lowering the paper. Someone was knocking, almost hammering, on his door.

He rose and stood facing the entrance. As he did so, the clock in the courtyard struck twelve.

'Who is it?'

The voice was his valet's: 'The Comte de Chalais and the Commandant de Valencay.'

'Admit them,' he said.

De Chalais and de Valencay; as they advanced into the room towards him he stiffened, and one hand crept to his side, searching for the sword he always wore, when in lay dress, and remembered that it lay unbuckled in his bedroom.

'You come at a late hour, gentlemen,' he said gently. 'What brings you?'

There was a pause; he noticed the distress on

Chalais' face, distress mixed with resentment, and the stern expression of de Valencay. At last the latter answered him.

'We come to save your Eminence from assassination,' the Commandant said. 'De Chalais, speak!'

The Comte wet his lips and glanced quickly at his friend.

'There is a plot to murder you,' he burst out. 'And I am in it. I told de Valencay and he said if I didn't warn you and ask your pardon, he'd expose me himself!'

Richelieu bowed to the soldier, his lips were smiling while his cold eyes considered the man who had witnessed his humiliation in Anne of Austria's room nearly three years ago, and remembered the mocking laughter which followed him as he left.

'I am indebted to you, Valencay. And surprised in you, Comte. I didn't know you were my enemy. Why should you seek my poor life?'

'The Duc d'Orleans seeks it,' de Valencay answered. Orleans was safe enough; and the Commandant despised him. He was outraged to hear of the plot, and determined to protect his foolish boyhood friend de Chalais from bearing the full consequences.

Orleans. Richelieu inclined his head in mock surprise. Orleans, and of course Anne. And after his death, no doubt the King . . . She must have consented to both murders.

'I forgive you, M. de Chalais,' he said gently. 'You have been led astray.' A further idea occurred to him; hadn't the spies watching Mme de Chevreuse in Brussels reported that de Chalais had become her lover? So she was in it too, of course.

'How did you intend to kill me?'

'A troop of the Duc d'Orleans' household are coming here, I was supposed to lead them. They were to pick a quarrel with your servants and run you through in the confusion.'

'Very ingenious,' the Cardinal admitted. 'No doubt they'd have sought me out so that they could murder me by accident . . .'

He could see that de Chalais was uneasy, he had betrayed everything and secured nothing from his enemy but a personal forgiveness. The Cardinal turned away from them and went to his desk; he wanted time to think; every revengeful instinct urged him to have de Chalais sent to the Bastille, but the gifts of insight and statesmanship warned him that verbal accusations of enemies like Orleans and the Queen were not enough. If de Chalais was punished, the incident remained nothing more than an attempt on his own life, and the real plot, which he suspected, the plot to kill Louis, place his brother on the throne, and probably, since she was part of the conspiracy, marry him to Anne – that plot would go undiscovered.

Even he dare not mention it to the King without proof, and he was certain that de Chalais did not know it. A show of weakness, mildness on his part now, might lull the conspirators into another attempt, and no plot of such magnitude could be conducted without letters.

He turned round and held out his hand to de Chalais.

'I pardon you,' he said. 'As a man and a Minister. You are my witness, de Valencay. M. de Chalais is under my protection; no harm shall come to him. In return for my pardon, Comte, you will ride with the Commandant to Fontainebleau and tell the King what you have just told me.'

'What of yourself?' de Valencay demanded. 'Orleans' men will come whether de Chalais is with them or not. Will you stay here to be killed?'

'I shall stay,' Richelieu assured him. 'But at least I know what to expect. Goodnight, gentlemen.'

* * *

'When they came to the house, he was in the hall, waiting for them.'

Orleans cursed under his breath. He was walking in the gardens at Fontainebleau with Anne, chaperoned by her ladies, who had been ordered to walk well behind, out of earshot.

'They were taken by surprise, the fools, and while they hesitated, he talked to them, bade them welcome, and then slipped out of a side entrance into a carriage waiting for him and was on the road to Fontainebleau. If there'd been a man of wits among them, he'd have run him through the body in the first few seconds! At the very moment I thought he was dead, the devil appears in my dressing room and hands me my shirt!'

'Now the King's given him a company of his own guards for his protection; as he escaped, everyone's lauding his courage and fawning round him,' Anne said bitterly. 'Dear God, what ill-luck! We'll never have him at sword point again.'

'We may,' Gaston retorted. 'I haven't given up, and nor have you, I know.'

'I'll never give up,' Anne answered. 'I'd as soon lose my own head if it would help to cut off his! We must stop him now, Gaston. Since this plot, the King is completely dominated by him. There'll be no end to his power, and God knows what harm he'll do to all of us.'

'I apologised,' Gaston sneered. 'I swore on the Testament I wouldn't plot again, and my brother believed me. I'll swear the Cardinal thinks we've given up. He even trusts de Chalais since that night.'

'Ah, he's mistaken,' Anne rejoiced. 'De Chalais would do anything to undo what he did and get back with Marie de Chevreuse. And I know the price of her forgiveness for this. If he trusts de Chalais, he knows little of men.'

'The Duchess will be back in Paris in a few days; it seems my brother has forgotten his grudge against her.'

Anne frowned; for a moment doubt shadowed her confidence.

'Have you ever known the King to forgive anyone for anything? Are you sure it's safe?'

'Perfectly,' Orleans assured her. Apart from the fright Richelieu had given him when he walked into his room at Fontainebleau when Gaston thought him safely assassinated, the whole affair had been passed over with no repercussions to himself. With the knowledge of his own immunity, all his arrogance and determination returned, stronger than before.

How weak his brother was, he thought contemptuously, and the task of removing him from the throne seemed even easier. The best preliminary was still to murder the one man who had nothing to gain and everything to lose from the conspiracy.

'As you said, my dearest sister, the good Cardinal is basking in the sunshine of my brother's favour and congratulating himself on his escape. I have promised to be a model of brotherly loyalty, you are not implicated, de Chalais has been forgiven; so we will strike again.'

Anne turned down a path into the rose gardens, it was a narrow path, just wide enough for Gaston to walk at her side; it was a warm and sunny day, some of the blooms had flowered early. Orleans stooped to pick one for her; they laughed lightheartedly for the benefit of the ladies-in-waiting who were trying to keep up.

'We need more allies,' Anne said quietly. 'No more pretence between us, brother; first Richelieu and then the King. Isn't that really what you mean?'

He smoothed back the lace cuff on his sleeve. 'It is.'

'Then we need a foreign power to back us; someone strong enough to accept you as King of France immediately, and the rest of the world will follow suit.'

'And who will give us such a guarantee?' Orleans questioned; there were times when the energy and daring of his sister-in-law annoyed him. It was politically so sound that he wished he had thought of it first.

'Spain will give it,' she said vehemently. 'The King my brother knows how I have been treated; he hates the Cardinal and will help anyone who can get rid of him! And we can approach Spain through the Ambassador at Brussels; he's a great friend of Marie's.'

'Most ingenious,' Orleans remarked. 'And I think the King's bastard half-brothers, the Duc de Vendome and the Grand Prior, would gladly join us. They feel our friend Richelieu has a mind to dispossess them of their frontier fortresses; I've told them so myself, on my dear mother's information. She's no idea how useful her confidences are, and Louis has never got out of the habit of telling her things.'

'It can be done,' Anne said. 'It must be done. I'll write to Spain this evening; I can smuggle the letter through to Marie. The rest is in your hands; but who's to do it this time?'

Orleans smiled. 'De Chalais. Who in the world would ever expect him to try again?'

* * *

Father Joseph was staying at the Capuchin Monastery outside Paris, when a plainly dressed cavalier called to see him. In the bare cell, with only the plank bed to sit on, Richelieu and his confidant held their secret meeting.

'You were right to do what you did,' the monk said. 'God guided you. I've heard rumours everywhere that the attempt on you was only the beginning. And more rumours, that the conspirators are laughing at you for your clemency.'

'I know,' the Cardinal said grimly. 'They think because I didn't ask de Chalais' life that they're safe to plot again. And that's the plot we must discover!'

Father Joseph bent his head; the Cardinal, looking more pale and strained than usual, was sitting on the bare boards of the bed.

After a moment he looked up and said, 'I think we'll find the key to it in Brussels; where Mme de Chevreuse is. A priest in her household writes that she is a constant visitor to the Spanish Ambassador and since he's neither handsome nor immoral, only politics would motivate their friendship.'

'Brussels . . .' Richelieu frowned. 'But how are we to know? We have no agents in the Spanish household.'

'Then we must plant one,' Father Joseph declared.

'I know just the man,' Richelieu exclaimed suddenly.

'A priest?'

'No, a layman, but I suggest he becomes a priest for a little while. A Capuchin, to be exact. You can train him in the ways of the Order and send him to Brussels in a few days. The Ambassador is pious; he'll never turn away one of the Order, and I can promise that the young man will win his confidence.'

'Who is he?'

'The Count de Rochefort, a member of the house of Rohan, but devoted to me and completely loyal.'

'Send him to me, and in less than three days he'll be on the road to Brussels.'

The monk on duty at the monastery gate opened the heavy door for the unknown gentleman a few moments later, and watched idly through the grille until his carriage passed out of sight down the dusty road. So little ever happened in the lives of the brotherhood that even a casual stranger's coming was an event.

* * *

The Marquis de Lainez had become so attached to the young Capuchin who'd called on him one day at the Spanish Embassy that he was genuinely distressed when the friar came to see him for the last time.

The Marquis had ordered supper for him, which the monk ate sparingly, refusing more than a sip of wine and water. It was the last of many friendly meetings, and de Lainez pushed back his plate with a sigh.

'I shall miss your company, Father.'

'I shall miss yours; do you know what it means to be a Frenchman who dreads returning to France?'

'If you're sure you want to go into a monastery in Spain,' the Marquis said seriously, 'I know I can arrange it for you.'

'No man can practise the religious life properly in France any more,' the monk said bitterly. 'The Cardinal has even corrupted the Capuchins. Oh, the freedom of Brussels, the happiness of being in your house . . . able to speak without fear. In France his spies are everywhere.'

De Lainez had heard the same complaint from many exiles, but there were few as bitter in their denunciation of Richelieu as this young friar.

After a moment the Marquis said slowly, 'You leave for Forges tomorrow then?'

'I do, and most unwillingly, God pardon me.'

De Lainez leant towards him across the table.

'Then perhaps you would do me a favour?'

'With all my heart!'

'I have some letters for friends in France,' the Marquis said; he hesitated and then went on. 'Will you take them for me?'

'Of course,' the friar said simply.

De Lainez rose and left the room; the man in the monk's habit heard the soft closing of a desk drawer; within a few minutes the Spaniard came back, holding a sealed packet in his hand.

'These are the letters, Father. They're very . . . personal. I know I can trust you to take good care of them.'

'The best care in the world,' the friar said gently. 'Where must I deliver them?'

'Someone will meet you at Forges. He will show you a letter from me, and you just give him the packet. That's all.'

It was quite dark when the monk left the house, after an affectionate farewell from his friend the Marquis, and the promise to come back to Brussels as soon as he could and then take ship for the sanctuary of Spain. Half way between Brussels and Forges, the monk met the courier of Cardinal Richelieu, and the letters of the Marquis de Lainez were opened in a little house on the roadside.

4

The Duchess de Chevreuse was back in Paris, and back in her old quarters at the Louvre. She was as gay and brilliant as ever, laughing about her recent exile, amusing everyone with stories of the English Court and the social life of Brussels. And under the disapproving eye of Madame de Senlis, she resumed her old intimacy with the Queen.

There was a relaxed and carefree air in the whole Court in the first weeks of the summer of 1626; even the Queen's existence was freer than before; the Duchess and the Duc d'Orleans spent hours with her, and no order came to forbid them. The Cardinal, watched over by the guards everyone thought so ridiculous in their special uniforms, seemed absorbed in his work, and avoided the public receptions. The King spent most of the time hunting; Marie de Medici assured the parents of Mlle de Montpensier that her son Orleans would agree to the wedding before the end of the year, and the Comte de Chalais resumed his relations with Marie de Chevreuse.

The Court began its summer progress; by the beginning of August the King and the Royal family were at Nantes.

Anne was sitting in the gardens sewing one sunny

morning; there was an air of calm about her lately that disturbed Madame de Senlis, who had seen her pride vent itself in fits of furious weeping only a little while before. Now she passed her time sewing, reading or enjoying the company of her brother-in-law and Marie de Chevreuse. Madame de Senlis, who knew her well, was very worried by this display of patience.

Anne sewed beautifully, frowning a little as she bent over her work; it was part of an altar cloth for her private Chapel at the Louvre. She had begun work on it many years before, when she first came to France. She looked up at the sound of someone running down the flagged path from the house; she saw it was the Duchess de Chevreuse, and the hands holding her needlework lowered slowly into her lap.

The Duchess stopped before her; she looked quickly round at the faces of Anne's women, all upturned in surprise. It didn't matter what they heard, she thought wildly, nothing mattered now.

'The King's half-brothers Vendome and the Prior have been arrested,' she burst out. Every drop of colour drained out of Anne's face. 'And they've arrested de Chalais!'

The Queen said nothing; she sat absolutely still. She saw that the resolute, reckless woman in front of her was trembling. She stood up, stiffly, the altar cloth falling under her feet.

'Where is the Duc d'Orleans?' was all she said.

'Shut up in his rooms, with the Capuchin Father Joseph,' Marie whispered.

Anne caught at the other woman's arm and held it.

'Then he is lost; and so are we.'

*   *   *

97

'I know your Royal Highness has been misled by others,' Father Joseph said gently; 'but the difficulty will be to convince the King.'

The heir to the throne of France stopped pacing up and down his bedroom and swung round to face the monk, standing before him, his hands folded humbly in his habit sleeves. Gaston's face was as white as his linen. The quiet interrogation had been going on remorselessly for almost two hours. The news of the other conspirators' arrest had paralysed Orleans, delivered in that calm voice by the man who was fast becoming almost as dreaded as the Cardinal himself. Chalais, Vendome and the Grand Prior. Everything must be known, Gaston said to himself, inwardly hysterical with fear, everything. The plot to murder Richelieu, that was nothing, but his proposed marriage with Anne . . . the 'abdication or death of the most august person in the realm . . .' The fatal words shrieked in his mind. They were in a letter, he knew someone had written them, but which letter and to whom; in the moments of his first panic he couldn't even remember.

'I'm innocent,' he stuttered; he'd said that over and over again, his mind writhing in the search for some means of saving himself.

Father Joseph nodded. 'I know you are, so does His Eminence. As I've been telling you, we're both convinced that this plot, this treason, has really been the work of others; that they hoped to use your Royal Highness.'

'That's true,' Gaston's voice rose in desperation. 'Before God, Father . . .'

'That's why the Cardinal sent me to you,' the monk went on. 'If you will only remember what was said to you, and by whom; if you confess everything freely before it's tortured out of these wretches, it will prove your good faith to the King.'

'My half-brothers . . . de Chalais . . . they'll be tortured?' The bastard sons of the great Henri IV, nobles of the Blood Royal, and de Chalais, scion of one of the first families in France, tortured like common criminals. Gaston could not believe that even Richelieu would dare such a thing. A look into Father Joseph's cold blue eyes assured him.

'They're not the only ones involved,' the monk reminded him. 'We have every name; we know every conspirator, great and small. And they are being arrested while we speak.'

'Oh, God!' Gaston stumbled to a chair and collapsed into it; after a moment he wiped his sweating face with his handkerchief. All the conspirators, great and small. Most of his gentlemen were involved; Anne, Marie de Chevreuse, and another bastard brother of the King, the Count de Soissons who wanted to marry the wealthy Mlle. de Montpensier himself . . . he was a new conspirator. Did they know about him too? Hope shot up in his heart; probably not, or he too would have been arrested with Vendome and his brother the Prior. Perhaps they didn't know about Soissons. If he told them that, if he gave that Cardinal-fiend another victim, as important as the others, he might help himself.

'My half-brother de Soissons . . . he talked treasonably to me,' he burst out. 'He said he wished the Cardinal dead! And the King.' His voice trailed off, trembling, and his frightened eyes blinked up at his inquisitor.

'And who else?' queried Father Joseph.

'I couldn't help it,' Gaston quavered. 'They came to me. . . . I'm the heir, what could I do? I never thought they meant it seriously.'

'Who else?' asked the monk's gentle voice.

By the time he left Orleans' apartments, Gaston had betrayed them all.

* * *

'You will have to pardon your brother,' Richelieu said. He sat with the King in the privacy of Louis' study; the house he occupied at Nantes was a large mansion overlooking the river, and the King's desk was drawn close to the window, so that he could enjoy the view even while working. The Cardinal had just placed a complete list of all the persons implicated in the conspiracy on the desk in front of Louis. The list was made out in Father Joseph's beautiful scholarly script.

He thought at first that the King hadn't heard him, till he suddenly looked up.

'They've all betrayed me,' he said slowly. 'All of them. I would never have believed it.' He stood up clumsily, his shoulders sagging, his face turned towards the windows and the sunny vista of river and garden. When he looked round once more the Cardinal saw he had been weeping.

'My mother came to me today, pleading with tears for Gaston,' he said dully.

'She's right, Sire,' Richelieu answered. 'The Duc is only eighteen; it's a foolish age. You've got to pardon him.'

'She loves him,' Louis muttered. 'But she never

loved me. I used to think she did, but it wasn't so. When I was a child she used to have me flogged for the least thing. . . . Now she comes whimpering for mercy for him. And she listens while they discuss who shall marry my wife when I'm dead.'

'The Queen Mother is only a woman, Sire,' the Cardinal argued. 'And women always listen; if she favoured your brother in her heart, that isn't treason.'

'She shouldn't have shown her favour,' Louis cried out suddenly; the grievances and repressions of his wretched childhood surged over him in a tide of pain and resentment. The sorrows of the boy burst out in the grown man at that moment; he turned towards Richelieu, shaking with emotion.

'Look at this,' he shouted, pointing at the indictment. 'Look at the names . . . my half-brothers, my wife, my courtiers! Merciful Jesus, who is there left for me to trust?'

The answer came quietly, accompanied by that level stare; Richelieu had risen; he picked up Gaston's confession and folded it.

'You can trust me, Sire. To the death.'

'I know that,' the King said. 'No wonder they wanted to murder you! Without you, they could have done what they liked. Oh, my friend, I know how much I owe you for this; for taking care of your King while others slept.'

The shock was wearing off; Richelieu recognised the signs of anger in the narrowed eyes, still red from the tears he had shed, and the sad, ugly mouth was pinched and cruel. 'What is to be done with the rest? I'll pardon my brother. I've no choice since he's my heir.'

'Imprison your half-brothers, Vendome, the Prior

and M. de Soissons, for life,' Richelieu said. He unfolded the list again and looked down it.

'Most of the Duc d'Orleans' suite is mentioned here,' he said. 'Take the six most influential noblemen and imprison them too. But I suggest that you execute the Comte de Chalais.'

The King looked at him; there was an expression of cunning in his eyes when he spoke.

'Chalais shall die. He and all the others shall be tried by a special Commission. And the same Commission shall try the Queen on the same charges.'

'And will you execute her too?' the Cardinal asked softly.

'She plotted my death,' Louis said savagely. 'And yours. She discussed re-marriage with my brother; her name is mentioned in those letters from Brussels.' He shook his head and smiled slyly at his Minister. 'No, my friend, you cannot save her this time.'

Richelieu laid Gaston's confession back on the King's desk. Twice Anne had condemned him to assassination; he thought of that pale beautiful face, and the implacability of her hatred; of the long duel already fought with the King to protect her. Fool, he said to himself bitterly. Fool to go on . . . The picture of the Place de Grève rose in his mind before he could stop it; the high-built scaffold draped with black, the ring of guards at the foot keeping back the pressing multitude of the common people, and from the windows of every building overlooking the square, the great nobles and their ladies craning forward, as blood-thirsty as the brutal populace; all of them waiting to see a Queen die.

When he turned to face the cruel, expectant gaze of the King he was quite calm.

'How long is it since a Queen of France has died on the scaffold for treason, Sire?'

Louis frowned; the question was unexpected.

'I don't know; what difference does that make?'

Richelieu shrugged slightly. 'Only that the charge and the trial will arouse a lot of interest. And you will have to convince all Europe, as well as Spain, that the sister of the King of Spain was guilty of something more than an intrigue against the life of a mere Minister, and a few words of indiscreet speculation about her future if you died.'

'But she's guilty! She was party to the whole conspiracy . . .' Louis insisted. 'You know it!'

'No, Sire,' the Cardinal answered firmly. 'I wouldn't plead for her if I thought she were. Would you have people say you were taking your revenge for Buckingham?'

Louis' face darkened with anger. 'They would not dare!'

'They would, Sire. The whole world would say that Louis the Just had condemned his wife because she had fallen in love with the Englishman.'

He turned his back on the King after that, leaving a long and uneasy silence between them. Louis hated Anne; he wanted her dead and up till that moment he had believed it possible to gratify his wish. The few words spoken so reasonably hummed in his brain. There was no proof. Do this, they said gently, and you will stand convicted of unmanly spite, you will prove to the world and to me that you are as weak and ignoble as you fear you are.

'Whatever you say, she shan't go unpunished,' Louis muttered. 'The Commission shall question her with the others.'

'I admire your wisdom, Sire,' Richelieu said. 'I shall inform them of the charges with which de Chalais and the rest are to be tried. Is that your wish?'

'It is,' Louis said. He turned back from the window, frowning and fingering the strings of his collar nervously.

Richelieu bowed in submission.

'May I withdraw,' he asked.

The King nodded. 'Once more, you have my gratitude, and my friendship, Armand,' he said awkwardly. The Cardinal bowed very low over his hand and kissed it. When he straightened up, the King was smiling.

'My friend. Go then.'

*　　*　　*

On 20 August Gaston Duc d'Orleans was married to the pale, plain little heiress to the Montpensier millions in a hurried ceremony in the Queen Mother's apartments, conducted by the Cardinal himself.

The King, Marie de Medici and the disgraced Queen Anne were seated under a canopy in a room half filled with courtiers, and as Richelieu's eloquent voice pronounced the blessing, the clocks all over the apartments began chiming midnight.

Gaston stood motionless, his eyes stubbornly refusing to meet those of his enemy who had protracted the ordeal by a gentle and lengthy sermon on the duties of the married state and the duties of Princes in general. Though Gaston's fear was ebbing away, he was still shaken; too shaken to do more than act churlishly towards the shy, stoop-shouldered girl at his side who had just added the Crown Matrimonial of France to her vast expectations. The marriage was the price of his forgiveness by Louis, and he had tried to make amends for his wholesale betrayals by asking that Chalais' life should be spared. A vague promise was conveyed to him by Father Joseph, while the date of execution was immediately set for three days after the wedding.

It was a nightmare, Orleans thought hazily; the news of the sentences imposed on the others had brought him to the verge of hysterics with fright, until the monk assured him over and over again that he was not going to suffer with them. Then this damnable marriage. Out of the corner of his eye he looked sourly at his bride: she was dark and pale and very small and her spine *did* curve, whatever anyone said.

He thought of his brief glimpse of Anne, white as her own satin gown, sitting on a low chair well away from the King under the canopy, and he reddened. She must know what he'd done. She must despise him for giving way to the threats of that fiendish Capuchin, and my God he was a fiend, he'd frightened him out of his mind – and now for standing before their greatest enemy and breaking his word to her by marrying Marie de Montpensier after all. Gaston hadn't dared to look up at her as they passed the dais, but he could guess at the identity of the devil who had suggested her presence there and the loan of her famous pearls to the bride.

Anne had been in bed and asleep when the summons came. She was woken by Madame de Fargis, pale and trembling in the light of the candle in her hand, and told that the King commanded her presence in his apartments immediately. For a moment Anne had thought she was going to be arrested, and weeping bitterly, she had refused to go. Then Madame de Senlis appeared. Her Majesty had nothing to fear, she announced. She was to be a witness at a wedding, that was all. And so Anne found herself seated beside her husband, Marie de Medici on one side, watching Gaston betray his promise to her and marry his little hunchbacked heiress after all. And there in the circle of light from an improvised altar, Richelieu waited for them. He avoided her, except for making her a formal bow, and mercifully didn't speak. But at a signal from him, Louis addressed his first and last words to her that night. She was to lend her pearls to Mademoiselle de Montpensier. De Senlis hurried away to get them, and Anne, her eyes suffused with tears, hung them round the bride's neck. She wouldn't look at Gaston, because she dreaded bursting into tears and rounding on him as a traitor and a coward. The old Queen watched the brief ceremony in gloomy silence torn between relief that her darling son had extricated himself from the plot, and anguish because he was marrying against his will and seemed unhappy. The officiating priest pronounced them married, but Anne scarcely heard him; she closed her ears to the voice of Richelieu, giving a sermon on the joys and duties of holy matrimony.

In spite of all the anxiety and this final humiliation, she was still safe. The King's half-brothers, nobles so powerful that they had been above the law, were languishing in Vincennes prison; de Chalais was under sentence of death, Marie de Chevreuse was punished, but she and Orleans alone had escaped unscathed. And not because she had defended herself well in front of the Commission. Anne had lost her head and wept, denying everything. The lords and lawyers appointed to try her, had bullied and abused in their attempts to incriminate everyone connected with her. She left the room weeping hysterically, to see her dearest friend Marie de Chevreuse waiting between an escort of two soldiers to stand her trial. They were not allowed to speak; bravely, the Duchess blew her mistress a kiss. The sight of Anne's distress strengthened Marie's vigorous courage. She defended herself brilliantly and boldly answered the angry questions of the King himself. She left the room under sentence of imprisonment in one of her husband's country fortresses.

But bullied, humiliated and disgraced, Anne yet remained Queen of France. And she knew that she owed her safety to the Cardinal.

Without looking at her, Gaston lifted the new Duchess d'Orleans' hand and kissed it formally; the ceremony was over.

'May God's blessing attend your union,' Richelieu said kindly; the words were directly addressed to the bride who stood hesitating, waiting for a smile or a gesture from her husband. The eyes of Orleans and the Cardinal met at last for a second; the Cardinal's were empty as if he were looking into space.

Orleans gave his wife his arm and together they turned to the dais to receive the blessing of the Royal family.

At last the Duchess d'Orleans knelt before Anne. She was very young and very near to tears. She kissed the Queen's hand and flushed, as Anne wished her happiness. By the time they left to be conducted to their bedroom the tears had overflowed and were running down her face. The only person who spoke kindly to her was the terrible old Queen Mother because a weeping bride would be sure to disappoint her darling son.

When they were alone with the bed curtains drawn round them, they lay side by side in silence.

Gaston wept a little himself from self-pity and useless rage. The plot had failed; he was no nearer being King and he was married to this silly little snivelling virgin, and his beautiful sister-in-law despised him. . . . Nearly all his gentlemen were in prison or exiled; several had fled. From now on, life would be dull in the extreme until he assembled an entourage as amusing as the last and that would take some time. And he was certain they meant to execute de Chalais, and de Chalais had been the gayest companion of them all. Suddenly an idea came to him. If he arranged to have the executioner abducted they couldn't carry out the sentence! Immediately he brightened. It was a brilliant idea, enough to restore his damaged reputation with Anne. That was vitally important; de Chalais didn't really matter so much, but if he managed to save him, people might forget that his own conduct had been less than brave. He smiled in the darkness; it would be amusing to arrange it and exhilarating to balk the Cardinal even for a few days. He became aware of a movement beside him and remembered his wife. The duties of Princes, he thought cynically. . . . Well, why not? . . . He turned towards her.

*   *   *

On 26 August the Comte de Chalais mounted the scaffold at Nantes; he was calm and almost jaunty. He retracted everything forced from him under duress in prison, admitting only the original plot against Richelieu which he had confessed at Fleury. There was a reason for his confidence in the face of death; word had reached him that Orleans and his friends had had the public executioner kidnapped.

De Chalais returned to his prison unpunished, while the crowds dispersed muttering their disappointment. The King was being besieged with petitions to pardon him. That afternoon Orleans played cards in his apartments and exercised his wit at the Cardinal's expense with all his old gaiety; people crowded in to congratulate him.

But at six o'clock that evening de Chalais was taken from prison for the second time. Two common criminals under sentence of death had undertaken to execute him, in return for Richelieu's promise of their own lives. Those who watched reported a scene of appalling butchery; in unskilled hands the axe struck de Chalais' body thirty-five times before it finally cut off his head.

The head of the man who had planned to kill Richelieu was exhibited on the City's North Gate, until the birds had picked it clean.

*   *   *

It was winter, and since Gaston's wedding, Anne had been as effectively banished as if she were in the Bastille.

The few friends who remained in her service had been dismissed, some even imprisoned, and replaced by spies and adherents of the Cardinal. Richelieu had saved her life, but he achieved it by condemning her to a twilight existence which was to last for ten years. In

the mornings she heard Mass in her private chapel, the
same chapel where she had read Buckingham's love
letters and burned them in the candle flames; then
she sewed, sitting by the window with either Madame
de Senlis, or a new and hated protégé of Richelieu's,
Madame de Fargis, in attendance. There was little
conversation; everything she said was reported to
the Cardinal. She played or sang to pass the time,
though she had little liking and less talent for music;
dined alone in the late afternoon, and then, if neither
her husband nor the Cardinal objected, she drove
out for an hour or so. The evenings were spent in
desultory talk between her women, in which Anne
seldom joined, or in reading aloud. Often the sound
of music drifted up from the great Hall of the Louvre,
where the King was holding a reception or a Ball, and
for a moment the Queen would look up, listening,
remembering the lights, the colour and movement
and gaiety which were forbidden to her, remembering
the times when Buckingham in all his splendour, had
crossed the floor to lead her out. The spies among
her women reported to their master that the Queen
often leant back and closed her eyes quickly because
they were full of tears. The most gentle and attentive
member of Anne's household was the Cardinal's latest
nominee, Madame de Fargis, the wife of the late
Ambassador to Madrid. Madelaine de Fargis was
not a pretty woman; she was marked by small-pox,
but she could, and did, boast of nearly as many lovers
as Marie de Chevreuse. She was witty and gay and as
good natured as she was immoral; she was friendly
to the Cardinal, who appointed her to take the exiled
Duchess de Chevreuse's place in Anne's household.

It was one of the paradoxes in Anne's life that she

fascinated women more strongly than men, and that the women who loved and served her so unselfishly were her opposites in temperament and morals. Her beauty aroused no jealousy, instead the sophisticated hearts of Marie de Chevreuse, Madelaine de Fargis and many others were touched by her distress and they were spurred on to help her at considerable risk to themselves.

One evening the Queen sat in her favourite position by the window, watching the sun sinking behind the roofs of the Louvre, staining the sky a gorgeous red. She sat very still, thinking with the cold desperation of helplessness that her final humiliation was the pregnancy of Gaston's wife. Even the plain, delicate little Duchess d'Orleans could bear a child in less than a year of marriage, while she, the Queen, remained barren and forgotten, the victim of Louis' aversion to the grosser side of matrimony. She shivered, remembering the miserable, distasteful episodes before he retired from her bed altogether, and her own dreams, shameful and persistent, of the young Armand de Richelieu, Bishop of Luçon, who was her almoner. She had often dreamt of him, obscene in his red Cardinal's robes, and cried out in her sleep in a phantasy surrender. Thank God, Buckingham had driven the man and what he symbolised out of her mind, and taught her frustrated senses the agony of conscious desire, and she had let Buckingham go without the proof of the love she had declared for him. Of all her life's regrets, that was the bitterest, that futile denial. Fear had prevented her, fear of discovery and death, but above all the fear of losing her position as Queen and the hope that one day the husband she loathed would die. . . . She looked out into the fading sunset colours, thinking then of Gaston. His schemes and his confidence and then the shivering betrayal of the people he had implicated. And his white face on the night of his marriage, imploring her forgiveness and understanding as he led his bride away. In spite of herself she gave it then; he and she had escaped with their lives at least while their friends went to imprisonment, exile and death; he was young and weak, as she recognised to her cost, and what chance had he against Richelieu and Father Joseph. She thought of that gaunt, gentle-voiced familiar of the Cardinal's with burning hatred; the monk turned spy and power diplomat, aiding and intriguing with that fiend who had ordered de Chalais to be hacked to death. With horror, she thought of those grey eyes as they looked at her across the long table where the Commission sat to try her, and the swift interruptions when some question came that she couldn't answer. And always the eyes, with a terrible message of encouragement in them so that she knew she was protected, and knew too that one day she would have to pay the price.

He wanted her, not humbly, from a distance, but with a desire that was the twin of hatred, and her own treacherous body leapt in response while her heart quivered with loathing of him and herself. She forced her mind away from him. Gaston . . . Gaston looking happy in the last months, braving the King to come and speak to her whenever he dared, but not too dissatisfied with his wife and eager for the child; already she was fading out of his sight. Buckingham.

Buckingham loved her still, more madly than when he left France. There were rumours that he had tried to return, that the quarrels between King Charles and Henrietta Maria were of his making, so that he could come back to Paris, ostensibly to negotiate, but in fact to resume his pursuit of Anne of Austria. Buckingham loved her. And she loved him, she insisted; she had never really forgotten him, even when planning to marry Gaston. But for weeks she had not dared to write to him, or allow her ex-lackey La Porte to smuggle in his letters to her. Everything she did and said was watched and her letters were supervised, except those addressed to her brother the King of Spain.

Her brother couldn't help her; he had protested at Louis' treatment but so long as Anne remained apparently free and unharmed, there was nothing he could do, except declare war on her behalf. And Spain was not ready for war yet; she was not ready to do anything more than finance plots for Richelieu's murder and build up a coalition with the Huguenots which she hoped would result in another civil war.

Thanks to the marital troubles of Charles and Henrietta Maria, the alliance between France and England which had alarmed Spain so much, now appeared likely to dissolve in war, unless a compromise could be reached. The devoutly Catholic Queen was resisting her husband's efforts to expel her priests and separate her from her French ladies, while Charles, normally mild and indulgent, succumbed to the influence of Buckingham, and would scarcely speak to his wife.

'Madame.'

Anne swung round, startled by a murmur at her elbow. To her annoyance she saw that the speaker was Madelaine de Fargis.

'If you must disturb me,' she said sharply, 'I must ask you not to creep up on me like a spy, Madame. I should prefer to hear you coming!'

Madelaine curtsied. 'I apologise most humbly. But as there was nobody in the room for once, I hoped I might have a chance to speak to your Majesty.'

In spite of the rebuke her brown eyes were friendly, and oddly beseeching. Anne had been puzzled by that expression for some time.

'What have you to say to me? Some message from the Cardinal?' she asked.

'No, Madame. I have a message from Madame de Chevreuse.' Immediately Anne froze with suspicion.

'The Duchess is a house prisoner; I am not allowed to communicate with her.'

'The Duchess has escaped to Lorraine,' Madame de Fargis announced. She laughed a little. 'She's been giving her husband the very devil, and everyone else as well. Now she's taken refuge in Lorraine and nobody can get her to come back.'

Marie, Marie was free . . .

'Why do you tell me this?'

Madelaine sank down on her knees before Anne, her plain, little face alight with feeling.

'Because I know how much this news must mean to you. Oh, Madame, Madame, I know I entered your service through the Cardinal, I know you must hate me for it, but I beg you to forgive me! I'm devoted to you.'

'You were sent here to spy on me,' Anne said quietly. 'How do I know that this is not a trick to bring worse suffering on me?'

Madame de Fargis shook her head. 'You don't,' she said. 'You have no proof but my word. But take it, Madame, please. I wanted to be a lady-in-waiting to you because of the honour – now I've served you and seen what you have to bear. Dearest Madame,

114

let me comfort you, let me help you!'

Anne turned away from her; the room was nearly dark and no one had bothered to come and light the candles.

'You know what my friendship has brought to others,' she said at last. 'Will you risk death, like de Chalais, you know how he died, don't you? You know what happened to some of the greatest nobles in France, because they tried to serve me instead of the Cardinal?'

'I don't care,' Madelaine said. 'If Marie de Chevreuse can serve you, so can I.'

'But how,' Anne questioned. Instinctively she knew the woman kneeling in front of her could be trusted, that Richelieu had made one of his rare and terrible mistakes when he placed her in Anne's household.

'By keeping you in touch with your friends,' came the answer. 'No one will ever suspect me.'

The Queen stood up suddenly and began walking up and down, clasping and unclasping her hands. It was almost a performance, but it bound the other woman to her with the strongest of all feminine ties: compassion.

'I'm friendless,' she whispered. 'You've seen how I live, insulted and restricted like a criminal! The King hates me and do you know why, de Fargis? Because he hates all women! I'm despised for being barren, while the Duchess of Orleans shows herself to the whole Court.' She turned, and Madelaine saw her hand move to wipe the tears away from her face. The gay, light-living woman, whose whole life had been irresponsible and tainted, even in those tolerant days, listened to the wretched outpourings of the virtuous Queen and nearly wept herself at being admitted to her confidence. The more Anne humbled herself, the more powerful her influence became. Marie de Chevreuse was living in exile in Lorraine at that moment because she had succumbed to similar scenes.

Madelaine came to her quickly, she took Anne's hand and pressed it to her lips. 'Don't, Madame, don't,' she begged.

'It's dark,' Anne said helplessly. 'No one has come to light the candles.' In a moment the lady-in-waiting ran to the door. A dozing lackey jumped as she banged it open.

'Tapers,' she ordered. 'Her Majesty wants light! At once, do you hear. Forget again, and I'll have the skin off your back!'

Within a few moments the room was filled with light, the curtains drawn; Anne sat down and gave her hand to Madelaine de Fargis.

'I trust you,' she said simply. A phrase was running through her brain, repeating itself over and over again, while she watched the servants obeying Madelaine's orders with an alacrity they no longer gave to hers. 'Tell her that if any danger threatens her, she has only to send me one word, and every soldier, ship and sword in England will be sent to her defence . . .'

The time had come to send that word, and to launch the men and ships of that promise against her husband and his Minister.

'I'll do anything for you, Madame,' her new friend said eagerly.

Anne looked down at her and smiled slowly.

'If I give you a letter, will you send it?'

5

England and France were at war. It had taken some months and the combined intrigues of the Duchess de Chevreuse from her refuge in Lorraine, where she made the reigning Duke her lover, the Duke de Rohan and his brother M. de Soubise, and Buckingham at his most determined to achieve it. They had all worked with tireless energy to bring their two countries into conflict, and the motives of all were at variance.

Marie de Chevreuse, Rohan and his brothers were concerned with destroying Richelieu by a war which Louis would lose, and by protecting the power of French Protestantism which the Cardinal was attacking. They pleaded with the King of England to protect his co-religionists, and because he was a deeply religious man, Charles took a sympathetic view. Marie de Chevreuse had made many friends during her stay as lady-in-waiting to the new Queen of England. She wrote to them all, including her old lover, Lord Holland, urging them to wage war on the sinister combination of Richelieu and Louis XIII. M. de Soubise left the threatened stronghold of La Rochelle and travelled to the English Court to beg for English ships and troops. The most powerful advocate of war was the Duke of Buckingham. He kept the letters Anne wrote to him in a silk bag tied round his neck; he boasted that they lay night and day over his heart. She had sent him the message that she looked on the future with despair; her tears left blots on the writing paper. Friendless, almost a prisoner, she had risked all to call his old promise to mind. He had said he would come to her with every man and ship in England. The time had come when such a course was her one hope. From that moment Buckingham had made up his mind to force his King into a war with France. He argued with great skill, prodding Charles' sensitive conscience about the plight of the good Protestants at La Rochelle, making the seizure of a few English coastal ships by France appear that England's dignity had been deliberately insulted. He joined his voice to the pleas of de Soubise, and the poisonous letters streaming into the Court from Marie de Chevreuse. His passion for Anne had become a mad obsession which had to be paraded. He took particular delight in informing every Frenchman who came to Court that he worshipped the Queen of France, and was leading the expedition to relieve La Rochelle on her behalf. War was declared and early in July 1627 England sent a fleet of fifty men-o'-war, and sixty smaller ships to the relief of La Rochelle. They transported an army of seven thousand men, guns, horses and supplies.

A Royal army of twenty-five thousand men were encamped before the seaport city of La Rochelle, and the King himself was quartered there. His commanders were the Duc d'Angouleme and the Marshals Schomberg and Bassompierre, but it was Richelieu who directed the siege, and took the rank of a lieutenant-general. He laid aside his Cardinal's robes, and dressed in officer's uniform, rode out among the troops and supervised the naval actions. He had created a Navy for just this purpose; to batter and storm the great bastion of French independence of the Crown. Father Joseph was with him, and they made their quarters in a small stone-built house called La Pont de la Pierre within a few yards of the beach. Richelieu liked to be near the sea; the brisk air agreed with him and the monotonous sea sounds helped him concentrate.

He had left nothing undone before the campaign started. He had barracks built for the army, they were given regular rations and pay. Consequently there was little sickness and few desertions, those twin hazards of any long campaign. And he encouraged Father Joseph to proclaim the war as a religious crusade, and loose his Capuchin friars among the troops, preaching and praying. It seemed to Richelieu that God had less and less to do in the affairs of men; he had never been naturally devout. The atmosphere of an armed camp suited him much better than the serenity of the cloister. He did not conceal his grow-ing agnosticism from the Capuchin; there were no secrets between them; they worked together in ab-solute trust.

They were together at the Pont de la Pierre when Richelieu received the news that Buckingham's fleet had sailed.

'I suppose it was inevitable,' the monk said. 'But it's a pity. Without help from England we'd reduce the Rochellais in three months.'

'It wasn't inevitable and I don't agree that it's a pity,' Richelieu said. 'Some wine, Father? It's an excellent Canary, I can recommend it.'

There were no servants to wait on them. Richelieu had read the day's despatches, given them to Father Joseph to read, and sent everyone away. The policy of France was made in the plain little room of the house by the sea, by the Cardinal who was losing his faith in all but the powers of this world, and the fanatic who now refused the indulgence of a glass of wine, for fear of weakening the powers of the spirit.

'I don't understand you, Armand. Why do you say it wasn't inevitable and isn't a pity?'

Richelieu took a long draught of the wine; he was tired. The King had exhausted him that day, insisting on laying the siege guns himself as if the war were a game of soldiers played in the Louvre. His fits of melancholy were taxing enough; his enthusiasm and enjoyment of the battle were an even greater strain. He closed his eyes, then opened them a little and squinted at the wine in the bowl of his cup.

'First it wasn't inevitable. All the pleadings of that traitor Soubise and the letters of that unspeakable woman Chevreuse wouldn't have moved King Charles to fight Henrietta Maria's country. No, no, the real author of this war is one man. Buckingham! Buckingham pulls the strings and King Charles moves like a marionette. He has spoiled their marriage with his vicious advice to the King and his petty cruelties to the Queen. And now he drags his King into a war of private vengeance. And vanity, of course. That fleet is sailing for one reason only. We wouldn't let him come back here and try to seduce the Queen of France! That's the only reason for it all. One man's insane conceit. As for it being a pity . . .' he drained the glass and put it down. 'We'll win, Father, and England will retreat from this enterprise poorer than before with considerable loss of prestige in the world. She'll be glad to conclude an alliance with us at a later date.'

'With Buckingham still at the King's elbow?' the monk asked him.

'Ah,' Richelieu said, 'now that's another matter. One has to think about this. Perhaps an opportunity may arise in the battle . . .' He left the sentence unfinished.

'You hope he'll be killed here?' Father Joseph said. 'A pious hope, my friend, if you'll excuse the word pious, in your present state of mind. How many leaders of expeditions ever get within sight of the enemy's guns? I can't think of many generals killed in battle. Buckingham will sail back to England, even if he leaves nine-tenths of his men floating in the sea.'

'I don't think it should be left to chance,' Richelieu remarked. 'Or the fortunes of war. I think we should make sure Buckingham does more in the service of his King than run up debts and cause trouble.' He paused and smiled. 'I think he should die for him. And I intend to see that he does exactly that.'

'This will be the second time you've shed blood. First de Chalais, now the Duke of Buckingham. At least the first was a just execution; this will be a murder. I can't absolve you for it.'

'I haven't yet confessed,' the Cardinal said coldly. 'Political assassination is not murder. He must be removed. To start with, my dear Father, you know that the King won't be reconciled to Queen Anne so long as he has cause for jealousy. And there won't be an heir to the throne but Gaston d'Orleans – God help us!'

'Then why do you keep this jealousy alive in the King's mind?' the monk countered. 'You've poisoned the King against his wife; you continue to do so. You insinuate things which you know are not true, so that he shuns her and keeps her a prisoner in the Louvre. Are you still pursuing your own private vengeance?'

'No,' Richelieu said. 'If I were pursuing my vengeance, she would be in the Bastille by now. Who do you think encouraged Buckingham to sail against us? Who has been writing him letters complaining that her life is a misery and only my downfall will deliver her – and what better way to get rid of me than lead an army against France and beat the King to his knees? No, I'm not pursuing any vengeance, I assure you. In fact she's the greatest traitor of them all.'

'You mean the Queen has been writing to Buckingham intriguing against France! Conniving with our enemies? How do you know this? How can you be sure?'

'I have spies everywhere,' Richelieu said. 'Madame de Fargis has betrayed me; she now works for the Queen's interests while she pretends to be serving mine. Letters have been getting through to Chevreuse, and to England. I arrested Lord Montagu when he was passing through Paris earlier this year. I suspected he was carrying some of these letters, before war was declared.'

'And what did you find?' the monk asked him.

'Mentions of the Queen and her correspondence with England. Enough, I assure you, to make the King insane with anger if I had let him see them. They were destroyed, of course, and Lord Montagu went on his way. A wiser man, I trust, after his experience in the Bastille. I must admit he was very brave. Very arrogant. The Queen will be better off without Milord Buckingham too. She may come to her senses and see where her destiny lies.'

'It won't lie with you,' Father Joseph said. 'Whatever you do, do it in full knowledge of yourself. You're a brave man, Armand, and I believe you are a great one. Everything you've done has been for the glory of the Faith and the unity of France; murder Buckingham if you must, but don't be tempted into it from jealousy of his relations with the Queen. If she isn't for him, she's never for you, this side of eternal damnation.'

'She hates me,' Richelieu said. 'I grow weary hearing how she mocks and insults me. So long as the King keeps her so strictly, I don't have to bear the hatred in her eyes when we come face to face. I don't understand it, my friend. What have I done to make her my enemy? Hasn't she sense enough to know that all I ever wanted was to be her friend, to help her?'

'Perhaps that is why she hates you,' the monk answered. 'Perhaps she fears herself as much as she fears you. She has used the foolish Buckingham for her own ends to get him to invade France. I don't believe she loves him. You and the King are alike in this folly. You're both jealous of nothing.'

'I believe she loved Buckingham and still does,' Richelieu said. It caused him such pain to admit it that he grimaced a little. 'But that's not why he must be assassinated. He stands between friendship with England, and we need that friendship. Buckingham's removal will be political, I promise you that. Whether I shall derive a little personal satisfaction from it, well, that must wait until I kneel before you in confession. Then you shall judge whether to absolve me or not.'

'How will this be arranged?' Father Joseph pulled his grey hood up to cover his head; the aquiline face looked out from under its shadow; it was gaunt from fasting and hours spent in meditation at the cost of sleep. Unlike Richelieu, he never tired.

'I don't know yet,' Richelieu said. He poured another glass of wine; he was abstemious in eating and drinking but the wine relaxed him and eased the tension headaches which tormented him at the end of a gruelling day. 'I have someone in mind. A distant cousin of mine, de Saint Surin. He's ambitious. And clever. He could be the person to arrange something. No wine, Father?'

'No wine, my friend. I recommend sleep instead. I'll leave you now. Since you won't pray and refresh your spirit, at least rest your mind. I'll come tomorrow.'

'Goodnight, Father,' Richelieu said. 'Pray for me, as I can't pray for myself. And never leave me; you're my only friend.'

'You have my friendship,' the monk said. 'But you must learn to accept loneliness; it's the price of being great in this world. Goodnight, your Eminence.'

*　　*　　*

'The news is bad, Madame,' Madelaine de Fargis had taken the place of Marie de Chevreuse in the Queen's oratory; now the two women exchanged secrets while they pretended to pray, and Anne received and read her letters from Buckingham and the Spanish Ambassador and the long effusions from the exiled Duchess. Anne turned her head, and let her clasped hands drop. De Fargis glanced behind her and said, 'We're alone, Madame; we can talk.'

'How bad is it?' Anne asked her. 'What's happened? I've had no word for weeks and I've been dying of anxiety. Has the Duke reached La Rochelle?'

'Yes, and he's given battle; the English besieged the Isle de Ré, but they couldn't reduce it!'

'That demon had it fortified,' the Queen almost spat the words out. 'He's prepared for this campaign for months before it started! What else, de Fargis, what other news?'

'The Cardinal's having a mole and fortification built to close the harbour; that means La Rochelle will be completely cut off from help by sea. I even heard a rumour that Buckingham was going back to England! I'm sorry, Madame, I did warn you it was bad.'

'He can't.' Anne got up and swung round; in her agitation she had forgotten the danger of a spy like Madame de Senlis walking into the oratory and finding her talking instead of making her devotions.

'He can't go back – he can't be so heartless! He knows what this campaign means to me. If he abandons me now, I'm condemned forever to this life of misery. I must write to him – de Fargis, you must get a letter out for me!'

For the first time her friend hesitated. She too was standing and she took the Queen's hand. It was cold and trembling.

'Remember Lord Montagu,' she said. 'Remember how we knelt in this very place and shivered, both of us, because of what we feared had been found on him?'

'I remember,' Anne said. 'It was a nightmare – don't remind me.'

'I must,' de Fargis insisted. 'You can't write a word to Buckingham now. We are at war with England;

if a single line from you was found while he is at La Rochelle – my God, Madame, I think the King would have our heads! No, my dcarest Madame, I love you too much to help you risk it. There's nothing to be done but wait. He won't abandon you; he came when you called for help. The man's besotted with love, he'll do all he can to win.'

'I hope so,' Anne said. She sank down on her knees again. 'I'm shut up here as if I were a prisoner. I won't endure it, de Fargis. Whatever I have to do, I'll do, but I won't submit to this treatment.'

'It's the Cardinal who requires submission,' the older woman said. 'It's he and he alone who can unlock the doors for you; his hand has turned the key, not the King's. I know something about his feelings. I was recruited by him to spy on you, and all the time he talked about protecting you from bad influences and guiding you because you were inexperienced and His Majesty was irritable and sus- picious, I could see he was beside himself with passion for you! He was as jealous of Buckingham as the King could ever be! I've known a great many men, Madame, and I promise you, I saw through him. The wretch is in love with you himself.'

'You're not to say that,' Anne said angrily. 'It's disgusting. He's a priest – it's sacrilege! And when I think of him – the impudence, the insult of it! Ah, de Fargis, I'd rather die than say a friendly word to him. And I shall let him know it. I have the power to hurt him, and if you're right, and he harbours some degrading feeling for me, then I shall make him writhe – I did before, when he came sneaking in after Louis made him First Minister, and dared to offer me his services. He left me crushed and humbled, and

126

from that moment he declared war. Very well. War it shall be – to the very end.'

'He must know that,' de Fargis said. 'You tried to have him murdered. He's hardly likely to forget.'

'I'd do it again,' Anne said; tears were falling as she spoke. They brought the generous-hearted Madelaine de Fargis to her side, anxious to comfort. She couldn't resist Anne's dependence upon her. The hauteur and hostility which made Madame de Senlis' post such an uncomfortable one because the Queen disliked her, was completely at variance with the warmth, graciousness and friendship she showed her friends. De Fargis was as captive to her charm as the exiled Duchess de Chevreuse. The Duke of Buckingham, engaging the impregnable fortresses on the Isles erected by the foresight of the Cardinal, was another helpless victim.

'If it's going to be war, then you need allies,' the lady-in-waiting said. 'Believe me, Madame, the Cardinal can't be fought alone. There's only one person strong enough to do battle with him, and that is the Queen Mother. And through her M. d'Orleans.'

'We saw the worth of Gaston last time,' Anne reminded her. 'He betrayed everyone to save himself. He can't be trusted. He talked of marrying me and making himself King, and now look at him! Married to that miserable hunchback for less than ten months, and now agitating to marry someone else! So much for his devotion to me.'

The little Duchess d'Orleans had given birth to a daughter the previous year, and died afterwards as unobtrusively as she had lived. She had been happy for the short time she was married; she spoilt her handsome husband and deferred to him in everything, so that he was quite agreeable to her. It was more than she had ever known from a man. Gaston hadn't pretended to mourn; he shed a few tears and consigned his infant daughter to the care of his mother, who lodged the baby at the Tuilleries where she was brought up by a certain Madame de St Georges. The widower had soon found himself madly in love with the pretty young Princess Marie de Gonzague Nevers, who was a débutante at the French Court. He had abandoned Anne as callously as he had betrayed de Chalais and his half-brothers.

'He's only devoted to himself,' Madame de Fargis said. 'But the Queen Mother holds him in the palm of her hand. So she does the King, only he has that cursed priest to turn to – you should make friends with Marie de Medici, Madame. Appeal to her, confide in her. She'll receive you because she's coming to hate Richelieu more and more. I'm sure of that. The signs are showing.'

'She abandoned me too,' Anne said bitterly. 'She brought Richelieu to Court in the first place. She made him what he is!'

'Precisely,' her friend said. 'And that's what she resents. She made him to be her creature; now he's gone over to the King. Ally with her, Madame. You may combine and bring the enemy down yet.'

'How can I?' Anne asked. 'She never sends for me, or comes to see me. I'm not allowed to go to the Luxembourg!'

'Leave it to me,' de Fargis said. 'I can go where you can't, and say what you mustn't. I'll drop a word in certain ears, and we shall see what Her Majesty makes of them. Come, Madame, we ought to go back now, or someone will get suspicious. Have courage – your lover is at La Rochelle, and you'll soon have the Queen Mother as an ally. Let us go back and listen to Madame de Hautfort's new verses. I swear they're excruciatingly dull, just like the last!'

'Dear Madelaine,' Anne turned to her impulsively, and kissed her cheek. 'How good you are. At least I'm lucky in my friends.' The plain little face blushed pink with pleasure; de Fargis had earned her bad reputation because she was witty and vivacious and men never found her dull. She very seldom cried, which her lovers also appreciated, but her eyes filled with tears after the Queen embraced her.

'We all love you, Madame,' she said shakily. 'We'd die for you, if need be.' A moment later the two women left the oratory. As the result of the idea Madelaine had put into her mistress's head, many were to die indeed, and hundreds were to disappear into keeps and dungeons all over the country. Others, and they included the greatest names in France, were to live out their lives in poverty and exile.

*   *   *

'Just because one is at war, there's no reason not to conduct ourselves like gentlemen. Sit down, Monsieur de Saint Surin. You'll do me the honour of dining with me?'

M. de Saint Surin swept the Duke of Buckingham a deep bow.

'The honour is mine, Milord Duc. I was encouraged to come and pay my respects by the number of French gentlemen on the side of King Louis who have done so, and been welcomed. It's surely the only way for gentlemen to wage war, as you say.'

Buckingham's flagship was anchored outside the harbour of La Rochelle, having withdrawn his fleet from the unsuccessful battles against the Isle de Ré and Fort St Martin, both of which held out for King and Cardinal with fanatical courage. The fortifications were superb and their stocks of ammunition were high. Richelieu enjoyed reminding the professional soldiers in the King's service that men fight better with full stomachs, enough gunpowder and cannon balls, and a stout wall between them and the enemy. Buckingham had gained nothing but casualties, and he had withdrawn from the fight to regroup and gain time to repair damage to his ships. He had also let it be known that he was ready to receive calls from gentlemen on both the Huguenot and Royalist sides and welcome them as guests aboard.

With this assurance, M. de Saint Surin had begun to carry out Richelieu's instructions. He had taken in every detail of the Duke's appearance; his cousin liked everything, relevant or otherwise, to be mentioned in his reports. Buckingham was dressed as if he were at Court in London. His suit was made of silver brocade and pale blue satin; he wore large pearls in his ears, and his long hair was curled and scented. De Saint Surin noticed that he also displayed a miniature of the Queen of France which was set into a bracelet and circled by large diamonds. This alone had made him stare, but when he accepted the Duke's invitation to dine and was led to his quarters on the poop deck, he could scarcely believe his eyes. The room was hung with silk; its furniture was magnificent, and the plate was solid gold. But at the far end, lit by gold candelabra and shrouded on either side by curtains of cloth of gold, there hung a life-size portrait of Anne of Austria.

As they came in, he saw Buckingham glance towards the picture, and instinctively touch the miniature on his wrist. In spite of his splendid clothes and jewels, he thought the Englishman looked pale and ill.

He sat down, and the Duke's personal servant came in with a dish of sweetmeats and Spanish wine. Buckingham paced up and down, seeming unable to sit or relax. Suddenly he turned to his guest.

'This miserable war is quite unnecessary, you know! It could end as far as England is concerned within twenty-four hours!'

'But Milord Buckingham, surely it needs a decisive victory for one side or the other – at least a willingness to mediate. Speaking for His Majesty King Louis, and the Cardinal Minister, they are bent on destroying La Rochelle. Nothing will move them from it.'

'The devil can take La Rochelle as far as I'm concerned, and every damned Huguenot in it,' the Duke burst out impatiently. 'Do you know why I'm here, Monsieur? Do you know the real reason? That is why!'

He pointed dramatically at the portrait. 'All I ask is the happiness of seeing the original again, just for a few moments. All I want is to visit Paris and kneel in her divine presence, warm myself in her beauty and grace.' He raised a hand, his eyes wild with emotion. 'Understand well, Monsieur de Saint Surin – I only beg to worship at her feet, to speak one word to her. Is that so impossible? Is that so great a price to pay for peace with England?'

'Why, I can't see that it is,' the Frenchman said. He had listened to the outburst with growing amazement;

the Duke spoke and looked like a madman. Only a madman wouldn't have seen the incongruity of any King agreeing to such a proposal regarding his own wife.

'Again and again I've tried to come to France,' Buckingham went on. 'Every time the King refused me. And do you know why? Because that beggarly priest has filled his ears with lies! Wait, have you been to Paris lately – have you seen the Queen?'

'Alas no,' the Frenchman admitted. 'I was in Paris two months ago. But the King has forbidden gentlemen to have an audience of the Queen. So I didn't see her, but I heard she was well and in good spirits.'

'Thank God,' the Duke said. 'Do you know, Monsieur de Saint Surin, before we give battle I kneel there, before her portrait, and I pray! You have your Virgin – I have Queen Anne.'

Richelieu's cousin wiped his lips with a lace handkerchief; it was an involuntary gesture of distaste which the Duke was too excited to see. 'I have a suggestion to make,' Buckingham said suddenly. 'Perhaps those in authority – the Cardinal even, don't realise how simple it would be to have my fleet turn about and sail for home! Perhaps my visit to Paris might be more acceptable now, with my guns battering their forts and my supply ships succouring the Rochellais – eh, Monsieur, what do you think of that?'

'It's possible, of course,' Saint Surin admitted.

'Then I charge you to give my message to Richelieu himself. Tell him that if I am chosen to negotiate the peace terms in Paris, the war with England will be over. Can you reach him? Will he listen to you?'

'Oh, yes,' the Frenchman smiled at him. 'I am

on close terms with him. I know he'll listen to any message I convey from you, Milord.'

'Then do it for me,' Buckingham commanded. 'As soon as we have dined, take my own barge to shore and speed at once to Richelieu!'

'Nothing,' his guest said gravely, 'will give me more pleasure.'

The dinner was laid for them and the Duke exerted himself to amuse and charm his guest; the food was palatable, though not to Saint Surin's taste, and he noticed with surprise that Buckingham drank ale, while he himself was served with the finest wines. Saint Surin was a man of fastidious manners and acute judgment; the man was visibly disintegrating. And the cause was looking down at them with painted eyes, the likeness showing a proud and beautiful woman without the frightening potency of the living subject's charm. She had destroyed this man, and in cold blood Richelieu's spy admitted to feeling sorry for him. The obsession had unhinged him. He was capable of any folly, any indignity in pursuit of his lamentable passion. Truly the great Cardinal was right. He must be removed. He was no longer sane.

Buckingham came out to see his guest disembark, and as they left the cabin, a man stepped out of the shadow where he had been waiting. The Frenchman bumped into him and moved back in alarm.

'Your pardon, sir,' the man said in English. 'My Lord! Your Grace! I beg a moment from you!'

Saint Surin understood English, and spoke it adequately. The man's broad regional accent made him difficult to understand. Buckingham scowled at the man; his face flushed a dull red with irritation at being intruded upon, and he made a contemptuous gesture. 'The devil take you, fellow! What do you mean by skulking round my cabin? Who are you?'

The man was young and he wore plain dark clothes with simple bands at the neck. He was a seaman, but his face was curiously white, as if he'd never seen the sun. 'I'm Felton, your Grace. I've waited here three days for a word with you – for pity's sake, sir, hear me out!'

Suddenly the Duke lost his temper; it was a common occurrence in the last few months. He cursed and shouted at whoever was near him at the time. His entourage were used to it.

'Go to hell fire, you impudent scut! Out of my way or I'll have you in irons!'

He took Saint Surin's arm and led him away. 'My apologies, Monsieur, the fellow's a Puritan by the looks of him. Pestilential scum they are, my ships are full of them! Come, you must be on your way before the tide runs.'

At the ship's rail, the Frenchman turned and looked behind them. The seaman who had tried to speak to Buckingham was still there, watching them. Never had Saint Surin seen such livid hate on the face of a man as he saw that afternoon. He had waited three days to be heard, and been turned away with insults and abuse. A Puritan, the Duke had said. He remembered the name as he sat in the barge on his way back to shore. Felton. He could be contacted, this young man with the pale face and the unanswered grievance, whatever it was. It was the merest chance, the slightest glint of intuition, but it was for this talent above all, his cousin Cardinal Richelieu had selected him. He ignored his promise to Buckingham and stayed within easy reach of the English fleet for the next five days. On the fourth day, his spies were able to tell him where this Mr Felton could be found when he came ashore.

*　　*　　*

'What do you want with me, sir?'

Saint Surin had paid the landlord of one of the few coastal inns for the use of his parlour that night; they were not to be disturbed, and the inn had been shuttered and locked against all other customers.

He faced Felton across a low scrubbed wooden table, the old wine stains making a pattern of blotches on it, and a stale strong smell of vine and garlic and coarse tobacco smoke permeated the whole place.

'Sit down, please,' the Frenchman said. He sat on the bench opposite the English officer, for such he now knew him to be. Buckingham's rebuke might have been addressed to the lowest ruffian on board his ship. The man was a lieutenant in the Navy.

'I repeat, sir – what do you want with me? Why am I invited to this place?' Felton looked round the empty parlour with suspicion.

'I asked you to meet me here,' Saint Surin spoke slowly in his stilted English, 'because I have a great desire to apologise to you.'

'For what? You've done me no wrong!'

'In France, it is considered wrong for one man to witness the humiliation of another. I saw you shamefully abused the other day. I desire to say I'm sorry and I have much sympathy for you. I would like you to count me your friend.'

'Thank you,' Felton said. There was a slight colour in his sallow face; he moved restlessly on his seat, unable to sit still or be at ease. 'You're a kindly man, to care for others so.' He leant forward suddenly. 'You saw that it was shameful, didn't you? You heard him tell me to go to the devil! What man of God curses his fellow man like that? What follower of the Truth dresses like a lackey of Beelzebub, drinks strong drink, swears vile oaths? Eh, sir – I promise you I'd done no wrong. I'd no greedy claim to make, nor no complaint. I wanted my due, that's all. Three days I'd waited, outside that cabin, and he sent me away like a dog. With you as witness to it!'

He bent forward across the table, his arms folded, his head bent. His eyes were wide and glaring at something. Saint Surin had never felt more ill-at-ease in his life.

'What was your plea?' he said.

The lowered head came up, and the fanatic stare met his.

'My captain was killed in our last engagement against St Martin,' he said. 'I wanted his command. I wanted to be promoted. It's my due.'

'Of course. Of course it is,' the Frenchman said. 'Does the Duke know what you wanted?'

'How could he, when he won't let me speak?' Felton demanded savagely. 'He's not just, that's the truth of it.'

'His heart is not in this war, my poor friend. You and the brave English out there on board the fleet, are fighting a religious war, are you not? Against the tyranny of Rome?'

'Aye,' Felton cried out. 'We're fighting anti-Christ in his red robes of Satan, with all the wickedness of Babylon throughout this land! We're shedding our blood to save our brothers of the Protestant religion – although, sir, they've still not seen the Truth as it really is! You're not of the Puritan persuasion, are you, you Huguenots?'

Saint Surin was able to follow enough of this outburst to answer it sensibly. He was a born, if not a particularly devout Catholic with a fastidious dislike of the gloom and dreariness of Mr Felton's version of the supreme Truth.

'We're simple Protestants,' he said. 'Fighting for our lives and our faiths. We do not want their heathen Mass, you see, and this is what they wish to force on us with bloodshed and terror. This Cardinal is the devil himself, they say!'

'I've heard of no Cardinal,' Felton muttered. 'I know only that these people worship at the feet of Baal. They must be wiped away, as God destroyed the idolaters of old. Not one must live to outrage God!'

'They will all live, if the Duke of Buckingham spoke truth to me,' the Frenchman said. 'He has no care for religion, Monsieur Felton. He cares nothing for you or his men or his country at home. He is an idolater himself!'

'What!' Felton demanded. 'He worships idols? Is he a spawn of Rome? Tell me, I beg of you!'

'He has a portrait of a woman in his cabin,' Saint Surin spoke slowly and carefully; the other was so excited that he could scarcely keep his seat. 'He told me he prayed before it. He also told me that he didn't care a curse for the good people in La Rochelle, and he'd make peace tomorrow. That is what he'll tell your King, when you return to England. He is a traitor to us all.' He gave a deep sigh, and the next moment Felton seized his arm. It was almost more than he could do not to recoil, but he let himself be grasped and both hands clutched in a tight grip, which he realised after a second or so, was a sign of the lunatic lieutenant's friendship. For lunatic he certainly was. What Saint Surin understood of his babblings confirmed the impression of the hollow-cheeked fanatic face which now leant so close to his own.

'No traitor lives,' Felton muttered. His lips were wet with saliva. 'No idolater profanes this world unpunished. So the Good Book says, and the Lord Our God speaks only truth. Will you be seeing him again, sir? Will you have a sight of him alone?'

'No,' the Frenchman shook his head. 'He dismissed me with the very words I've told to you. He cares nothing for religion or the people suffering in La Rochelle. He won't receive me a second time. He told me so.'

'Then you can't do it,' Felton said. He sank back, releasing Saint Surin, much to his relief. He seemed to sag physically in sudden gloom. 'You can't kill the monster. He must go on living, doing Satan's work.'

'I can't get near him,' the other said softly. 'But maybe you can. One day, my dear friend Monsieur Felton, he'll have to see you and hear your plea to be promoted.'

'Yes,' Felton said. 'Yes, he must. That command belongs to me. It's my right,' he repeated angrily. 'No one shall have that ship but me.'

'Then you must be patient and persistent also; you must bear his insults and though you are driven away, you must return. He will grow tired of abusing you. You will get in to see him, and that will be your opportunity. Are you a brave man, Monsieur Felton?'

'I think so.' For a moment the crazy shadows lifted, and the young man looked calmly across at Saint Surin. He answered simply and modestly.

'I've never run from danger, that's for sure.'

'That I believe. I believe that God has indeed chosen an instrument brave and – *fort* – I don't know the English word at this moment. But it means more than strong. It's a thing of the spirit. You have this, my friend. You have the courage to kill the Duke of Buckingham and stop him doing any more evil in this world. I believe, as you sit before me at this moment, that God has marked you for this deed.'

'Am I His instrument?' Felton said slowly. 'Am I to do the work of His hand?'

'You are,' Saint Surin said. 'You, Monsieur Felton, are the Englishman who will save England. By one blow.'

'It shall be delivered then. I will strike it. He is a great persecutor of our Puritan teachers,' Felton said quietly. 'All manner of evil is told against him. But I had heard nothing of idolatry, not till you told it me.'

'I spoke the truth,' Saint Surin said. 'You will rid the world of a very wicked man, my friend. You will be one of the deliverers of your people. I beg of you, don't let your courage falter or your heart go soft.'

Felton stood up. The sweat shone on his forehead and two trickles ran down his temples onto his cheeks. His eyes were wide and staring, their pupils dilated into tiny specks. He put his hand into his coat, and Saint Surin saw the glitter of a long thin knife blade in the smoky candlelight. 'I shall strike to the heart, sir. Be comforted.' He walked to the door and then turned. 'Be comforted, and have faith. Watch and pray, sir. God will open the way for me. And I will kill His enemy.'

The next moment he had gone through the door into the darkness. Saint Surin took a deep breath, and on an impulse made the sign of the Cross. 'Patron!' he called out, 'bring me some wine – hurry! And have my horse brought round to the door.'

Ten minutes later he was riding hard on the road to the Royal army and the Cardinal's house at La Pont de la Pierre.

6

'It is so good of you to receive me, Madame.' Anne
knelt in a deep curtsy before her mother-in-law.

The old Queen held out her hand for Anne to kiss
and smiled on her. There was a core of human kindness in the fierce Florentine; she had never needed to
fight Anne because the girl Queen had never been a
rival for her power. She had been what she still was
as a woman in her twenties. A dependant, a suppliant.
The Queen Mother had formed all her friendships
with people who came seeking something from her.
The most fatal of these had been the man who now
undermined her authority and was in open control of
the King's mind. Richelieu. The very name made her
gather spittle and expectorate like a fishwife. But at
least he was at La Rochelle, directing the battle, while
her dismal son stayed with him playing soldiers and
making a nuisance of himself to the generals. That
was Marie's opinion of the King's participation in the
war. It was due to her frustration at not having him in
Paris where she could bully him, while the Cardinal
stayed at the siege. Like the serpent in the fable,
Richelieu had insinuated himself into Louis' councils
and confidences, and he knew only too well how unreliable his position really was. A long period alone

with his mother and his brother Gaston and all their malcontent friends, and the wretched King would have abandoned his Minister as the price of his own peace of mind. Richelieu made the war so attractive that Louis spent most of the year at La Rochelle.

When he did return to Paris for short visits, the Cardinal was on his heels. Marie smiled warmly at her daughter-in-law, and pointed to the window seat. They were in the Luxembourg Palace and she had given Anne an audience because her darling Gaston begged it. The poor creature was dying of boredom in the Louvre surrounded by Richelieu's spies, believing herself abandoned by everyone. She longed to come and see her mother-in-law and be satisfied that she was not forgotten by her too. Marie couldn't refuse her favourite son, whatever he asked. Besides she was also bored, and the months had dragged on since the scandal and de Chalais' death, until it was nearly two years, and surely time Anne was forgiven.

'You look pale, my daughter,' she said. 'Too much time spent brooding. You should be near La Rochelle, where Louis can visit you.'

'I asked,' Anne said. 'But His Majesty refused me. If I'm pale, Madame, it's from weeping, and from loneliness. Am I never to be reinstated?'

'My son's a weakling, and weaklings are usually vindictive when they know they're safe. He's punished you for lighting a gleam in Buckingham's eye. So – then he thinks you've done the same with Gaston and behold, he's like a madman with jealousy! Pity he pays you no mind himself! I've told him so, over and over. But of course he doesn't listen to me now. There's another voice murmuring day and night into his ear!'

'I know,' Anne said. They faced each other, sitting in the window seat, with the view of the Luxembourg gardens behind them.

'That voice whispers on and on, poisoning his mind against me. Suggesting new suspicions, thinking out new tyrannies to break my spirit. But it won't be broken, Madame. Not so long as I have your friendship and affection to sustain me!' Anne turned her head away and wiped the tears which had come up at her bidding. The old Queen patted her arm; she was too emotional herself not to be moved, even though it was only superficially.

'I'm your friend, my dear daughter. Gaston and I are both in sympathy with you. I feel you've been shamefully treated, and I agree with you about who's really to be blamed. That viper's at the back of all your trouble with my son!'

'Can't you plead for me?' Anne murmured. 'The King loves you so deeply; he owes everything to you, Madame, all the years you ruled the country while he was a boy, your selfless devotion to his interests – he must listen to you, if you intercede for me?'

The Queen Mother frowned; a deep line scored between her brows and ran down each side of her mouth, furrowing the plump cheeks.

'He owes me everything,' she said. 'But he's forgotten it. He sent me away once, when he let them kill my poor Concini. Oh, he was only a boy then, but he agreed to it all. He's never been grateful to me, Anne, only envious, because I've statecraft and he's a fool. Now he doesn't listen to me any more. And you know why? Because your viper is the same as mine; he's sunk his poisoned fangs into us both!' She got up, pushing Anne back into her seat as she tried to follow protocol and rise with her. 'They planned to attack La Rochelle without a word to me till it was about to be declared! Imagine that! Imagine the insolence, the affront to me, his mother! And then he sent for me, that wretched son of mine, and sat there hangdog while the villain of a Cardinal explained it all – oh, so smoothly, so humbly, and asked my blessing on the enterprise! I wasn't even told, till they were ready. By God, daughter, I'm growing tired of that man. You ask me to intercede for you with Louis?' She swung round to face Anne; her thick hands dragged at her ropes of priceless pearls, twisting them round and round in her agitation. Her face was red with anger, and as was her habit, she turned quickly aside and spat.

'He wouldn't listen to me, because of that devil. If Richelieu's against you, then you'll go on suffering. I advise you to throw yourself at his feet the next time he comes to Paris, and beg *him* to forgive you for Buckingham and Gaston! I swear it'll be more effective than any argument of mine.'

'Many people have said that to me,' Anne answered. 'I'd sooner die than do it. I hate and despise that creature; he's an upstart who should be destroyed.'

'Those are strong words,' the old Queen said. 'Take care they're not repeated to him.'

'He's heard them plain enough,' Anne retorted. 'I've never hesitated to say what I thought of him and express my loathing for the man. You made him; you elevated him and trusted him, and now he changes sides and casts you off, to suit himself. Madame, you shouldn't submit to it. We, as Queens of France, should join together and remove this creature. Alone, I'm helpless. But with you, we might constitute a danger that the Cardinal couldn't overcome.'

'Ah,' Marie said. 'Ah yes; the mother and the wife. It's strong enough to daunt my son – given the opportunity! Without the Cardinal to support him. My God, daughter, we must combine, you and I. I've right on my side to press reconciliation for you. A mother's wish to see a happy marriage and an heir for France. Not that you'll get one, my child. I know where Louis' fancy lies and it's not with you or any woman. De Luynes knew that, the cunning pimp. But never mind, never mind. Appearance is the thing. I shall make a stand on it; insist that you're released from these restrictions.'

'And then I can be useful,' Anne said eagerly. 'I can see the Spanish Ambassador, enlist my brother's influence in Spain, assist you in a thousand ways to bring that scoundrel down into the gutter. Oh, Madame, you've always been kind to me since I came to France! Help me now, and we may both be happy!'

'I will, I will,' Marie de Medici promised. 'And remember this, my daughter. It's not as if he'll live for ever; we talked of this before. My son's a weakling in body too, as well as character. One day, one very happy day, France may have another, better King. And he'll be free to marry.' She patted Anne's cheek, and nodded, enjoying her own thoughts. 'That is the day to hope for; the ultimate solution to our difficulties. But until then, let's bend our energies against our friend the Cardinal. Let's occupy ourselves with him!'

'From this moment,' Anne said solemnly. 'We are one, Madame. Let him beware of us.'

*　　*　　*

For the first time in three years Louis sent word to his wife that he was going to visit her. The Marquis de Saint Villere, who was a gentleman-in-waiting, appeared at the Queen's ante-chamber and solemnly informed Madame de Fargis that His Majesty would honour them in an hour's time. Madelaine ran to the Queen with the news, and immediately Madame de Senlis and her other ladies began to suggest what their mistress should wear, and what the King might be offered to eat, as excited as a flock of birds over a handful of corn.

Anne, with de Fargis beside her, held up one hand and stopped the tumult. 'You are too noisy, Mesdames,' she said coldly. 'You make my head ache. It is now four o'clock; I have dined, I have changed my costume for the evening, and there seems little point in changing it again. His Majesty dislikes fuss; he also detests eating between meals. Be good enough to calm yourselves. There's no cause for this excitement.'

After three years he was coming. Her first impulse was to go to her bedroom, say she was ill, and bolt the door in his face.

'His Majesty is very fond of marzipan, and he enjoys Madeira wine,' Madame de Senlis said boldly. Her glance held the Queen's for some seconds before she felt it wiser to look away. The first visit from the King in three years, and this was no cause for excitement. She determined to write those exact words in her report to Cardinal Richelieu. The Queen refused to yield an inch, either to make herself more attractive to her husband, or even to show that he was welcome by the extra courtesies of the sweetmeats and the wine. Even Madelaine felt that Anne was being unnecessarily rash in showing her resentment so openly.

'Show him you've taken some trouble, Madame,' she whispered. 'For God's sake, this could be very important to you – and that wretch de Senlis is going to repeat every word to our friend!'

'Very well,' Anne said under her breath. 'Order whatever His Majesty fancies,' she said to Madame de Senlis. 'And I suggest you change your own gown; that green is very drab.' She turned away and went into her salon, followed by de Fargis; there the two women settled by the window where the light was clear, and embroidered while they waited.

'What does he want?' Anne said. 'Why in Heaven's name does he decide to come here at this hour and make a public show of it? Madelaine, I'm frightened! It's not because he wants a reconciliation, that I'm sure of – it must be because he's got something unpleasant to say!'

'Hush,' the lady-in-waiting said. 'It's nothing like that. It's your friendship with his mother – that's the cause of it. That and the fact he's left Richelieu at La Rochelle for a few days and come to Paris alone. Be nice to him, Madame, be gracious! I know how you feel, and how much you have to forgive, but he's the *King*! Don't drive him away, I beg you.'

'I'll do my best,' Anne said. 'But it won't be easy for me, Madelaine. You'll stay with me? Close to me?' She depended on Madame de Fargis as completely as she had once done on Marie de Chevreuse; that forbidden friendship still flourished by means of letters; Anne knew that Buckingham's fleet had returned to England after three months spent uselessly battering at Richelieu's forts round La Rochelle, because the Duchess wrote to her. She had last heard that he was returning with a second expedition.

'Have courage, Madame,' de Fargis said. 'I'll be close by you. Wait! I think he's coming now!'

When Louis came into the room there were four gentlemen with him; he walked slowly towards his wife, who had risen from the window seat, and after a hesitation which he couldn't help but notice, Anne moved to meet him. All her ladies were with her, and as he entered they sank to the ground in deep curtsies. He had almost turned back before Anne's apartments, he hadn't wanted to come near her, and yet some motive which was too complicated to understand, drove him to do the thing he most disliked. His mother had been reproaching him for hours on end, with virulent abuse of his past actions, and the purpose of this pitiless tirade was to reconcile him outwardly with his wife. He had refused at first, and been surprised at his own courage in doing so, and withstanding the furious emotional storm which broke over his head as a result. He had been away from Marie de Medici for a long time and he found himself able to oppose her. But that was in the beginning. His confessor had joined the chorus, led by the strident maternal voice, urging him to show kindness to a wife he hated and who he knew hated him. And had dared to make him look a fool with Buckingham and then his own brother. He had almost refused them all, when he remembered that, but the effort was too much for him. He felt depression advancing on him like a black, blanketing cloud, and there was no Richelieu there to rescue him, make him feel strong and in the right. He had given way, morose and grudging, and come to see Anne. And he had the upper hand, which gave him confidence. He had just heard a piece of very gratifying news, and gone to share it with his mother, who was also very pleased to hear it. And on the strength of this, she had prevailed upon him to see his wife and promised him that he would find her penitent, anxious to please him and visibly declining because of his disfavour. He had secretly hoped she was right. It would have made him very happy to see his wife chastened and downcast; it would have satisfied his thirst for vengeance against her, and even allowed him to be clement if he felt inclined. And as his mother kept repeating, his life was lonely and without affection; if she were really changed, and showed a little warmth, a little understanding – he might see her more often, lift the restrictions on her life.

He had come to her with all these motives inextricably mixed up, and as a result he stammered so badly when he first spoke that he was forced to stop and pause. She knelt before him in a deep curtsy, her glowing red head was bent and he could see the white nape of her neck and the glittering clasp of her necklace. These were said to be erotic points in women, the nape of the neck, the small of the back where the spine hollowed out, places which roused men and were secret, more stimulating than the exposed breasts which were the fashion. He felt a sense of distaste when he looked down at her. The sexual side of marriage had filled him with self-disgust and a sense of failure which increased his shyness and inversion. He had to be positive with a woman; the initiative lay with him, the action itself could only be performed by him, and he had never plumbed the depth of his own nature and inadequacies, until he tried to make love to the woman kneeling in front of him. He gave her his hand and she raised it to her lips. But she did not kiss it.

'I bid you welcome, Sire,' Anne said. He lifted her to her feet, as protocol decreed a King must do with his Queen after she has made her obeisance, and then he let her hand drop and stood awkwardly.

'I hope you're well, Madame,' he said at last. His eyes roved everywhere, without once resting on her face.

'Very well, Sire,' she answered. 'And happy to see you here. After so long an absence.' He did look at her then; though the words were warm, the tone of voice was cool and noncommittal.

She had changed very little; his mother had prepared him for a pale and dispirited prisoner, whose nights were spent sleepless and her days in tears and crushing ennui. Instead he saw his wife had never looked more beautiful, or less of a suppliant. She bloomed with health and her brilliant blue eyes were as cold as ice when she looked at him.

'Won't you sit down with us, Sire? We would be honoured.'

It was so stiff and formal, so perfectly correct, that he felt as if he were a stranger being given audience. Her women were all staring at him, and his dour face darkened with an embarrassed flush. He made a gesture and Anne swept in front of him to the place where two chairs were set, with a table and lackeys to serve wine and comfits.

His gentlemen followed at a distance, and when the King sat down, Anne spread her skirts wide and took the place beside him. The members of their household were then free to mingle and talk at a distance. Only Madame de Fargis stayed nearby as she had promised the Queen. And she prayed silently that some spark of sense would make Anne smile at him, or instil a little gaiety into the halting, stilted conversation.

He refused the wine, and Anne did the same. He nibbled at the marzipan, and said nothing for minutes on end.

'Have you been hunting?' Anne enquired. She could feel Madelaine willing her to make an effort, and with a bad grace she decided to try. Hunting was his favourite sport. If the weather was too bad to hunt outside, flocks of birds were released in the great Hall and the King shot them indoors.

'Yes, I went out yesterday and had a fair run. And again this morning. But I miss Richelieu; he's good company at the chase.'

She felt herself stiffen as if he had suddenly slapped her face. She was too hostile to realise that the remark was not deliberate. He often said exactly what he was thinking at the time, and he had just thought how much he missed the Cardinal.

'It's a strange sport for a Churchman,' Anne said coldly. 'Almost as strange as waging war.'

The King considered her for a moment without answering. Anger began to stir in him. 'He's an expert at both,' he said. 'Our enemies are almost beaten to their knees. The Cardinal closed the harbour and nothing can get in or out of La Rochelle. The siege will soon be over. And he has done much to gain the victory. I've played some part myself. You may have heard of it.'

He was so proud of his excursions into the field that a word of flattery or interest might have altered the whole course of their interview. Had she praised him, he would have forgotten that she had criticised the Cardinal. He would have told Richelieu what she said afterwards because he took a delight in repeating insults to his friend. It irked and humbled the Minister on whom he depended, and Louis often encouraged jokes and sneers among his entourage which were at the Cardinal's expense. But his wife was an exception. He wanted nothing controversial or independent from her. Anne answered his last remark, and Madelaine de Fargis winced as the first words came out.

'I've heard nothing of your doings, Sire. How could I, when I'm kept incommunicado from the outside world? Have you performed great feats of daring at the battle? I must congratulate you!'

'I have done nothing, Madame,' Louis said slowly, 'but prosecute a war against my subjects who refuse their lawful obedience to me. I won't tolerate rebellion; it's no matter to me where it comes from, high or low. I will be obeyed.' There was such a dull dislike in his eyes that Anne blushed.

'It's easier to rule by kindness, Sire. There are some spirits that can never be broken this side of the grave.'

'How odd,' he twisted his mouth into a smile. There was no humour in it. 'You quote the Cardinal, Madame. Almost his exact words. And for these people, the grave is the place where they shall find themselves.'

'Is that why,' she said suddenly, 'I am condemned to a living one, because you fear my brother the King of Spain too much to kill me?'

At this point de Fargis began to move away out of hearing. The King's voice was low; Anne spoke so that only he could hear her.

'You reproach me?' he said. 'You are Queen of France, you live in state in my Palace. You are forbidden to meddle in politics or to expose yourself to undesirables. That's all I have imposed on you, and it's a light punishment for your betrayal of me with Gaston. We'll not mention the Englishman. We'll not mention any of that.'

'I was innocent,' Anne said fiercely. 'I did nothing against your honour with the Duke. I did nothing against it with your brother Gaston. I deny it all!'

'You discussed my death,' Louis said flatly. 'That was treason. Only Richelieu saved you.' Again the mirthless smile appeared. 'He is afraid of your brother and Spain. He shields you constantly because he doesn't want a conflict with your country. I have no such fear. Remember that.' He got up and Anne sprang out of the chair as if she couldn't wait to see him go.

'I came to exchange a few civil words with you,' he said.

'I received you, hoping to hear them,' Anne retorted. 'We have both been disappointed. I beg your pardon, Sire. You haven't been amused.'

'No,' he said slowly. 'I have not. Nor encouraged to return. I bid you good day, Madame.'

Again she curtsied, again the meaningless touch of their hands which this time did not lift her to her feet. The King turned and walked away without looking back.

Madame de Fargis rushed to her mistress. 'Oh, Madame, Madame, what happened? Why did he leave like that?'

'Because he threatened me with death,' Anne said. 'And I refused to be intimidated. De Senlis! Have that

153

horrible dish of comfits taken and thrown away. The smell of it disgusts me.'

In his own apartments Louis sank back into a chair, while his gentlemen stood round, waiting for him to speak or send them away. It was quite twenty minutes before the King looked up from some dark reverie, and addressed the Marquis de Saint Vallère.

'The Queen complains that she hears nothing from the outside world. This should not be, Saint Vallère. Go back and deliver this piece of news. Tell Her Majesty that the Duke of Buckingham is dead. Say that he was stabbed to death. Just as he was going to embark for France once more.'

In all the years that they had served her, the Queen's women had never heard her weep as she did that night. The door to her bedroom was shut in their faces, and the sound of bitter sobbing came from within, as if she were crying the tears of a lifetime into her pillow.

De Senlis scowled and tried to make some criticism, but the other ladies, headed by Madelaine de Fargis, silenced her fiercely.

There was something about Anne's total collapse into grief that touched even the most hostile heart. For such a proud woman, so careful to hide her feelings, the shock of De Vallère's message took a dreadful toll. She had heard him to the end, her colour fading, one hand holding the chair back for support against her sinking limbs. When he had left she fainted into Madelaine's arms. And it was Madelaine who heard her bitterly accuse herself of bringing Buckingham to his death. 'It was my fault,' Anne wept, again and again, 'I wrote to him, I asked his help! He only fought France for my sake, because he loved me. Oh, Madelaine, Madelaine, what a nightmare . . .' She turned away from her friend, hiding her face, her body trembling violently with grief, and wildly said the words which could have meant her own death if Louis ever got to hear them.

'I loved him,' she said. 'I loved him with all my heart! I wish I were dead too.'

And then she sent Madelaine away and ordered her women to leave her alone. The sound of her grieving went on until the dawn broke.

De Fargis was the first to intrude upon her. She found Anne deathly pale, her eyes swollen with weeping. 'Madame, Madame,' de Fargis said. 'You mustn't do this! You must calm yourself; the King will hear of it!'

'I know,' Anne answered. 'It is too late for tears, Madelaine. Nothing can bring Buckingham back; nothing can take my guilt away. I know I dare not show it now. Last night my heart broke for him. This morning, it must appear to have healed.' She held out her hand and pressed that of her friend. 'Only you know that it's not so,' she whispered. 'He was so brave and splendid. May God receive his soul!'

*　　*　　*

On 28 June, 1629, Richelieu concluded a peace treaty with the Huguenots of France. La Rochelle had been conquered, and when Louis entered the city in triumph the previous October, it was a city of the dead, only a hundred and fifty-four men remained capable of firing a shot. The civilian population had been driven out by their own garrison, because their supplies were dwindling, and the Royal troops had stripped and robbed the miserable thousands of old men, women and children and driven them back again. They died under the walls of their own city. The Rochellais had fought with a tenacity which the Cardinal couldn't help admiring. His feeling was not shared by his King, or by the more extremist elements in the Church. Louis was incapable of generosity to an enemy; his nature was too jealous to admit that there was much virtue in others, even his friends.

Richelieu, disregarding the pleas of Father Joseph, treated the defeated Protestants as a political, rather than a religious force.

He stripped them of their legislative independence, razed their fortresses to the ground, and won them over to the King by guaranteeing their religious liberties. The conflict between them had been caused by lack of secular loyalty to the Crown. This could not be tolerated; the cold-hearted ferocity with which Richelieu had pursued the war was only matched by the innate tolerance and justice which he showed in dictating the peace. His object was to unite Frenchmen round the throne, and eventually to extinguish the independent dukedoms like Lorraine which existed within French territory, and unite them all under the rule of the King, accountable to him alone.

Peace was concluded with England in April. After Buckingham's death the fleet he had prepared set sail again, but sighting the mole and fortifications which now cut off La Rochelle from the sea, the English ships turned about and returned home. King Charles was now anxious to make peace; his Parliament was showing such signs of disloyalty and independence that he wished to dismiss it, and this could not be done while he was at war. One of the conditions of that peace, and such a small point that Richelieu couldn't hope to refuse it, was a pardon for the Duchess de Chevreuse. So powerful was her influence with the English Queen Henrietta Maria, and so influential her admirers, that this was a definite stipulation of the peace negotiations. The Cardinal acceded, as he always did, with apparent willingness, and Marie appeared at the Louvre in triumph, to throw herself into Anne's arms, and dazzle the whole Court with tales of her exploits while an exile.

Within ten days of her return, the Duchess received a personal letter from the Cardinal de Richelieu, inviting her to visit him at the Hotel de Richelieu, which was already one of the most magnificent houses in Paris. It was a short note, written in terms of sinister humility, considering that after the King its author was the most powerful man in France. It offered Marie de Chevreuse an olive branch, which, as she said to the Queen, undoubtedly contained a mass of poisoned thorns. She dared not refuse the invitation, and besides, she was afire with curiosity. She sensed a challenge, and this was something her intrepid spirit and boundless egotism could never resist. Twenty minutes later than the time the Cardinal suggested, dressed in a gown of gold brocade, her famous breasts impudently exposed to just above the nipple, the Duchess made her entrance to the Cardinal's private study.

Richelieu came to meet her; the Episcopal amethyst gleamed on his right hand. Marie curtsied and kissed the ring. The Cardinal raised her with both hands, and then making an elegant bow, kissed her hand in return. He had always thought her beautiful, though it was an intellectual judgment. The voluptuous quality of her appeal had never moved him as a man. Marie de Chevreuse could have stood naked before him without arousing a flicker of interest. But as a personality she fascinated him.

She was one of those rare women, mercifully rare, in his opinion, who was chemically attractive to most men, regardless of their normal preference for type. Men who adored brunettes fell in love with the Duchess as helplessly as others who desired their ladies meek and feminine. She was amusing, that was indisputable; she possessed enormous vitality and health when so many of her contemporaries were worn out with pregnancies and often ailing. She had spirit and dash, rather like an impetuous young man, and a hearty enjoyment of the bawdy aspects of life. He had read some of her letters to the Queen with astonishment at the coarseness she displayed. She was his enemy, and as such he sat and made a careful study of her. She in turn was taking her measure of him.

Marie sat down in a large gilded Florentine chair. A footstool in the same style was placed for her by a lackey in the Cardinal's livery, and another lackey came to her side with a gold salver on which there was an exquisitely chased Spanish ewer and cup, also made of gold.

'It's a warm day,' Richelieu remarked. 'I thought you might like to try my special remedy. Sherbert; it's a favourite drink in the East, where they prepare it cooled and serve it several times a day. It was a present to me.'

'Like the charming little set of ewer and cup, I expect,' the Duchess smiled at him mockingly. 'I'll try some with pleasure, my dear Eminence. Won't you keep me company?'

'I intended to,' he said. He also smiled, and there was mockery in his eyes too. A second lackey had come to him with a salver, ewer and cup exactly like the first. He took the sherbert and sipped it.

'I like it,' he said. 'It refreshes and it leaves the head clear for work. And I assure you, my dear Madame, I work very hard in His Majesty's service.'

'I'm sure you do,' the Duchess said. 'I'm no idler myself, you know. Inactivity would be my death.'

'Over-activity could have the same result,' Richelieu said gently. 'I despaired of your health several times in the last two years. But I must say,' he added, 'that I have never seen you in such splendid state, and your beauty – ah, my dear Duchess, you're justly famous for it. Now that I see you here before me, I shall have to forgive all those victims of yours who have made so much trouble for me. And I must forgive you too, or every gallant in France will be calling for my blood.'

'Every gallant in Europe,' the Duchess corrected him. If he wanted a war of words then he had a worthy opponent. She sat back at her ease, sipping the delightful drink, and showed that she wasn't afraid of him in the least. He understood this, just as he understood something else, for the first time. The woman's vanity was unbelievable; it could only be forgiven because it was so manifestly justified. The reason for her enmity was two-fold. He had never fallen a victim to her, and she had no basic liking for men. Her emotional attachment to the Queen was the most genuine feeling of which she was capable. Men gratified her and pleased her self-conceit; men were the means by which she exercised her love of power and her passion for danger and intrigue. But they meant nothing to her. He smiled, and the smile was returned; it was like two duellists saluting before they engaged.

'I should find it easier to join the host of your admirers, Madame, if you could do me one small favour – just to make up for all the ill turns others have tried to do me on your behalf.'

'That would depend, your Eminence, on what you ask. I'll do my best, of course, but I can't promise anything.'

'Ask the Queen to intercede for me,' he said. To the Duchess's astonishment the cold sardonic face had softened.

'The Queen is so restricted,' she said curtly, 'that she sees no one and no one sees her. With whom can she possibly intercede, Eminence? Especially for you, who seem so able to provide for yourself!'

He received the insult with a gentle smile. 'I'm only a servant of the King, Madame,' he said. 'It's the King who provides for me, but he can't help me in this. I had hoped that the Queen might; I had hoped even more that you could persuade her.'

'You haven't yet told me what she is asked to do,' Marie de Chevreuse retorted.

'She has the Queen Mother's confidence,' Richelieu explained, as if the Duchess weren't closely involved in the endless plotting and discussions taking place at the Luxembourg Palace. 'I appear to have lost it. I visit the Queen Mother and I see that she's displeased with me. Her anger weighs on me, Madame. I suffer on account of it.'

He was going to suffer a great deal more, the Duchess thought at that moment, by the time Marie de Medici had finished with him. And the snake knew it. He had every reason to feel that he was out of favour; the old Queen could hardly speak to him she was so hostile, and she bullied and wheedled the King night and day with complaints against the Cardinal. It was typical of the man that he dared approach the Queen he had persecuted and humiliated for the last six years, and try to make an ally of her. She sat back and waited for him to go on.

'I've noticed how close the Queen and the Queen Mother have become in this last year. And I've been happy to see it, very happy, I assure you,' he said coolly.

'Indeed,' the Duchess said. 'I can imagine your joy.'

'Then you understand how anxious I am to be on good terms with both these exalted ladies,' Richelieu announced. 'Whom the King loves, I love also. Mother and son are very close.'

'But husband and wife are not,' the Duchess interrupted. She couldn't endure the false humility much longer. He was mocking her with every word and her inflammable temper was about to explode. Perhaps that was what he wanted. She had never hated any man as much as she did Richelieu at that moment. No man had ever subtly assumed the mastery and kept it, while the initiative had long since slipped away from her.

'Let us speak frankly, my dear Eminence. You ask me to ask the Queen to speak in your favour to Marie de Medici? I can scarcely believe you're serious. My mistress has been humbled and hounded by you for six long years. She's the most wretched Princess in Europe, the most neglected, the most persecuted. And you are responsible. How can you possibly ask anything of her?'

Richelieu didn't answer immediately. He got up and stood in front of the Duchess, looking down at her, his hands clasped behind his back.

'You want frankness, Madame,' he said softly. 'Instinct tells me not to trust you. Reason assures me that you are biased and whatever I say will be dismissed. However, I shall try. I am not responsible for anything that has made the Queen unhappy. She is to blame, and so are you, and all those like you, who encouraged her to snub the King, to flout his wishes and embarrass his honour with the Duke of Buckingham. That was the beginning of her sorrows. She made the King jealous. I know the excuses, Buckingham's indiscretion, his vanity, I know them all because, by God, Madame, I've had to use them often enough to stop the King from really punishing her!'

'She did nothing,' Marie said hotly. 'And he still reproached her with it again the last time he saw her!'

'She was caught struggling in the man's arms after making a rendezvous with him. That was not very Queenly – or discreet! She arranged to have me murdered, this is not relevant of course, I'm only a humble priest and the King's servant and I've no right to bear malice on that account, but she went further still. She agreed to a plot which meant the King's death and her marriage to his brother.'

He stepped close to her and his pale eyes blazed.

'She was guilty of treason then and she's been guilty again. And it was I who saved her! I and I alone who hid the guilty evidence of her love letters to Buckingham, her intrigues with England. I haven't persecuted the Queen, Madame. I've saved her life. Now you may go and tell her that, and doubtless you will sit and laugh together and make fun of me. It doesn't matter. It distresses me . . .' He paused, and the sudden flare of anger disappeared; he was himself again. The cold smile reappeared, the voice resumed its smooth, self-deprecating tone. 'It distresses me deeply that the Queen should be my enemy. I have wanted to gain her favour for a long time, Madame, and I felt that now, at this moment, I saw an opportunity to approach her through you.'

'By asking her to do you a service,' Marie said scornfully. 'My God, Eminence, don't you think it might be more appropriate if you did one for her?'

'That, my dear Duchess, is what I'm trying to do,' Richelieu answered.

'You're an intelligent woman and a loyal friend. I admire you for that; I admire you for the love you've shown the Queen, and the risks you've taken to please her. Even though they were foolish and brought disgrace upon her and exile on you. Not to mention poor M. de Chalais, who suffered such an unpleasant death, for the same reason!'

'You were responsible for that butchery,' the Duchess said. She got up and they faced each other.

'He would have butchered me,' the Cardinal said. 'Hélas, Madame, I had to protect myself. This is what I'm trying to tell you. I shall always protect myself because I'm necessary to the King and to France. If you really love the Queen, persuade her to pacify Marie de Medici. If she can't or won't do this, then warn her not to join in this particular cabal against me!'

'Speak plainly, Eminence,' the Duchess said. 'Whom do you threaten? I must make my warning clear if it's to be effective.'

'I threaten no one,' Richelieu moved away from her. He had tried and failed, and he knew it. Further talk was a waste of time. 'I want to be on good terms with the Queen Mother and with the Queen. Give Her Majesty my humble respects and ask her to show me a little favour when next we meet. I shall accompany you to your coach, my dear Duchess. A thousand thanks for this agreeable hour we've passed together!'

'You're too kind,' Marie said coldly. She was not used to being dismissed. 'I'll give all your messages to the Queen, but I can't say how she'll receive them.' Anger and malice prompted her to thrust at the enemy where she was sure it would wound him most deeply.

'The Duke of Buckingham's death was a great shock to her. Innocent though she was, she felt a certain compassion for the poor man. His devotion was so great.'

Richelieu walked with her through the marble vestibule and out on to the step. There he turned and kissed her hand.

'It was also unwise,' he said. 'It cost the Duke his life. Farewell, Madame.'

Marie looked into the light eyes, so pale and green in the bright autumn sunshine, and found herself unable to answer. He had arranged Buckingham's murder. And he had let her know it, deliberately, as a warning. For the first time in her life, the Duchess felt afraid. When she sat back in her coach she shivered, as if she were suddenly cold.

7

'He's coming,' Gaston d'Orleans said. He had posted
M. de Jovre at the door of his mother's ante-chamber,
to signal the King's approach. Marie de Medici came
quickly to her younger son, and threw her arms
round his neck. 'Be firm, my dearest boy,' she said.
'We know what you want, and by God, we're going
to make him give it to you! And he'll give that
scoundrel's head to me, before I've done with him!'

'I'll be a rock,' Gaston promised. Mother and son
looked very alike in their expression of vindictive
determination. They had spent the morning in con-
ference with Anne, and the subject was the one which
had united them all for the past year.

How to force the King to dismiss and arrest his
hated Minister the Cardinal. Marie had decided that
the time had come when Louis could be persuaded, as
she termed her method of violent emotional bullying.

War with Spain and the Empire had been concluded by the Treaty of Ratisbon, after a campaign
in which France had been victorious. There was no
further need of Richelieu's diplomatic skill; he could
be sacrificed. And if the King wanted peace with
his mother, his brother, and an enduring peace
with Spain, then he must immolate his Minister.

Marie had invited Louis to visit her that afternoon in order to present this ultimatum to him. Anne had decided to stay in the Louvre and not attempt to take part; her husband's dislike of her might act in Richelieu's favour if she were present at the interview. But she had the personal assurance of the Spanish Ambassador Mirabel, that Spain would regard Richelieu's downfall and arrest as a guarantee of French good faith.

'His Majesty the King!' The usher announced Louis, and the double doors of Marie's audience chamber were opened wide.

Louis had been very ill the previous September, and as he lay in agony from an internal abscess, his mother and his wife had combined in the sick room, exhorting and demanding that the seemingly dying man should send away his only friend. Louis, in such pain and so debilitated that he lacked the strength to argue, had promised to dismiss Richelieu, only to gain time and a little peace. He had recovered and promptly gone back on his word. The Cardinal was higher in his favour than before, but fear of his mother and dread of the violent scenes she made, counselled Louis to conceal the extent of his reliance upon the Cardinal. He still had the Minister, he hadn't been faced with the awful responsibility of conducting the peace negotiations, and he hoped to placate his mother with lies and vague promises until she grew tired of her vendetta against Richelieu. It was a vain hope and in his heart Louis knew this; he knew, even as he walked through into her audience chamber and met the cold glare of his mother's eyes and the obstinate supercilious gaze of his brother, that battle was going to be joined yet again. He had known, and yet he came when she sent for him as if he were a boy, rather than a man and a King. He was still weak and suffered badly from depression as a result of his illness and the knowledge that he was the loneliest of men. Nobody cared for him; even on what they thought must be his deathbed, they had harassed him and bullied him, impervious to his sufferings. He had said very little but he bore a bitter grudge.

Marie came towards him, and they saluted each other coldly. He couldn't remember one occasion in his childhood when his mother had kissed him or shown him a single gesture of affection.

Gaston kissed his hand, making the act of homage so casually that it was like an insult. The King's face flushed, and he stood awkwardly with his gentlemen surrounding him, waiting for his mother to say something. 'I would like to see you alone,' Marie said. 'As mother and son, and brother to brother. If your Majesty pleases!'

'Of course,' he said wearily. 'Gentlemen, retire outside and wait for me. Now, Madame, before we begin, I must beg you not to start our meeting with a hostile attitude. I see by your face that you're angry; I see by Gaston's that he's sulking. I swear to God, I can't bear any more scenes!' He slumped back into a chair and stared at them one after the other, before he concentrated on his shoes, as he usually did in moments of stress. Marie advanced towards him; she had grown so heavy that the floor shook under her. He looked so dull and miserable that she longed to hit him, or shake him into life. He had always aroused this desire to hurt him physically, even as a tiny child. She couldn't resist slapping and pushing the spindly little creature every time she saw him.

'Your brother isn't happy,' she announced. 'And I'm not happy either. That's the first thing. He's not being fairly treated.'

Louis raised his head. The black eyes were filmed with boredom; they showed nothing of his feelings.

'My brother is Duc of Orleans, he has towns, possessions, riches, and permission to do as he likes. What more must I give him?'

'I want to marry Marie de Ganzague de Nevers, or Marguerite of Lorraine,' Gaston announced. 'I want your permission to choose between them. I married before because you forced me into it, now I insist on making my own choice!'

'And,' Marie de Medici continued for him, 'Gaston should have the fortresses and government of the Isle de France, Soissons, Coussi, Charny, Laon and Montpellier!'

'Anything more?' the King enquired. 'A marriage with one or other of the most eligible Princesses in Europe, one with a father who hates me – Lorraine, and the most important fortresses in my kingdom. Why don't you ask for my crown brother? Isn't that what you really want?'

He stood up suddenly. 'The answer is no! No to both.'

'Wait,' Marie's fat strong fingers seized his sleeve and held him. As she conceived it, she had tried to be temperate, tried to reason with him. Now she lost her temper. Hate for him and passionate love for her other son flared up in her at this refusal. And even more at the sarcasm, the signs of defiance he had dared to show her.

'You dismiss Gaston's claims, as if he were a nobody. He's your heir. You talk about the crown

168

of France – you fool, how easy it would have been to tear it off your head, if that was what he wanted. You talk about Gaston as if he were greedy, or a traitor – just think how loyal he's been to you, how he's resisted the temptation to *take* all, instead of asking for a little! Now listen to me. I said Gaston's demands were the first thing. So, we'll come to the second. You've broken your word to me. Richelieu is still in office. I've waited, and been patient . . .' Her voice rose to a shout, carrying beyond the closed doors into the crowded ante-chambers. 'I've waited for you to do what you promised. And you've done nothing! Your brother and I and your wife, and Spain itself, are all united. You must get rid of this priest! We demand it, as the price of peace between us!'

'And my peace?' Louis had never shouted back in his life. It was the first time and for a moment it silenced his mother.

'Who cares for my peace, my well-being? You harass me night and day to get rid of the best servant I've ever had. You insult him, you ridicule him; you encourage my brother to do the same, and you torment me with this promise every time I see you. It was dragged out of me when I was too ill to resist. I refute it, absolutely. Richelieu stays with me. And if you cared for me at all . . .' he suddenly began to stammer, overcome by emotion, and to his intense shame and hurt, he saw his mother and Gaston exchange a contemptuous smile at his expense.

'If you had any affection for me,' he went on, mangling the words until he had to stop, and fight for control over his stumbling tongue. They waited, enjoying his embarrassment, and at last he finished, cutting the angry speech into a few words.

'You'd think of my welfare. You wouldn't want to separate me from the Cardinal.'

'He's a traitor,' Gaston burst out. 'He's only serving himself, enriching himself, taking power for himself! Do you think we've forgotten how he murdered de Chalais? How so many of our friends are in prison because of him? Ah, my brother, the time has come when you must choose between him, and our mother and me and all your subjects. We won't endure his arrogance, his interference. He must go!'

'Either he goes,' Marie announced at the top of her voice, 'or I do!' She allowed herself to burst into tears. She cried noisily and wept copiously, abusing and accusing at the same time. 'You're an ungrateful son; I've done my best for you, I've kept the crown on your head for all the years after your father's death! I've sacrificed my life for you, and what's my reward? Where's the gratitude, the love you ought to show me? You break your promise to me, you prefer this upstart, this miserable treacherous intriguer, to me, your own mother!'

Louis stood speechless in front of her; he felt as if he were being buffeted by tidal waves, as the fierce, contorted face loomed large in front of him, pouring out tears like water. The voice assailed him, the burden of violence and reproach was like a physical pain.

He was accused of preferring Richelieu to her. Richelieu, who never made him feel as she was doing, an inferior, an ingrate, a boy man who'd never grown up. Richelieu had never harassed him, or worried him, or emphasised his own role at his King's expense. Richelieu was his buffer against a malignant, treacherous Court. She had made the accusation, and suddenly he saw how true it was. He *did* prefer

Richelieu to her. He preferred him to all of them.

'Will you dismiss him?' Marie demanded. 'Will you promise me now, in front of Gaston, that you'll have that devil safe in the Bastille before tomorrow morning?'

'If you don't, brother,' Gaston said, coming to his mother's side, 'I personally shall know how to defend myself.'

'And I shall leave you! I shall leave the Court and abandon you completely!'

Louis hesitated. The issue was clearer than it had ever been and yet he tried to temporise once more, because it was his nature.

'For my sake, Madame and Gaston, I beg of you. Forgive the Cardinal, and receive him back into your favour. You shall have your bride, my brother – I'll give you the Isle de France if you insist, but stop persecuting the Cardinal!'

'Never,' Marie de Medici said, and Gaston echoed her. 'Never!'

'Cling to that creature, and you will find yourself friendless and deserted by us all,' his mother threatened. She moved near to him and involuntarily Louis quailed.

'Come, what's your answer? We're waiting!'

For a moment Louis hesitated; he was almost on the point of giving way and letting them take his Minister from him. His head ached violently in reaction to his mother's attack; his tongue felt so swollen in his mouth that he doubted if he could even answer. The temptation came, and suddenly he overcame it. When he spoke he did so without a trace of stammer.

'Richelieu stays, Madame. That is my final word.'

He turned and walked to the door; he rapped upon it with his little gold-headed cane, and instantly it was opened and he was surrounded by his household. He felt safe, protected. He turned and bowed to his mother who stood in the middle of the room, one hand on Gaston's shoulder, glaring at him. Louis went out and the doors closed.

'Liar! Deceiver!' Marie roared after him, and swore in Italian. 'We won't be turned aside, my son,' she said. 'Not by that ungrateful dog, who owes me everything. We'll carry out our plan. Come; let's go to the Louvre and tell Anne what the next move is in this little game. And a bloody game it's going to be,' she added. 'Just let him wait, that sullen wretch, with his beloved Cardinal! Before we're done, he'll wish he'd kept his word to me.'

Anne had spent the afternoon in such an agony of suspense that she had walked the length of her suite of rooms, from her bedchamber to her oratory to the audience chamber where no one presented themselves on the King's prohibition, down the gallery looking out on to the gardens which were grey with rain and stripped of colour in the dismal February winds, up and down and backwards and forwards, waiting for the messenger from the Palais Luxembourg. It was quite late when the Queen Mother and Gaston d'Orleans were announced. Immediately the Duchess de Chevreuse came to Anne's side, followed by Madame de Fargis. It was fortunate that the two women, both so diverse in character, were united in their devotion to their mistress and were not in the least jealous of each other. 'My God,' Anne whispered. 'What has happened? Why have they come themselves?'

'You've won,' Marie de Chevreuse said. 'That must be it. They come in triumph – you know what a boaster Gaston is!'

Marie de Medici swept into Anne's audience chamber, her younger son hurrying a few steps behind her, and with a single imperious command, sent Anne's ladies to the far end. Even the Duchess de Chevreuse bowed before the formidable old Queen and retired.

With a dramatic gesture, Marie held out her arms to embrace her daughter-in-law

'What happened,' Anne implored. 'What did the King say?' Her mother-in-law was furious, Gaston stood biting his lower lip and scowling; failure was evident from them both.

'He refused,' the old Queen said. 'He went back on his promise and walked out of the Luxembourg!'

Anne slipped out of the hot, clutching embrace of the woman who had shown her such scant kindness in the past, but was, perforce, her only powerful ally. Marie's breath smelt strongly of garlic; Anne's nerves, already so overwrought by the long waiting, made her feel faint and nauseated.

'I never would have believed it,' she said. 'I thought he really meant to keep his promise, when the Cardinal wasn't so essential to him – I hoped and prayed that for once, he might be man enough!'

'Bah,' Marie de Medici exploded. 'Man? What kind of a man has he been to you, eh? He's an impotent spineless weakling! Gaston, tell the Queen everything that happened – every word that passed. I'm so outraged that I can't trust myself to go through it again!' She sank into a chair, and began to fan herself, breathing heavily through her nostrils, eyes flaming as she listened to Orleans' account of her scene with her eldest son.

'He's wedded to that fiend,' Gaston said at the end. 'Nothing will separate them but force.'

'Force?' Anne, also seated now in a half circle, glanced quickly at the group of women in the far corner of the room. They were too far away to hear anything, and mercifully the old Queen had kept her voice at a low pitch.

'What do you mean, force? What are you planning?'

Orleans' handsome face lit up with a smile of triumph. 'I'm going to slip out of Paris tomorrow, go to Orleans and raise my standard there. I shall send letters to the exiled Princes, to Rohan, the Duc de Montmorency and de Bouillion, calling on them to join me in a war to drive Richelieu from power. That is the only course left now!'

For someone who had betrayed de Chalais and all his friends so quickly at the last crisis in which the King and Richelieu were involved, Anne felt that Orleans was the least dependable of anyone in France to lead a civil war against the King. But there was no alternative. Vain, stupid, venal and a coward, he was still the heir to the throne and in spite of his faults, he was generally popular. And the shadow of the Queen Mother loomed over him, large and forceful, backed by the authority of a ten-year Regency. It might succeed; especially if her influence with her brother the King of Spain persuaded Spain to send money and even troops to their assistance.

In moments of crisis Anne had given way to tears and even fainted; these outward signs of nervous strain were not indicative of cowardice. She was brave and she was resolute by nature; she proved herself to be so in the next few moments. No one could hear; she had to trust the callow Gaston and the unscrupulous Marie de Medici. But again, they were her only hope. So much depended upon the success of this rebellion. With Richelieu in power, Anne had nothing to hope for but a continued existence in the twilight, the neglected wife, childless and suspect, the victim of one man's rejected love. He had punished her savagely for that rejection, and now she knew from Marie that his vengeance had reached as far as England, and taken the life of Buckingham, because he had succeeded where the Cardinal had failed. Any means were justified in getting rid of him, and any allies were acceptable.

'I'll write to my brother,' she said. 'You'll need money, Gaston, and perhaps even men too. I'll ask for them. Spain will help us!'

'Excellent,' Marie de Medici said. 'There's a woman of mettle for you, my son – that's a worthy Queen of France! How will you get this message through? If your Ambassador is seen making his way here again, Richelieu will scent something.'

'I can go to my convent,' Anne said. 'Everyone knows I spend some hours there nearly every day. Nobody will suspect the Val de Grace as a meeting place. I'll receive Mirabel there. If you can get a message to him, Madame, I'll be at the convent tomorrow, at one in the afternoon. I'll wait for him there.'

'I'll get the message to him,' Marie said. 'But be careful, my daughter. If that fiend discovers you have any part in this we could all be ruined!'

'I'll be discretion itself,' Anne promised. 'I trust Madelaine de Fargis and Marie de Chevreuse. I'll need their help, but I shan't tell them everything.'

'As you decide,' Gaston said. All the way from the Luxembourg his mother had been telling him how brave he was and how well fitted to rebel against the King and drag him off the throne. His ego was so swollen by her attitude that it only needed the enthusiasm of Anne to puff him out completely. He would have undertaken any enterprise, however rash or doomed it might turn out to be. He had asked for a rich wife and sufficient geographical vantage points to make him the most dangerous rival to his brother's power; the demands had been refused, and he was able to assuage his pique by the grander plan to seize the crown of France and marry Anne himself. And looking at her in the flickering candlelight, her rich hair glinting as if it had taken fire, her lovely face flushed and animated with excitement, Gaston forgot about the two eligible Princesses he had thought of marrying, and fell in love with Anne all over again. He thought of his brother Louis with contempt. Married to so much beauty and spirit and unable to enjoy it, unwilling to challenge and tame such a glorious creature – Gaston imagined himself in all his manly splendour arousing and consoling the ardent widow, and was ready to dare anything. The attitude of his mother was more calculating, though no less violent.

'Gaston must go secretly. He's left the Court before and then come back. It mustn't seem more serious than that. In the meantime you, my child, will secure Spain's support. I shall raise money everywhere, and prepare to flee to join Gaston when he gives the word. You must stay with the King, of course. How else,' she added, patting Anne's arm, 'will we have any source of information?'

'I'll stay,' Anne said. 'I can be very useful. Your headquarters can be the Convent at Val de Grace, for meetings, letters, everything. I'll do everything in my power to help you, my dear brother.'

Gaston took her hand and kissed it; on an impulse he turned it over and kissed her palm. 'You've suffered long enough,' he said. 'It's time we got rid of more than just a meddling priest. You're going to be the happiest, most adored Princess in all Christendom. Leave it in my hands.'

Marie de Medici got up.

'Go to the Val de Grace tomorrow, and I'll get word to the Spanish Ambassador to meet you there. We must leave now, my daughter. My miserable son has a reception tonight, and we must be there, Gaston and I. We will be gracious and pliant with the King, and nobody will suspect that by this time tomorrow, France will be on the edge of civil war!'

Two years earlier Anne had founded the community of the Val de Grace and built them a convent on the outskirts of Paris. Bored and almost without hope, the Queen had turned to religion for relief and consolation. She had spent the enormous sum of thirty thousand livres on building the convent, and chosen the Superior herself. Her motive at the time had been untainted by a desire for political intrigue. The world had abandoned her, and in an interlude of despair, Anne had tried to flee the world. But hers was a restless spirit; incapable of admitting defeat or accepting injustice with patience, Anne spent more time in the Val de Grace discussing her grievances with the Superior, than she did in the prayer and meditation she had originally intended. Anne had chosen Luisa de Millay as head of the community because she had a close affiliation with Spain, spoke Spanish, and was a congenial companion for the Queen. The friendship which sprang up between the pious nun and the unhappy turbulent Queen of France was on the same level as the devotion of Marie de Chevreuse and Madelaine de Fargis; the spiritual and the worldly became her passionate admirers, prepared to help her at any risk to themselves.

Anne had her own suite of rooms at the Val de Grace and a private oratory. It was in that oratory, before a crucifix sent by her brother the King of Spain, that she told the Ambassador Mirabel of the plot against Louis and the Cardinal.

They spoke in Spanish, Mirabel asking a question here and there. How much money would Gaston need? Was it their intention to stop at pulling down the Cardinal if their armies were successful?

Anne hesitated. 'I must know, your Majesty,' the Spaniard said softly. 'Spain cannot be compromised through ignorance.'

'I don't know what my mother-in-law will do,' she said. 'She hates the King; she's always wanted Gaston to succeed him. I can't be definite, but if Orleans wins the war, I don't think Louis will be King of France for long. I've written everything to my brother.'

The Ambassador bowed. 'It will be on its way to Madrid one hour after I leave here,' he said. 'And his reply will be brought here to you. All letters, all messages are to come to you through this convent.'

'It's perfectly safe,' Anne assured him. 'No one will watch me here, the nuns and the Superior are devoted to me. You'd best go now, Monsieur Mirabel. I'll leave in an hour, and return in two days. I'll have more news for you then.'

'Until then, Madame.' He bowed low over her hand. He admired her spirit, and only hoped that it was equalled by her caution. As a diplomat he didn't underestimate the brain and energy of Cardinal Richelieu. It would need more than a community of nuns and one lonely woman to outwit him.

Two days later, Anne paid her visit to the Val de Grace; she carried letters from the Queen Mother to Gaston, now ensconced in his dukedom at Orleans, apparently indulging in a fit of sulks, to the Prince de Rohan, and to the Duc de Bouillion. In all these letters the old Queen abused the Cardinal and reviled her son the King for his weakness and adherence to the Minister's disastrous policies. Between them they were ruining the country and alienating Spain to the point where the hard-won Treaty of Ratisbon was becoming a farce. Her Majesty therefore encouraged Gaston in his purpose with profuse affection and unstinted praise for his bravery and devotion to herself, and besought the other nobles to help her younger son.

Mirabel's messenger had come and left with this explosive correspondence, including a long letter from Anne herself to Orleans, in which she added her sentiments to his mother's, enjoining firmness and promising that she, too, would know how to show her gratitude when their great enemy was punished with the ruin and death he had decreed for so many of their friends.

On her way to see Marie de Medici in the Luxembourg, Anne found herself in the ante-chamber face to face with Richelieu.

It was nearly six months since they had met; he had encountered her once, after the King's illness, and made an attempt to speak to her which she frustrated by walking away before he could say anything. In that time she had almost brought him down, or so she believed. Now, his downfall might be a matter of weeks or at worst, months, while Gaston's armies rallied and marched on Paris. And he knew nothing of it. There was no escape this time; they were both at the Luxembourg for the same purpose, to see Marie de Medici. He came up to her deliberately, and as she met the large grey eyes, so coolly fixed upon her face, Anne felt her colour rising. He never seemed to change; for once he was in his red Cardinal's robes, the skull cap on his head. There was a little grey in the neat beard which hadn't been there six months before. The handsome, hawk face was a little thinner, a little tired about those piercing eyes, but that was all. Fear and loathing swept over her as he came close. The guilty colour ran up to the roots of her hair, with an instinctive gesture she put out her hand as if to ward him off, and before she could stop him, Richelieu had taken it in his, and she felt the touch of his lips on her skin. It seemed as if she had been burnt by that kiss, as if the contact, however slight and cloaked in formality, were more passionate, more dangerous than the mad embrace of Buckingham so many years ago. And her body almost betrayed her again. She had an impulse to scrub and scrub at her hand to wipe that cold kiss off her hand, as if his lips had left a mark upon it.

'This is a very happy chance, Madame,' he said. His voice had always been low, with a persuasive quality. She had never heard the harshness, the sharp sarcasm with which he was known to flay others.

'I was going to pay my respects to you after seeing

the Queen Mother. May I be permitted to do so now?'

There were half a dozen people in the room; a few noblemen and their wives, a priest, and a member of the Cardinal's household. All were watching them, afraid to come near yet longing to know what was being said by the Queen and the Cardinal, who hated each other so bitterly.

'I can't prevent you, since your own sense of delicacy doesn't,' Anne retorted. The Cardinal bent his head as if to apologise. Eight years ago she had insulted him loudly and publicly so that everyone could hear. She had spoken in a whisper this time. She had learnt that much, at least.

'My sense of delicacy is as sensitive as any man's who comes in contact with you. I'd rather die at your feet than make you angry.'

'Then why don't you go away?' she demanded. 'You know your presence is an affront to me!'

'Alas, you make that clear at every opportunity. It grieves me, Madame.' There was a slight, mocking smile on his face, but there was a look in the eyes, usually so ice clear and self-contained, that was very like pain. It was pain, she knew it, and the knowledge made her strike again.

'One blessing came out of my miserable restricted life,' she said, 'and that was the fact of seldom seeing you, my Lord Cardinal, or having you thrust yourself upon me. I have been lonely, neglected and watched as if I were a criminal instead of Queen of France. I know you're responsible for my humiliation. I tell you now, so you need never trouble me again with your deceitful words – I shall never forgive you! Is that clear enough?'

'Nothing could be clearer.' He answered her calmly, in the same gentle tone of voice. But she had wounded him, because he looked away from her to hide it. 'But I sent you a message by the Duchess de Chevreuse. I hoped, through her mediation, to mend our relationship – to gain your forgiveness at least, if not your friendship. I'm sure she gave it to you.'

'She did,' Anne said. The warning had daunted even the Duchess's reckless spirit for a while. 'Tell her not to join in this particular cabal against me.' She had not only joined it, but her help was an essential part of its success.

'And it would seem,' he made a gesture towards the Queen Mother's inner audience chamber, 'that you took no notice of that message. Tell me something, Madame. Why do you hate me so?'

It was a whisper, and now the eyes were on her again and the fierce forbidden hunger blazed at Anne. Nothing had changed between them. He was still in pursuit, and she was still trying to run away from him.

'You know why,' she said slowly. She put one hand to her cheek; there was no colour in it now. 'You're the same man as you were at Tours; you have the same unspeakable disregard for your estate and mine. That's why I hate you, and why you torment me.'

'If I torment you,' he said, 'it's because you leave me no alternative. I've never wanted to hurt you; I wanted to be your friend, your guide – you made me your enemy because I'd committed a crime in your eyes. But was it such a crime for Buckingham? For that puppy Gaston? Why must I never be forgiven, Madame?'

'Because you're a priest,' she whispered. 'God

forgive you, you horrify me, you repel me. . . . Leave me, for pity's sake!'

Richelieu made her a deep bow, one hand outstretched. The big Episcopal amethyst gleamed with the movement.

'I'll leave you. Too many eyes are on us, Madame, and you know how jealous the King is where you're concerned. Or rather you don't really know, because I've shielded you with all these torments you complain about. I've sheltered you, because of course you're right. I am the man I was that day in the Chapel at Tours when you drove me away with your reproaches, when you shrank from me as if it were the devil at your feet, saying how much he loved you. I've kept you safe from others Madame, but I've saved your life at the same time. I'll make one last attempt to warn you. Don't throw in your lot with the Queen Mother or her son. Farewell, Madame. I fear it may be quite some time before we meet again.'

At that moment a page came out of Marie de Medici's room; the boy walked up to the Cardinal, bowed, and handed him a note.

Anne watched him read it; she trembled where she stood, her heart was racing with fear and the tempest of emotions he had roused in her. Fear and self-loathing were the strongest; they smothered the persistent, dangerous flicker which had once so nearly burst into a consuming flame.

He looked at her and smiled. 'I won't deprive you of the pleasure,' he said, 'of knowing that it's my turn to be humiliated. Her Majesty sends me away unheard. Again, farewell Madame.'

He turned, and with his usual politeness, bowed and saluted everyone in the room who had witnessed his dismissal without audience. He left with the resigned air of a man already fallen from favour. Anne hurried to the window; down below she saw the Cardinal's coach with its escort of guards, the King's precaution against murder after Chalais' clumsy plot. Within a few minutes the figure, dimly visible in the darkening light, clothed all in scarlet, came down the steps and entered the coach. It drove away in the direction of the Louvre. Anne knew that he had gone to see the King.

*　　*　　*

'What must I do?' the King muttered. 'She's my mother, Richelieu – what *can* I do?'

They sat in semi-darkness in the King's private ante-chamber; a log fire blazed in the grate, hissing as rain spattered down the chimney, and the light of the flames was the only light Louis would permit. Richelieu understood his reason. The King couldn't restrain his tears, and while his Minister might suspect, he mustn't see his sovereign's weakness. Richelieu had been talking for almost an hour. His quiet voice had gone on and on, reminding Louis of old wrongs, old intrigues and humiliations, occasionally resurrecting some particularly painful childhood memory. He was trying to persuade the King that he must arrest his mother.

Louis sat crouched down in his chair, his head hanging, his hands nervously opening and shutting on his knees.

'Sire,' the Cardinal said, and his voice was full of pity. 'Consider your position. Your brother has fled to Orleans; you have seen copies of the letters he's sent to the Huguenot Princes, your half-brothers, and even to the Duc de Montmorency, urging them all to take up arms against you. I've shown them to you because I had to convince you what was happening. Your throne and your life are in danger. And you've seen the Queen Mother's letters, too.'

'I know, I know.'

The unhappy man opposite Richelieu writhed and twisted in misery and indecision.

'But you know my mother! She doesn't think like you or I do. She's impulsive, violent! She may have written things to Gaston, but that doesn't prove she'd actually *help* him rebel against me. Words are cheap, Richelieu, you've often quoted that to me, and these are only words.'

'Alas,' the Cardinal said. 'May I go back a little while?'

'If you must,' Louis said. 'As the King I must listen to you.'

'When the Duc d'Orleans married Mademoiselle de Montpensier, she brought a great dowry with her, including some magnificent jewels. The Montpensier diamonds were among them, weren't they?'

'Yes, yes, of course they were. They were willed to the child, if it was a girl. My mother keeps the diamonds for her.'

'They are the little Princess's inheritance, bequeathed by her dead mother,' Richelieu said. 'Entrusted to the Queen Mother by you, Sire. Well, she has sold them, and sent the money to your brother at Orleans to buy arms. Here is the bill of sale.'

After a moment the piece of paper drifted to the ground; Louis' fingers had opened, letting it slip through them. It lay at his feet, the name of the Paris jeweller plainly visible. His mother had pledged her own grand-daughter's inheritance to finance a rebellion against him.

No wonder she wanted him to dismiss Richelieu. Then he would have been completely at her mercy, and the mercy of his brother Gaston. They would have had him assassinated, poisoned. He didn't speak, and while he waited, Richelieu stayed silent and motionless. He had only told the truth. Marie de Medici was so deeply implicated that the bill of sale for the diamonds was only one of a dozen documents he had acquired which proved her guilt. But psychologically it was the most damning. Equally damning were the intercepted letters of Anne to her brother the King of Spain, but this was not the time to use them. Richelieu had still not discovered how the Ambassador Mirabel received them. When he did, he would uncover all Anne's secrets. He had excluded her completely from his talks with the King. No suspicion attached to her. It was Marie de Medici who must be pursued and destroyed. The Queen's turn would come later.

'Richelieu!'

'Yes, Sire?'

'I agree. My mother must be restrained. How shall it be done?' Louis had risen; in the flickering firelight his face was dark and sullen, the eyes reddened by tears. The Cardinal stood before him.

'Order the Court to go to Compiègne,' he said. 'It can be done there. The details are painful for you, Sire. Leave them to me. I'll deal as gently with Her Majesty as if I too were her son.'

'So be it,' the King said. 'But let it be soon. I can't endure suspense.'

'In two days we can leave for Compiègne,' Richelieu said. 'And within the week it will be done and you will have come back to Paris. More surely King of France than when you went away.'

* * *

The forests of Compiègne were one of the finest hunting grounds in France; the countryside was beautiful and February was a crisp dry month, ideal for the chase. On the 17th, the King, his household, Anne and her ladies, and Marie de Medici, travelling in great state and saying loudly that she was only coming because she couldn't trust her son alone with Richelieu, arrived at the Royal Palace. Anne had been uneasy at the sudden order to leave Paris, and she was unable to convince Marie that she should stay behind in the Luxembourg and not travel out of the capital. She couldn't give a reason for this advice, because nothing prompted it but instinct, but the instinct had its origins in the sight of Richelieu leaving the Queen Mother's Palace, dismissed and humbled. There had been something ominous in the shadowy figure driving away in his coach, and the coach turning towards the Louvre and the King. The King was not himself either. He was always gloomy, always bored, and as hostile to Anne as ever, but there was a furtiveness in his manner to his mother which Anne had never seen before. He did his best to avoid her, he spent the first day at Compiègne in the saddle from dawn until it was too dark to ride, and the Cardinal was hardly seen at all. Anne spent the time with her mother-in-law, sewing and talking about the news from Gaston.

'All goes well,' the old Queen said. 'De Bouillion's agreed to join him, and you know he's approached Montmorency. It'll take time, my daughter, but when Gaston's armies march, there'll be an end of all our troubles. I think that viper knows it; he's hardly put his face outside his rooms since we came here!'

'The King worries me,' Anne said. 'He's not himself, Madame. Something is weighing on him.'

'Decision,' Marie said contemptuously. 'He can't wipe his own nose without hesitating. I've given him a choice . . .' she banged her plump fist on the chair arm, 'Me and Gaston, or the Cardinal! And he can't bring himself to tell the creature he's dismissed. Tomorrow I'll go to him again and tell him Gaston won't come back so long as that devil remains in office. After all,' she went on, 'if Louis gets rid of him, there needn't be a civil war. But he won't, he won't,' Marie said. 'He's too weak, too spineless. We'll have to fight, my dear, and in my heart I think that's the best way.'

Anne went on sewing as she answered; the long needle stabbed in and out of the cloth like a tiny dagger. 'It's the *only* way, Madame. We've declared war on the Cardinal, and it's not a war which can end in truce. But I just wish we were in Paris. I don't like this place; there's an atmosphere, a sort of foreboding in the air. I can't feel comfortable.'

'Bah, imagination is playing you tricks,' the old Queen said. She was a believer in fortune tellers and astrologers, and all had assured her that the future held a long period of calm for her. She pictured herself secure in Paris while her adored Gaston marched in triumph on the city, her son Louis cowered at her feet, and the Cardinal revealed his secrets in the torture chambers of the Bastille before losing his head in the Place de la Grève. She laughed and patted Anne's arm.

'All will be well, my daughter. I feel it here, in my heart. You have presentiments of trouble – I sense only success. Perchance Louis may fall off his horse tomorrow and break his miserable neck! That would solve everything!'

Anne dined alone in her apartments that night; the King waived etiquette at Compiègne and dispensed with the stiff public meals which were part of Court ritual at the Louvre. Anne ate very little and discouraged even Madame de Senécée from talking. Madelaine de Fargis and Marie de Chevreuse were in Paris, and Anne consoled herself for their absence with de Senécée, who was an amiable, rather silly gossip, but devoted to her.

'I'm tired,' Anne said. 'Ladies, we will retire early.' She washed her fingers in the golden bowl full of rose-scented water, said grace, and left the supper table, followed by her attendants. In her bedroom Anne stood while each lady performed her duties in undressing her, taking off her jewels and locking them away, brushing her abundant hair, and robing her in a long nightgown of the finest lawn, with Mechlin lace at the neck and wrists.

Anne mounted the steps up to her bed, took the chamber-stick with its single taper inside the curtains, and ordered the hangings to be drawn. There was a small book of devotions under her pillow; she tried to compose herself by reading a few pages, but the words danced in front of her, making no sense at all, and in despair Anne threw the book aside and blew her little candle out. All was dark and quiet. Her ladies-in-waiting had left for their own quarters where they slept in a dormitory. Her tirewoman de Filandre lay in the tiny closet attached to her room, and Anne could hear the muffled sound of snores. All the Palace slept, but sleep couldn't come to her. Marie de Medici was wrong. Something was going to happen, and it was sure to be the doing of Armand de Richelieu. She never allowed herself to think of him in anything but terms of bitterness and disgust; she mocked him and encouraged her friends to do the same, but at that hour, alone in the dark, silent bedroom, Anne had to admit that he seemed invincible. But he was weak with her because as he had said that day at the Luxembourg, he hadn't changed. He was still the suitor consumed by hopeless passion, who had knelt at her feet in the Chapel at Tours. She could feel the luminous green eyes upon her, conveying that in spite of all that had passed between them, he still loved and still pursued. Anne found herself trembling. He never gave up. His hates were relentless, his vengeance persistent as eternity. And to those he loved, like his niece Mme de Combalet, men who served him faithfully, the Capuchin Father Joseph – to these he showed the same steadfast face, as strong in love as he was in enmity. Many times she had been advised to show him friendship, tempted with the vision of power and influence which she would enjoy with Richelieu as her ally. It only needed a few kind words, a smile, a little gracious act from time to time and she could have been the most brilliant Queen in Europe. Louis couldn't stand against him; Richelieu had insinuated himself into that gloomy, indecisive mind and gained control of both the will and the emotions. At the same time he remained humble and subservient, acutely sensitive to the King's irritable pride. As she thought of Richelieu, Anne realised with terror that she had allied herself with creatures of straw in Gaston and Marie de Medici. Neither was a match for the Cardinal; the old Queen was brave enough, but her intrigues were clumsy, her motives transparent. Gaston was a shallow popinjay, puffed up with pride one moment and cringing with fear the next. Richelieu would win, and this time his victory would be decisive. Anne knew it; she drew back her bed curtains and watched the dawn come up through the windows and waited. It was only partially light when the first loud knocks sounded on the door of her ante-chamber, and Madame de Filandre burst into her room, stammering that the King himself was outside, demanding that his wife should get ready to leave the Palace within the hour.

Trembling, Anne sprang up, dragged on her robe de nuit, and ran to the ante-room. The Chancellor Chateauneuf came forward and bowed. The room was full of her women, still in their nightclothes, weeping and whispering. They watched the Queen, as white as her own linen, but still composed and dignified. Her voice didn't tremble when she spoke to the Chancellor.

'What does this mean, Monsieur? Am I to be arrested?'

'No, God forbid, Madame,' Chateauneuf answered. 'His Majesty and the Court are leaving for the Capuchin Monastery nearby. He commands you to go there, with your ladies. I assure you, you are in no danger. It is the Queen Mother who is under guard.'

'The Queen Mother! The Queen Mother has been

arrested! This is an outrage – I don't believe it,' Anne cried out; she turned to the cluster of women behind her. 'De Senécée – go to her Majesty's room at once!'

'No, Madame.' Chateauneuf held up his hand. 'The rooms are surrounded. The King forbids you to see or speak to his mother, and commands you to join him immediately. I advise you most strongly – do not disobey! The Queen Mother is at the filial mercy of the King. She won't be harmed. Come, ladies. Make the Queen ready!' He bowed once more and went out.

By seven o'clock that morning, the Palace of Compiègne was empty of all but Marie de Medici, her household and a strong guard under the command of Marshal D'Estrée. Anne drove in silence through the woods, taking the winding road to the Capuchin Monastery where Louis waited with his Court. It had been accomplished without a sound, or a cry of protest. Marie was a prisoner, and she had been enticed to Compiègne, where she was isolated, so that she could be confined without a public scandal. Richelieu, Anne said to herself, as the coach rattled through the early morning; Richelieu had accomplished the impossible. He had turned the mother-ridden King against Marie de Medici at last. She had lost her most potent ally, and now she too would stand defenceless.

'Madame,' de Senécée leant forward and whispered to her mistress. 'Madame, are you sure we should obey? What if this monastery is but a trap, a place where you will be imprisoned? Shall I divert the coach?'

'No,' Anne said. 'I think Chateauneuf told the truth. The Cardinal is not ready to dispose of me just yet. And if it is a trick – I'm a Princess of Spain, and I don't flee from anyone. Look, there is the Monastery. In a few moments we shall know our fates.'

She was brought to the King in the choir of the Monastery; the Abbot himself conducted her.

The King looked very yellow and drawn, and his eyes were haggard as if he had been weeping. She looked everywhere without seeming to do so, but there was no sign of Richelieu.

'You have been told what has happened, Madame,' Louis said abruptly. 'To protect my mother from intrigues, and to safeguard the peace of the realm, I have left her under the surveillance of M. D'Estrée, while the Cardinal and I persuade my brother Orleans to return to us. Her Majesty will be well cared for, and treated with the most tender courtesy by M. D'Estrée. It is my hope,' he hesitated, stammering, as emotion overcame him, and then continued with a visible effort. 'It is my hope that Her Majesty will resolve her difference with my dear M. de Richelieu and return to Court. For now, Madame,' his dark eyes glowed angrily at Anne, 'I have decided that you too should be protected from bad influences. Madame de Fargis will be dismissed. I present Mademoiselle de Hautfort in her place!'

Anne stood immovable; there were tears in her eyes which she was too proud to shed in front of him. They were tears for the fierce old woman left behind at Compiègne, a prisoner condemned by her own son, and tears for the blow that had just been struck at her, the dismissal of Madelaine de Fargis. She saw a woman move forward out of the crowd surrounding the King, and sink before her in a deep curtsy. The face that was raised to hers was strikingly beautiful, and very young. The blue eyes were large and limpid.

'Your Majesty's devoted servant,' said Mademoiselle de Hautfort softly. 'I beg you to receive me into your household.'

'Since the King commands it,' Anne said coldly, 'it shall be done. Rise, Mademoiselle, and take your place among my ladies.' She turned to Louis. 'Sire, I must protest at the harshness of what has been done to Her Majesty the Queen Mother. She had always shown me kindness, and my heart breaks for her in her humiliation.' The tears came then, and flowed down both her cheeks. She curtsied to the King and turned away. As she did so, she saw in astonishment that he was watching the new maid of honour de Hautfort with an expression she had never seen since the death of his old favourite de Luynes.

Slowly the Court re-assembled for the journey to Senlis, where the King intended to stay for some days. Anne asked the Abbot for some water, and was shown into his own rooms in the monastery, where wine and fresh fruit were put in front of her. She couldn't eat anything, and the wine made her aching head swim. De Senécée came flustering round her, white lipped and tearful, begging her to eat something and be calm. In the background the new maid of honour stood with her hands clasped and her eyes cast down, silent and unobtrusive, and as lovely as the new morning.

Impatiently Anne sent her women to wait outside, and once alone she gave way and wept for some minutes. She felt an overpowering sense of loneliness and helplessness. De Fargis, whom she loved, was being sent away. Marie de Medici was a prisoner; even Gaston, useless though he was, was still a friend and he was far away. She heard the click of the latch and the door opened. Richelieu stood in the doorway, and without speaking he came into the room, closing the door very quietly behind him. She felt the colour flood into her face, and sprang up.

'How dare you! How dare you come in here without permission!'

'I asked the King,' the Cardinal said gently. 'He agreed that I should speak to you. Don't cry, Madame. Certainly don't cry for the Queen Mother; she's only been kind to you to suit her own ends. She would abandon you without a qualm. She isn't worth your tears.'

'You have no heart,' she accused him. 'You're without pity! Leave me alone!'

'When I've delivered the King's message,' he said. 'And it's *his* message, not mine. You are not to write to the Queen Mother or to send messages to her. You are not to involve yourself in any way on her behalf. That is his command.'

'*You* give the commands,' Anne said bitterly. 'You have persuaded him to imprison his own mother! He's no more than your puppet.'

'He's a man who has never been loved, Madame,' Richelieu said quietly. 'Such people are very cruel when they're roused. Don't rouse him now. Don't play at politics this time.'

'I shall do as I think fit,' she blazed at him. 'I'm not afraid of him, or you. I've nothing to fear!'

'No,' he agreed. 'Because I've suppressed your foolish correspondence with Gaston. You turn pale, Madame,' the thin lips smiled at her, 'and well you might. Madame de Fargis was a fool; her folly nearly ruined you. I warned you before and you wouldn't listen. Don't join this particular cabal against me.'

'I'll work against you as long as I live,' Anne said. 'I'm not a liar, Monsieur Cardinal, nor am I a coward. You've tormented me, insulted me, persecuted those I loved for a reason too shameful to admit! I shan't forgive it. I won't forgive it!'

'It is *you* who are ashamed, not I,' Richelieu reminded her. 'My love for you has been your only shield for twenty years. It will go on protecting you whether you wish it or not.' He bowed very low to her, and left the room as quietly as he had come into it.

The Court stayed a short time at Senlis, while the King hunted, and signed the orders for exile and arrest which the Cardinal presented to him. All those who were friends of the Queen Mother were either imprisoned or ordered to leave France. Madelaine de Fargis was accused of High Treason, but she had fled from Paris, and the Court which sat in judgment upon her pronounced sentence of death in her absence. She was beheaded in effigy in the Place de Carrefour de St Paul. Madelaine was one of the few to escape the angry vengeance of the King and his Minister; quick-witted as ever, she fled at the first reports of the arrest of people she had known and with whom she had acted as courier for her mistress the Queen. She found a refuge in Holland, where she lived in poverty and isolation, the victim of her devotion to Anne, who used her undiscovered post bureau at the Convent of the Val de Grace to send her what money she could spare, and carry on her lone and desperate fight against the Cardinal Richelieu.

8

On 10 July Marie de Medici climbed down a rope ladder from her window at Compiègne and escaped to Brussels. The news caused consternation to the King, whose courage crumbled at the thought of his mother free and in a position to revenge herself upon him, and renewed hope to Anne and all the Cardinal's enemies. Only Richelieu seemed unaffected by the news; if he showed any emotion it was relief when he heard that the Queen Mother was safely in Brussels under the protection of the Infanta Beatriz. He seemed no more concerned when Gaston finally declared open rebellion against the King, and with the support of the Ducs de Montmorency, de Bouillion and many splendid cavaliers, gathered his troops to invade from Languedoc. Gaston had also defied Louis by marrying Marguerite de Lorraine, and at this moment Spain announced her intention of invading France on behalf of Marie de Medici, and actively aided Gaston with money and volunteers.

The situation appeared very grave, almost desperate. It was remarked that the Queen spent more and more time at the Val de Grace, and when she wasn't shut up there with the Superior and her nuns, she clung even more closely to the Duchess de Chevreuse.

'Madame, if you're going to the Val de Grace, may I come with you?' Marie whispered the request to Anne as she was helping at her morning toilette. 'No,' Anne murmured. 'It's too dangerous. You mustn't ever be seen there. My motives aren't suspected. You would be noticed immediately! Ah, thank you, de La Flotte, you may retire to the ante-room. Madame de Chevreuse will serve me now.'

When her ladies had retired, Anne turned impulsively to her friend. 'Why do you want to come, Marie? Has something happened?'

The Duchess laughed. 'It has indeed,' she said. 'I long to tell you every detail; I thought we might be truly private at the Convent. But perhaps one shouldn't mention lovers in a holy place!'

'Oh, Marie,' Anne exclaimed. 'Be serious. You are always having lovers!'

'But this one is quite special,' the Duchess said. 'As a man he's a stupid bore, and clumsy as an ape, but politically – ah, my darling Madame, I could hardly do better if I were sleeping with the Cardinal!'

'Who is it?' Anne demanded. 'Hurry, tell me. We can't delay in here alone or we shall be reported by that wretch de Senlis again!'

'Last night I seduced the new Lord Keeper of the Seals – Chateauneuf himself, no less! He had been making overtures for some time. I decided to encourage him a little, just to see what happened. He became like a dog, drooling in anticipation. Ugh, I can't tell you how awful he is to have in one's bed – but he's besotted. And he talks, Madame, he talks like an old woman after he's been made happy!'

'My God,' Anne said in a low voice, 'Marie, how dangerous this is – he carries all the Cardinal's secrets.

He's his devoted servant. He's present at the most private meetings.'

'Exactly,' the Duchess said. 'Don't worry, Madame. You can trust me. I'll be discreet, and I shan't probe too deeply until I've got the wretch completely at my mercy. And he shall be, I promise you. The poor ape is already beside himself with passion. And self-satisfaction too. To be *my* lover – that will be fame indeed for such a creature!'

In spite of herself, Anne laughed. 'You're impossible,' she whispered. 'Dear Marie, no one else could have done such a thing. But he could be invaluable – we would know everything!'

'Precisely,' the Duchess said. 'And when Spain invades France, you can give them Richelieu's plans in advance.'

'Yes,' Anne said. 'Through the Val de Grace I can send information direct to Spain. If Spanish arms join with Gaston, and they win, Richelieu will fall. It's dangerous; terribly dangerous for both of us. But it'll be worth the risk! You have my blessing, Marie. Long live the love of M. de Chateauneuf. Follow me into the other room, we've talked long enough. I'm going to the Convent this afternoon, and I can send word to Mirabel.'

By the end of the year Gaston d'Orleans raised his army and joined by the Duc de Montmorency, the most famous gallant and brilliant victor of La Rochelle and other battles, engaged the armies of his brother, the King, and the Cardinal de Richelieu. Gaston's troops, much vaunted for the quality and numbers, turned out to be a ragtag collection of Walloons, Spaniards and French renegades, and with typical lack of discipline or judgment, Gaston advanced three days earlier than agreed with Montmorency. Spanish forces were mustered on the French frontiers but until the success of the rebellion was assured, they did not move. And at last the confidence of Richelieu was justified. However strongly Louis' subjects deplored the harshness of his Minister and disliked the idea of the King driving his mother into exile, they liked it less still when both Mother and brother turned against the crown and invaded France itself with mercenary troops.

Two armies under the command of Marshals Schomberg and de La Force set out to do battle with the rebels under Gaston and Montmorency. The Royalist armies routed Gaston, who fled from the field without attempting to rally his forces, and Montmorency fell wounded and was taken prisoner. The campaign was over, and the King and his Cardinal were victorious. Those who had escaped capture and might still be tempted to rally round the miserable Gaston for another attempt, were discouraged by the execution of the Duc de Montmorency. Other heads fell too, prison gates opened and closed on some of the most illustrious names in the kingdom. Those whom Richelieu and Louis could not convict on a capital charge, were disposed of by the dreaded lettre de cachet, which imprisoned them without appeal for as long as the King decreed.

Gaston himself joined Marie de Medici in Brussels. The Infanta Beatriz, who had given them shelter, was plagued by their incessant reproaches and quarrels and the petty bickering of those who were in exile with them. Marie de Medici occupied herself with writing letters of virulent abuse to the King in France, to her relatives and to foreign embassies all over Europe in which she reviled Richelieu and abused her eldest son. The letters satisfied her restless passion for revenge, but they were without influence in the power politics of the world. She was no longer in France, and as an exile she was of no consequence. The Cardinal, usually so adept at keeping prisoners in prison, had been deliberately careless in the way he had guarded the Queen Mother, and she had played into his hands by fleeing from Compiègne and sinking into a backwater in Brussels as the pensioner of the Spanish Government.

In this dull circle, presided over by his mother who spent her time weeping or fulminating against fate, Gaston soon wilted, and even the charm of his wife Marguerite of Lorraine failed to please him for long. He became bored. He pined for the brilliance of his old life at Court, for the excitement of his duels with the Cardinal – after all, *he* always got off lightly – for the pomp and splendour of his position as heir to the throne. He was short of money, and his doting mother couldn't hope to supply his needs out of her meagre treasury. She too got on his nerves. He decided petulantly that his plight was entirely her fault. He wasn't disloyal to his brother; he had been misled. He sent a message to Louis asking to be forgiven and allowed to come home.

If the old Queen Mother was a spent force in exile, the heir to the throne was a profound anxiety to the Cardinal. At any moment he might have to be summoned back to France to take the Crown if Louis died. He was a natural focus for every malcontent. It was obviously safer to have him in Paris divorced from the influence of his mother and his friends, where the power of Richelieu and the King could insulate him from political intrigue.

Gaston received the enormous sum of half a million livres to settle his debts, the promise that his marriage to Marguerite would be acknowledged, and he would be forgiven and welcomed back at his brother's court.

In September, Gaston fled from Brussels without saying goodbye to his wife or his mother, and hurried to St Germain, where he literally threw himself at Louis' feet. His relief was enormous. He agreed without a murmur that from that moment he would be the Cardinal's devoted friend, and abandoned his mother's cause as heartlessly as he had done his friends in the rebellion. He came to see Anne, a little hesitantly, trying not to remember the last time they met, when he had promised such great things, and hinted they would marry. He hoped she would forgive him, like everyone else. When he saw her, he brightened; her beauty shone with greater lustre than ever; she glittered like a goddess in the midst of her brilliantly dressed ladies, and advanced towards him with one white hand held out to be kissed. Gaston forgot his wife in the same instant. He stepped forward, swept his sister-in-law a magnificent bow and kissed her hand. Anne looked at him, and smiled. Blood had flowed in torrents because of him; men like Montmorency had died on the block as a result of his treachery and boasting. She herself had trusted him twice, and twice been betrayed. He had even abandoned his mother.

'Welcome back, Monsieur,' she said in French. And then as he stood smiling into her eyes, she added one word in Spanish.

'*Perfidio!*' Then she turned her back and walked out of the room.

A chill had settled over the Court, which had its origins in fear of the King's Minister. Death and imprisonment had overtaken the highest nobles guilty of intrigue against the Cardinal. The Queen herself seemed completely isolated from the tumult which had just taken place. She spent much of her time at the small country château at St Germain des Prés, when she wasn't ordered to accompany her husband on his campaigns or his hunting trips. Otherwise she kept her small Court at the Louvre, patronised her Convent at Val de Grace more frequently than ever, and submitted without protest to her husband's public infatuation with her maid of honour Mademoiselle de Hautfort.

It was impossible to believe at first. Even Anne sought some other motive in the sudden appearances of Louis in her apartments after the rebellion was crushed, and his sojourns amongst the embarrassed women which lasted for an hour or more; during these times he seldom said a word. He merely sat and stared at the beautiful de Hautfort, who blushed and edged into a corner, taking care not to look up and meet the silent, obsessive stare which never left her face.

The King could not be in love. He had never shown the slightest interest in a woman before; his dislike and awkwardness with the whole female sex was too well known for anyone to take this odd infatuation seriously. It was ridiculous that he should haunt Anne's rooms and suddenly insist on her accompanying him everywhere, just because he wanted to stare at Mademoiselle de Hautfort.

But so it seemed, and by the spring he had so far advanced in this odd courtship that he summoned the girl and made her sit beside him. They talked about her life in the country, which flowers she preferred, and other innocent subjects. It was ridiculous to everyone at first, and then disturbing. But Anne, usually so proud and careful of her dignity, bore this added humiliation with surprising meekness. She did not persecute the unwilling object of her husband's doleful fancy. She treated de Hautfort kindly, and indeed teased her good-naturedly about her effect upon the King. And she was genuinely unconcerned about the odd situation which had developed because Spain was on the point of declaring war on France, and Anne was in the midst of the most dangerous and vital intrigue of her life.

*   *   *

Since 1631 Catholic France had been the active ally of Protestant Sweden and the German States who were in revolt against the Hapsburg Emperor Ferdinand, and French policy was therefore in inevitable conflict with the interests of Spain. Within two years the Swedish King Gustavus Adolphus had proved himself the greatest soldier in Europe; the Emperor Ferdinand suffered such a series of defeats that the war raged on the frontiers of Alsace, and when Gustavus Adolphus died on the battlefield of Lutzen, the intervention of the Spanish Hapsburgs was needed to save the Empire from extinction by its enemies. French troops fought side by side under the terms of the Swedish Treaty, following the policy of Richelieu which was to reduce the power of Spain and the Empire and thereby increase the influence of France until she became the premier power in Europe.

Spanish support for Marie de Medici, who was a permanent refugee in Brussels, and for Gaston's miserable rebellion, had so exasperated the King that he agreed to an alliance with Holland against Spain. Spain's reply was to declare war on France and invade Picardy.

Richelieu remained in Paris, shut up in his magnificent house the Palais Cardinal, so endangered by popular hatred for the war which was ascribed to his policy that he dared not show himself in the streets for fear of being stoned by the people. He worked without pause; he hardly slept and he ate his frugal meals at his writing table, sending couriers all over France, waiting for news of the invasion. Rumours spread through the city that he was ill, even dying, and the bright spirits forgot caution and expressed their joy at the prospect. Loudest among these were Marie de Chevreuse and her infatuated lover Chateauneuf. But they were ill-informed. Their enemy was silent, but not because he was about to leave the world. On the contrary he had never been more actively engaged in its affairs, and he shared his tremendous burden of work with his confidant Father Joseph. The monk had grown much older and more frail, though the fanatic fire still burned in his eyes, and the same fierce determination took his weary body on exhausting journeys across the length and breadth of France. They sat together as usual in Richelieu's private cabinet in the splendid house, and unlike the luxury and opulence of the public rooms, the cabinet was small, plainly furnished and comfortable. A large fire always burned there throughout the years, because Richelieu felt the cold. They had eaten, and the remains of their supper stood on the table.

'You've eaten nothing, Father,' the Cardinal said. 'Most of the food is on your plate. You mustn't fast at this time, I forbid it. I need your strength; France needs it!'

'France needs you, not me,' the monk said. 'You know what your enemies are saying? That you're sick to the death, lying here eaten by illness, dying of fear – do you know that's what is being spread about Paris?'

'I neither know nor care,' Richelieu said. 'I've more to occupy me than the stupid tattling of a lot of vapid courtiers. For these are the rumour mongers aren't they? Just as always; they've nothing to do in their country's time of danger but try to pull me down! Let them gossip – they'll see how dead I am as soon as we've driven the Spaniards back!'

'You're right, of course,' Father Joseph agreed. 'The only thing that matters is victory against Spain. By the way, would you call M. de Chateauneuf a vapid tattler? He's talking louder than anyone these days. So is the Duchess de Chevreuse. But this is not important, as you say.'

He leant forward and stirred the fire till the flames leapt up and the heat spread out, warming his cold limbs. The coldness in his body was not the chilliness of a slim man, like the Cardinal. Age and sickness were at work in him, and death was creeping after him like some faint shadow, growing darker and nearer every day. He had only a short time left to serve God and Richelieu, and he knew this.

'How do you mean,' the Cardinal said suddenly, 'Chateauneuf is talking? Father, I know you, when you have something hidden in your mind, some suspicion – what is it? Tell me!'

'Chateauneuf and Marie de Chevreuse are lovers. Spain is so well informed of every move we make that she seems likely to win the war in a few months, isn't that so? When you confer in council with the King, who is always present? The Lord Keeper of the Seals, M. de Chateauneuf. Who declared himself your devoted friend, and now goes round rejoicing because he thinks you're about to die or be dismissed? Who has the Queen's most intimate friend as his mistress – M. de Chateauneuf! I'm an old man, Eminence, and perhaps I've seen too many intrigues in the past not to imagine one now where probably none exist. But my senses tell me there's a connection here.'

'You think Chateauneuf is passing on State secrets?' Richelieu asked him. 'You think he's betraying our plans to Marie de Chevreuse and she is telling the Queen, who in turn – My God! My God, what a fool I've been, Father! How blind, how stupid!'

He struck his forehead with his clenched fist and sprang up from his chair. The monk watched him silently, as he moved round the room, pacing up and down, his mind working through the proposition and the possibilities, digesting, rejecting and divining further still.

'Spain is too successful,' he said suddenly. 'I should have known this. I saw it before my eyes, and I refused to see. We have a spy at Court, Father, and I tremble to think who it must be. So highly placed and so well informed, that it could only be one person. We suspect who the informant is – Chateauneuf! That miserable traitor I befriended, raised to the highest office – trusted with my innermost secrets! By the living God, Father, I'll get to the end of this. I'll have him arrested tomorrow morning, and his house searched. If I know these people, they always commit themselves to paper. His mistress will have written to him, that strumpet that I allowed to come back to Court because I thought she'd learnt her lesson. She'll have sent him letters. And he'll have kept them. We shall know all, by this time tomorrow!'

'"All" will involve more than the Keeper of the Seals and the Duchess de Chevreuse,' Father Joseph said at last. 'Are you prepared to find the Queen is betraying us to Spain?'

'Of course,' Richelieu said impatiently. 'I've never underestimated her. Of course it's the Queen who is passing the information at the last stage.'

'Will you arrest her too, if you discover proof of this? The King will be delighted, especially since he fancies himself in love at last.'

'The King would be overjoyed,' the Cardinal said. 'But it's not something I shall leave to His Majesty's judgment; I feel it's a little too warped where his wife is concerned. No, Father Joseph. I shall deal with Queen Anne. In my own way. But first I must have proof. Will you believe me if I tell you something?'

'I will,' the Capuchin said gravely. Richelieu came close to him; he was no longer angry, no longer even coldly sarcastic as he had been a moment ago, talking of Anne. He was quiet, almost humble.

'I'm not really concerned with Chateauneuf or that harlot Chevreuse. Their treachery to me means nothing. I'm not even thinking about the Queen at this moment. All that matters is that Spain will beat us in the field if this betrayal isn't stopped at source. I'm only thinking of France, now, Father. Nothing and no one else is important.'

'I believe that, Eminence,' the monk said. 'We will begin with Chateauneuf.'

The King paid a visit to St Germain-en-Laye; he was restless until he could join his troops in Picardy, and yet unable to ignore the advice of the Cardinal who insisted that it was still too uncertain for him to go there. What would befall France if her King were captured by the enemy? Louis took refuge in hunting and set off for St Germain, leaving Anne and most of the Court behind in Paris. Richelieu remained in the city too, though the Council members and the Lord Keeper of the Seals followed Louis and conducted the business of government at the small country château. Anne ordered her carriage as usual and accompanied by de Senécée, made her daily visit to the Val de Grace. She was dressed in a flowing cloak of dark blue velvet, the hood pulled over her head, and inside the lining of this cloak she carried half a dozen letters hidden in a secret pocket. It was a fresh morning, and yet Anne was tired. She had spent hours talking to Marie de Chevreuse in her apartments, and written her letters in the privacy of her bed when she was alone. The one addressed to her brother King Philip was long and full of details which the Duchess had passed on to her the previous night. It contained news of troops on their way to reinforce the armies of the Comte de Soissons in Picardy, and an assurance that the governor of the town of Corbie, a key fortification barring the road to Paris itself, would capitulate easily if he were attacked. Besides the military information, Anne had poured out her feelings to her brother, begging him to proceed against France and deliver her from the ignominy of her position as its Queen. For twenty-four years she had lived with a husband who neglected and despised her, refused to live with her as a man, and allowed his Minister, Spain's bitterest enemy, to humble and persecute her out of spite. She wrote of the death of the Duc de Montmorency, and on this page the writing was blotted by tears. He had been beheaded for his part in Gaston's rebellion, and this was done in spite of many petitions for mercy, including one from the Pope himself.

He had been misled by Gaston, she went on, pausing for a moment to repeat her contemptuous insult, perfidio, and when captured he was almost dead from wounds. He was a simple-minded man, beautiful to look at, with a generous heart and a trusting character. All his great military services to the King had been discounted; he had been sentenced and butchered for this one act as an example of pure terrorism by the Cardinal. It was also said that he had been found wearing a bracelet set with her miniature when he was captured and this had placed him beyond clemency. Such was the evil heart of Richelieu, whom she besought her brother to destroy. Without him, the letter repeated, underlined and scored in places for emphasis, without his malignant, perverted influence, her husband Louis might see his duty, and treat her as a Consort instead of an enemy. She had written many similar letters to her brother; the others, addressed to the exiled Marie de Medici and to the Spanish Governor of the Netherlands, were very similar in tone. Anne possessed a rare gift – she was as articulate and moving on paper as she was in the flesh. She could arouse passions in her letters as strongly as when the person she addressed were standing before her, exposed to the force of her personality and the stimulus of her beauty. In the letter to her mother-in-law, Anne mentioned the infatuation of the King for her maid of honour Mademoiselle de Hautfort, and with a generosity of which most women were incapable, said that she didn't blame the girl. She did nothing to encourage Louis, and everything to avoid giving offence to her mistress. But it was another painful humiliation that Anne had to bear, and everyone at Court was talking about it. As the coach made its way slowly through the narrow streets and turned off towards the Convent, Anne's tiredness and depression began to lift; there would be other letters at the Convent, left there by her faithful La Porte, the valet who had been dismissed after Buckingham's visit and still remained secretly in her service. These letters, carrying news from the outside world, were the very stuff of living to Anne. They broke the barriers Richelieu had erected round her; they gave her a sense of excitement and action, so that in spite of all appearances, she wasn't a voiceless cypher, caged like a bright-coloured bird in the Louvre, but a woman and a Queen who had never given up the struggle to be free.

At the gates the Abbess came to meet her; she curtsied deeply and kissed Anne's hand.

'I'll go to my oratory at once,' the Queen said. 'De Senécée, you will please wait in the gardens for me. I want to pray alone.' The oratory had been specially built for Anne's use; by the side of the altar there was a little cleft in the wall, covered by a curtain. She went to it, and drew out a packet of letters. There was one from Spain, in the handwriting of Cardinal D'Olivarez, her brother's Minister and favourite, and two from Brussels. For the next hour she knelt in the little oratory reading them, and then put them away in a carved vestment chest which had been placed at the back for this purpose. Leading off the oratory there was another small room with a writing table and materials. Here Anne wrote answers to the letters she had received and put them back into the secret niche in the wall. Before Spain invaded France, Mirabel the Ambassador used to come for an audience. Now he had been recalled and an official named Gerbier, who worked in the English Embassy, had taken his place as direct contact with Spain. Even Marie de Chevreuse considered this was dangerous and had tried to argue Anne out of meeting the man, but she was obdurate. It would need the combined powers of Europe to detach her miserable husband from the Cardinal. She risked all in order to gain all. The meetings with Gerbier continued, and La Porte acted as courier, leaving letters for her at the Convent gate, and taking them from the same place for despatch abroad.

While Anne occupied herself at the Convent, Chateauneuf had an audience of the King at St Germain-en-Laye, and having been graciously received by Louis, took his leave and left the apartments. In the corridor outside the King's rooms he was seized by the Cardinal's special Guards, and taken away under arrest. At the same time a detachment of the same Guards forced their way into his house in Paris, accompanied by three under secretaries of State, and removed three large coffers full of papers.

Late that evening the Cardinal's coach left for St Germain-en-Laye. Out of the mass of correspondence, he had found exactly what he predicted to Father Joseph, a packet of love letters from Marie de Chevreuse. They were indiscreet enough to destroy both her lover and herself, and to indict the Queen of France for the ultimate in crimes against the State.

9

'The Queen must know by now,' Louis remarked slowly. 'She must be terrified of what this means for her.' He faced Richelieu in his little audience chamber at St Germain; he had been woken by the Minister's arrival at midnight, and received him in his robe de nuit, silencing his gentlemen who protested that even the Cardinal should wait till morning. But in the last ten years since their association began, Louis had developed a nose which could scent out trouble and bloodshed as keenly as one of his own hunting dogs. And he enjoyed it, like war. He had begun to revel in the violent upheavals which shook his throne, because they always ended in success for him and death for others. He became excited, and forgot to be bored. He could hardly wait while his gown was put on him, to hurry out and hear what Richelieu had to tell him. Together they had read Marie de Chevreuse's letters to her lover. She too was an articulate writer; some of the more florid passages turned the King a sulky red with embarrassment. Others, where she referred to Richelieu, were so unspeakably coarse that it was difficult to believe a woman of education and birth had ever written them.

'How they hate you,' Louis murmured from time to

time as he read, and Richelieu only bowed his head without replying.

Then they had come on the political letters, full of support for Gaston in his rebellion, for the Queen Mother, for Spain, for all the enemies of France and Richelieu. And Anne's feelings had been quoted in full, with reports of conversations they had had, and letters which the Duchess had smuggled out for her. In one she remarked that this post office was no longer necessary, as her mistress had established another source, faster and safer than herself. At this point Louis raised his heavy eyes and looked at his Minister.

'What source? Do you know what this means?'

Richelieu only nodded, and made a gesture, begging the King to read on. Now the letters were finished; they were stacked in a neat pile on the table beside Louis' chair.

'She must be terrified by now,' the King repeated. 'Chateauneuf arrested – his papers taken. And the Duchess de Chevreuse.' He looked at the letters and shuddered. 'What filth lies in the minds of women, Richelieu. The way she speaks of you . . .' He could never resist causing the Cardinal a little pain, inflicting a harmless snub. It reduced him a little.

'A harlot, using a harlot's language,' the Cardinal shrugged. 'As you say, Sire, the Queen must indeed be terrified.'

He watched Louis carefully as he spoke, and he detected the quick gleam of pleasure in the dull eyes. Anne was what really interested the King. He sensed an opportunity which had so far evaded him, a chance to strike at her with all the bitterness of his perverted nature. And he could be righteous now, because he had concealed it from himself under the guise of loving someone else; he worshipped the beautiful, talented Mademoiselle de Hautfort with the passion of a man who knows that only words will ever be asked of him. Her virtue made her safe, and because she was safe and he would never have to become her lover, Louis could delude himself that he hated his wife because she was a barrier between them.

'She will be more frightened still by tomorrow morning. I anticipated your order, Sire, and ordered the arrest of the Duchess de Chevreuse. The Convent of the Val de Grace is under observation now. I believe it's the source of the Queen's correspondence mentioned in one of those letters. But watching is not enough, Sire. Nor, I suspect, will we get anything out of the Duchess. I doubt if torture would make her speak against the Queen, and we would lose time while it was being tried. I need the right to search that Convent. It can't be entered without the Archbishop of Paris's authority, and I would prefer him to give it to you, rather than me.'

'I'll demand it,' Louis said. 'I'll write to him tonight, and you can get his authority tomorrow. The Val de Grace! The convent where the Queen pretended to spend her time in prayer, in piety! It shall be razed to the ground, I'll have those damned nuns sent to cloisters where they'll learn the meaning of discipline!'

'We must make sure,' Richelieu said softly. 'Don't judge the Queen in advance, Sire. She could be guilty of writing to her brother, in defiance of your commands, I know, but not of sending information, or fomenting treason in your subjects. We mustn't take the babblings of the Duchess as a final proof.'

Louis looked up at him and smiled. 'Ah, my friend, you can't play fox with me. You think my wife is spying against France. That's what brought you here in the middle of the night; that's what you really think, and so do I. You want the proof to put before me, isn't that so?'

Richelieu looked down, away from him. 'I pray to God it won't be found,' he said.

'I pray to God it will,' Louis stood up suddenly. 'I know I can't have her executed, Richelieu, because you won't let me. But there's a fortress at Le Havre where she can go. No one escapes from there.'

He watched the Cardinal carefully. There were times when his Minister's attitude towards the Queen puzzled and angered him. She hated Richelieu; she had encouraged attempts on his life, supported Marie de Medici in her efforts to ruin him and allied herself with everyone who worked against him. Louis knew that in spite of his mild, reasoned manner, Armand de Richelieu was ruthless and bitterly vindictive. He had punished the least disloyalty to himself or his sovereign without mercy or regard to past services rendered. Yet he sensed that the Cardinal was hesitating, unwilling to agree even to life imprisonment for a woman whom they both believed to be guilty of high treason.

'You don't answer, my friend,' he said. 'What excuse can you make for her if she's been spying for Spain? How can you persuade me not to punish her this time?'

Richelieu looked up; he looked into the King's eyes and his own were cold and without a flicker of emotion.

'If the Queen is guilty, Sire, I'll arrange for her imprisonment in Le Havre myself. You have my word.'

'No mercy this time then?' Louis demanded.

'No mercy,' Richelieu said.

'Then proceed, proceed,' the King stood up and held out his hand; there was a slight flush on his sallow cheeks. 'Neglect nothing, Richelieu, protect no one. I want the guilty brought to trial, no matter who they are!'

* * *

Only two candles burned in the Queen's private cabinet in the Louvre. The curtains were drawn, and a fire flickered in the grate, casting a monstrous shadow of the woman sitting in a chair, her eyes closed against the feeble light, a handkerchief soaked through with tears in one listless hand.

Anne was alone; for forty-eight hours she had been shut up in the château at Chantilly by the King's order, unable to leave her rooms or receive anyone from outside. Chateauneuf was a prisoner; Marie de Chevreuse, her loving friend and ally, was a prisoner in one of her own husband's country fortresses, enduring God knew what interrogations at the hands of the King's officials. The fear of what was happening to her friend drove Anne out of her bed at night, walking the room till dawn. And now the worst blow of all had been delivered. After she had dined, or pretended to do so, because she couldn't eat or sleep, Anne saw Madame de Senlis approaching her. Of all her ladies, this was the only true adherent of the Cardinal, and her loyalty to him had never wavered. She curtsied to the Queen and said quite simply, without preliminaries, 'Madame, they have arrested La Porte. He is in the Bastille.' Then she curtsied again and withdrew.

If they had taken La Porte, then it was only a matter of time before they wrung her secrets out of him. Anne knew the rigours of the torture chamber too well to imagine that anyone could endure them indefinitely. He would betray her because he must, and so the Val de Grace would be invaded by the Cardinal's agents. She thought of that vestment coffer in the oratory and the mass of letters it contained, and almost fainted.

Letters would be waiting for her, left there by Gerbier, the English embassy official who was her link with Spain. These too would be discovered. Her advice to her brother to attack Corbie and march on Paris, her denunciations of Louis as a husband, her entreaties for help against Richelieu – all would be found in irrefutable proof that in French eyes she was a spy and a traitor, whose penalty under the law was death. She had sat alone in the half dark room, weeping hysterically, reproaching herself for the fate which had befallen Marie de Chevreuse, whom she genuinely loved, and for poor faithful La Porte. He had carried Buckingham's love letters to her in the years gone by, and her letters to him. She had brought destruction and death to everyone she touched. She had risked all to gain all. But instead of gaining, she had lost. She heard the door open, and didn't trouble to look round.

'Who is it?'

'De Senécée, Madame.'

'Why do you come in? I said I was not to be disturbed.'

'Madame,' the voice was so low it was almost a

whisper, and still it trembled. 'Madame, the Cardinal himself is here! He wants to see you.'

Anne got up; she moved slowly as if the effort were too much for her.

'Bolt the door. I won't see him.'

'Madame,' de Senécée whimpered, 'he anticipated that reply. He has a squad of guards with him; he says he has the King's authority to break down the door.'

'So,' Anne said after a moment. 'So, he comes to make the arrest himself! Very well; I shan't deprive him of that pleasure. Go and tell him I'll receive him in a few minutes. Summon my ladies, de Senécée, and get me ready.'

Nobody dared to speak in the bedroom, as Anne stood in the centre of the room, now brilliantly lit with candles, and stepped into a dress of purple velvet, with a high collar of stiffened lace framing her head. She chose the emeralds which had come to Isabella of Castile from the Conquistadors, and rubbed a little colour into her white cheeks. She made a gesture and the women moved quickly away from her; all but the relentless Madame de Senlis were in tears. Anne stepped to the long polished steel mirror on the wall and examined herself carefully. She was going to leave that room as a prisoner; very well, she would also leave it as a Queen and a Princess of Spain.

She turned to Madame de Senécée, who was choking into a handkerchief, and managed a pale smile.

'Don't cry, my poor Amélie. I'm not afraid. Be good enough to have a cloak ready and a change of clothes packed for me. Now, will one of you please admit the Cardinal?'

When he came into the room, he didn't speak. He bowed very low to her, and turning to her ladies, told them to leave the Queen alone with him. Anne waited silently till all had curtsied one by one and gone. Now the room was full of lights and the fire blazed round fresh logs. It might have been the setting for an intimate reception, such as she used to give for Marie de Chevreuse and a few friends. Richelieu was wearing cavalier costume; he carried his broad feathered hat in his left hand.

'Where are your guards, Eminence?'

'Guarding your Majesty. I see you received my message from Madame de Senlis? La Porte was arrested this morning and taken to the Bastille. Letters from you were found on him.'

He stepped closer to her, and with a sudden gesture, threw his hat on to a chair.

'This isn't the time for formality, Madame. Nor for standing up when everything about your circumstances says you should sit down. We must talk, you and I, and it will take some time.'

'I have nothing to say to you,' Anne said.

'No?' To her surprise he smiled. Then he shook his head, as if he were arguing with a child.

'You are a very brave woman, Madame, and a very obstinate one. But I feel sure that you aren't also a fool. Only a fool would continue to fight me at this moment. Let me put it to you. You are discovered, Madame. I have letters, written by you, which could send you to the Place de Grève!'

'I'm not afraid of death,' Anne said slowly. 'It would be a relief after my life these twenty years. You can take your revenge upon me, Eminence, I shan't resist you now. You've seized my friends, you'll have them tortured and then killed when they're no further use to you. I'm happy to die with them.'

'I believe you,' Richelieu said seriously. 'I believe you'd bear it very bravely and die with great credit. But the King has other plans for you. How would you like to spend the rest of your life shut up in one of the oubliettes in Le Havre? Ah, I see you've heard of the place. You're young, Madame, and strong. You could live years in such a hole, groping in perpetual darkness, eaten by rats! That is what His Majesty suggested to me, only the night before last.'

She turned away from the cold green eyes and the thin, mocking smile. She was trembling so much that she was forced to sit down.

'I'm going to order some wine for both of us,' Richelieu said. He was completely at ease, completely in command. He rang Anne's bell and gave the order to a page. When it was brought he poured a glass and gave it to her.

'You had better drink this,' he said. 'Your colour is quite gone. Now. Let us make the position clear. You have committed treason.'

She half left the chair, and then sank back before the cold, accusing stare. 'I deny it. Any letters you've found on La Porte were forgeries. I never wrote them!'

'They are in your writing,' Richelieu said. 'They contain information about the fortifications in Picardy and advice to the King of Spain on how best to defeat France. You haven't spared the King, if I remember. Is it true that he hasn't visited you at night for fifteen years? How foolish you were to write about Mademoiselle de Hautfort; you know how sensitive His Majesty is. Need I go on?'

'I deny it,' Anne repeated. 'I deny everything.'

'I expected that you would,' the Cardinal said. He

seated himself, crossing one slim leg over the other, and sipped his wine.

He considered her in silence for some minutes. He had come determined to break her, or failing that, to remove her to Compiègne under guard till she could be brought to trial. Now the second alternative seemed so impossible that he wondered how he had ever considered it seriously. She was so beautiful it hurt him to sit and look at her. Desire welled up in him, and it was mixed with hatred and anger and a love which abhorred seeing her white-faced and in tears. He couldn't abandon her even now, and having admitted that, he felt renewed. He had been harsh with her, threatening, sarcastic. Now he moved his chair close to her, took the wine cup from her and refilled it, and spoke very gently.

'I have an order from the Archbishop of Paris, authorising a search of the Val de Grace. Already La Porte has admitted collecting letters there. Madame, for the love of God, why do you think I'm here?'

Anne pressed one hand to her throbbing head. 'To enjoy your triumph over me. To arrest me. If you were less cruel you'd do it and have done.'

'You're wrong, Madame,' Richelieu said. 'I came to try and save you if I can. It isn't the first time, you know that. Buckingham – Gaston d'Orleans' rebellion – I've stood between you and the King for all these years. I stand between you still. And you know why!'

'You told me,' she said, 'at the monastery at Compiègne. You said your love had shielded me.'

'I also said it would go on, whether you wanted it or not,' he said. 'And it will, Madame, because I find that I love you as much as I ever did. Nothing can change that now.'

She did not look at him; she felt the burning eyes upon her and she began to cry. Still the soft, insistent voice went on.

'Louis hates you. For twenty years he's longed to get rid of you because of his own failure. I've stopped him, Madame. But you've gone too far this time. I uncovered the intrigue because I had to, or risk France being conquered by Spain. I couldn't risk that even for you. Now the King knows too much to be fobbed off. He knows about the Convent, about La Porte, he knows you've been writing to Spain. It's only a matter of days before he discovers everything that you've been doing, till other letters are found like the ones La Porte had in his pocket when he was arrested. And I swear before Almighty God that the King will wreak twenty years of spite upon you! Le Havre, Madame. Darkness, stench, vermin – oblivion! I'm not threatening you now, I'm trying to make you see what will happen to you, unless you listen to me. I can help you. I can save you from it all.'

She had sat with her eyes shut, fighting the words and the images, fighting the sense of growing helplessness as he talked on. Now she forced herself to look into his face, and to see the answer to her question there even before she asked it.

'What is your price?'

'Your trust. Your submission to me personally. I've waited a long time, Madame, and suffered a great deal in my own way. Those are my terms and nothing less will do. I'm not asking you to love me. In return I'll save your life and within a year you'll know what it means to be the Queen of France and the friend of Richelieu.'

'The mistress of Richelieu,' Anne said slowly. 'That

is what you've wanted for all these years, isn't it? I must do that, or you won't help me.'

'Those are my terms,' he said quietly. 'You may not find them as unpleasant as you think. I told you, I'm not expecting to be loved.'

'You want me to submit to sacrilege?' Anne cried out. 'I won't do it. I'd rather throw myself at the King's feet and beg for mercy! I'll tell him what you've proposed to me – I'll confess everything to him! Then if I suffer, Eminence, you'll suffer with me!'

He shrugged, and the little smile came back to his mouth. 'You're very naïve, my dear Madame. Have you really been married to the King for twenty years and learnt nothing about him? Don't you know that he is so jealous of you that it's a sickness? You imagine he'd relent if you poured out a tale of my efforts to seduce you, if you knelt before him, admitting how you had tried to betray him and even succeeding in tempting his own Minister away from him? If he believed you, he'd have you burnt alive for fornicating with a priest. Because that is how he'd see it! Oh, I should suffer too, but I doubt if that would console you in the end, supposing of course that you proved cleverer than me, and I couldn't persuade His Majesty that this was yet another attempt to put between us, and accomplish Spain's desires by getting rid of me. Come! No more heroics, no more phantasies. Be sensible, and make your peace with me. You must admit,' he said gently, 'that I'm a very patient man.'

Anne didn't answer. Everything he said was true; she could see the hopelessness of her position, even as he exposed it, step by step. Mercy from Louis; understanding, forgiveness from Louis . . .

She covered her face with her hands. 'God help me,' she said. 'What can I do? I'm lost.'

She could have accepted death. She could have borne the humiliation of a trial, the public exposure of her treason, and then the penalty itself with the courage and dignity of her royal race. Anne was not a coward, and the threat of execution would not have moved her. But the dungeons of Le Havre were a nightmare. To live in darkness for the rest of her life; sinking to the lowest level of physical degradation and filth, tormented by vermin, stalked by the huge ferocious prison rats. She raised her head and looked across at the man who waited, his large eyes fixed upon her as if their gaze transmitted the force of his tremendous will. 'I will make him kill me,' she whispered. 'I'll confess to things so terrible that he will have to kill me.'

Richelieu shook his head. 'He won't do it,' he said. 'He's very cruel, didn't you know that? He'll keep you alive so that you can suffer. He's enchanted with the idea of Le Havre and what it means for you. He'll only think of extra miseries to punish you. Tell me, will you be compromised when the Val de Grace is searched?'

'I shall be ruined,' Anne said. 'Everything is there, in my oratory.'

'And La Porte? He is in your confidence completely?'

'Yes,' she said again. 'He's served me secretly since Buckingham left France. He knows everything.'

'In that case,' Richelieu said, 'we had better make sure that the searchers at the Convent find nothing important. And that La Porte doesn't suffer the rigours of a full interrogation.'

'What do you mean,' Anne said. 'What are you saying?'

'I'm thinking of how you may be saved from this situation,' Richelieu answered. 'You have agreed to my terms, Madame, and I know it. You are being sensible, are you not? Imprisonment for life, or the chance to come into your own as a Queen, and as a woman too. You've made the choice; that's understood. Now, let's arrange the details. You must make a full confession and sign it, so that I can put it before the King.'

'A full confession! I'll be condemned at once!'

'A full confession on some points, not a confession in full,' the Cardinal amended. 'You must admit writing to your brother the King of Spain. Louis knows you've done this. You must admit it, but swear that the letters contained only personal news, from sister to brother. You must admit writing to Madame de Fargis, but again only to ask how she was faring in exile. The same of your correspondence with Marie de Medici. Admit you disobeyed and saw the Ambassador Mirabel at the Convent, but that nothing political ever passed between you. That's all you need say in your submission. The rest can be left to me. The King's got the scent, and he must find something wrong to satisfy him, but not wrong enough to do anything about it. He will have to pardon you, because your faults will turn out to be trifling ones after all. He'll be very disappointed, very frustrated; but I shall persuade him to be generous to you. I've done it before, many times.'

Slowly Anne stood up; it was agreed, resolved, and yet she hadn't said a word. He was showing her the way out, and because of him she knew that it was all possible, and she would escape unscathed.

'You can get word to the Val de Grace,' she said.

'But you'll need something the Abbess recognises comes from me, or she won't touch my papers. Here, take this ring; she knows it's mine.'

He took the ring from her, and for a moment their fingers touched. It was an uncut ruby in the shape of a heart, with a border of pearls and diamonds ending in a crown above the stone. Richelieu slipped it on to his little finger and admired it for a moment. He smiled.

'You've a brave spirit, Madame,' he said. 'It soon recovers. We will do very well together, you and I.'

'One thing,' Anne said quickly. 'I've one thing to ask of you. Let Marie de Chevreuse go free!'

'Impossible,' he said. 'She's been so foolish, so indiscreet that I can't possibly excuse her.'

'You can do anything you want,' Anne said fiercely. 'You can save Marie too; if you want the last part of your infamous bargain fulfilled by me, then that's *my* price, Eminence. Marie goes free!'

'Very well. She shall escape. So will your friend La Porte.'

Anne turned away from him; she hadn't expected this generosity, and it overwhelmed her for a moment. She wiped away tears, and when she looked at him again there was a softness in her face which he had never seen before.

'Thank you,' she said. 'I love them both. I can't let them suffer while I escape.'

He came to her then, and taking her hand in his he bent and kissed it. 'They won't be harmed. I promise you. And when I come to you, I shall show this.' The ruby gleamed on his finger. 'I'm not asking you to love me, Madame. Only to let me love you. And it may not be as disagreeable as you think.'

'I don't understand you,' Anne said slowly. 'How

can you bear to touch me, knowing how I feel? How can you force yourself upon me?'

'Because pride is a cold bedfellow,' Richelieu said. 'I have none left where you're concerned, Madame, and what I have is satisfied by having you depend on me at last. As for your feelings towards me – I have an instinct they may change in time. Now you can leave everything to me. I shall come back tomorrow with my secretary and a draft submission admitting your faults. You will have to be humble, Madame, and contrite. No one must suspect that you and I have made our peace just yet. And it is made, isn't it?'

'Yes,' Anne said at last. 'It is.'

* * *

On 18 August, the Archbishop of Paris, the Chancellor Seguier, two Secretaries of State and a guard of soldiers, appeared at the Convent of the Val de Grace with an order to arrest the Abbess and search the building. Watched by the weeping nuns the King's officials broke open the vestment chest in the Queen's oratory, and also examined the papers found in a small writing desk in the room leading off the oratory itself. A great many documents and letters were taken away under seal, and read by Seguier and the Secretaries. After a whole day spent looking through them, they reported to the King that they had found nothing dated later than 1630, and that there wasn't a single incriminating word as regards politics or the campaign then being fought against Spain. At the Convent, the Abbess thanked God that she had had plenty of time to dispose, not only of the Queen's letters, but even of the ashes which were all that was left of them. And in the torture chamber at the Bastille, Anne's old servant La Porte faced his inquisitors, the Chancellor Seguier among them, and admitted on his knees that he had carried letters from Her Majesty the Queen to the British Embassy on one occasion eight months previously, and collected a packet for delivery to her. He denied ever having used the Val de Grace as a post bureau, and though the Chancellor bullied him and the instruments of torture were pointed out to him by all his questioners, La Porte refused to add another word to his statement, and no other pressures were applied to make him change his mind.

His admissions were found to agree exactly with the statement which Anne had written and signed and which had been presented to the King by the Cardinal Richelieu. There was no proof of any conspiracy or of any crime graver than a petty disobedience of the King's command not to write to her brother, or her exiled friends.

The King had suddenly removed to Chantilly, but Anne had not even seen him. During her interviews with Richelieu she answered his questions in the presence of independent witnesses who could report back to the King. He had made no sign towards her since that night in her room. He was humble, respectful and seemed diligent in his pursuit of the truth. Only the news that nothing had been found at the Val de Grace, and that La Porte had not been tortured, assured Anne that she had not imagined the interview and the pact that had been made.

By the end of the month, though she had never seen Richelieu alone, or detected the slightest sign of warmth or conspiracy in his manner, Anne had proof that he had kept his promises to her in full. She received an angry, insulting letter from Louis himself, forgiving her for disobeying him, but forbidding her to visit any convent in the future, or to write any letters to anyone except under strict supervision. It was a long way from the oubliettes at Le Havre, but it was the best he could do. Surrounded by her ladies, Anne read the letter and began to cry. She had followed Richelieu's advice very closely in the last harrowing weeks; she had humbled herself so deeply that she felt overcome with self-disgust. Her tears were of shame and humiliation as she read the spiteful letter. Richelieu had not exaggerated. How he hated her; how he would have delighted in putting her away for ever. She looked up and saw Mademoiselle de Hautfort watching her; the girl glanced away quickly and blushed. He wasn't man enough to have a mistress, he wanted to pretend, to play act.

'Madame,' de Senécée approached her. 'His Eminence is in your audience chamber. Will you receive him?'

'Yes, of course. Come with me, and you too, de Filandre.'

He bowed very low to her, and kissed her hand. The two ladies-in-waiting stepped back, after curtsying to Richelieu, and he led Anne to the window where they could talk.

'You have his pardon,' he said. 'I couldn't help the insults; he insisted on them.'

'I am sure he did,' she said. 'Is it all over now? Has he done trying to trap me?'

'He's tried and failed,' Richelieu said. 'You're safe now. I see you've been crying, Madame. Believe me, there's no need. We're returning to Paris; the news of the campaign is very encouraging. Spain is being

231

driven back. We shall have peace by the end of the year. I have some news I thought would please you.' He smiled at her, and made a little gesture, signifying his annoyance that they weren't alone. 'The Duchess de Chevreuse has had the good fortune to escape. The King had sent an order confining her to the fortress at Luches; there are oubliettes there too, you know. But alas, my dear Madame, someone must have warned her, because she disguised herself as a man, and set out for the Spanish border. We'll never catch her now.'

'Thank God,' Anne whispered. 'And La Porte?'

'One year's imprisonment, no more. He shan't be too uncomfortable, I promise you. But don't try and get in touch with the Duchess. She's safe now, and you must banish her out of your life completely. Will you promise me that?'

'How can I help it?' Anne answered. 'It seems I owe you everything. I can't accustom myself to the feeling. But if I thank you, it will be false, can you understand that?'

He nodded. He seemed unable to take his eyes away from her face for a moment. The sense of his nearness was overpowering, in spite of the fact that they were watched by two of her women.

'I can understand it. You don't have to thank me. Farewell, Madame. I shall claim my reward in Paris.'

In all women there is a capacity to become resigned to a circumstance however abhorrent, once that acceptance is inevitable. To Anne, after twenty years of unremitting resistance to one man, her surrender was almost a relief. The danger which had threatened her, the violent emotional strain of trying to outwit Richelieu, had exhausted her mentally and physically. Deprived of the support of Marie de

Chevreuse, who might have mocked her into a fresh defiance of the Cardinal, Anne sank into a miserable lethargy, through which she sought to escape the final sealing of the bargain she had made with the Cardinal.

He talked of love, but not in the impassioned words of Buckingham; he made no florid gestures; he spoke of her seduction as if it were an evening playing cards, and yet the sensuality played round them both like lightning in a storm about to break.

Her spirit rebelled constantly; her pride and her conscience cried out again and again that she could still withdraw, betray her promise to him now that he had kept all his promises to her. But the temptation was enfeebled by a sense that what was going to happen was no less than fate. It was useless to resist, futile to ignore the fact that she needed Richelieu to survive. Without him, she would have perished, and all her friends with her. There was no one strong enough to stand against him; she had tried them all, and all had failed. The greatest failure was her own. He would come, and she would submit. She had learnt how to absent herself from her own body when Louis first consummated the marriage. What Richelieu enjoyed would not be Anne of Austria, but an inanimate victim, slack and unresponsive as a sawdust doll.

Madame de Senlis was dozing on a window seat, her embroidery half slipping off her lap; it was her duty to undress the Queen and remain with her till the candles in her bedroom were blown out, but the Queen hadn't sent for her, and it was long past eleven. De Senlis was tired; she was not a young woman and her life since she was placed in Anne's service hadn't been an easy one. She had remained loyal to the Cardinal and

233

borne the hostility of her Royal mistress and the other ladies as best she could. She had hoped a few months ago, when the Queen was under guard at Chantilly, that at last her own servitude would end with the Queen's imprisonment or return to Spain, but the danger had passed. The King still came to visit his wife, but he hardly spoke a word to her, beyond the most formal greeting; he merely retired into a corner with Mademoiselle de Hautfort, and sat mumbling a few stilted sentences, or didn't speak at all. The Louvre was gloomy and life there was monotonous. She longed to retire from it all.

At a quarter to midnight she was woken by a page. For a moment she thought the Queen's bell had rung, but the boy only bowed and handed her a folded slip of paper, with the Cardinal's red seal stamped on it. De Senlis got up, yawning, and opened the note. Suddenly her mouth sagged, and was immediately covered by one hand in a gesture of alarm; she made a series of little noises, expressing astonishment, excitement and fear. There was a door in the Queen's bedroom which opened into a secret passage from another part of the Louvre. This door had been kept locked, and she was in charge of the key. No one ever used that entrance, it was unlikely that Anne herself even knew about it. De Senlis was instructed to unlock the door, and make certain that the Queen was not disturbed during the night. A gentleman, too exalted to name, intended making use of the passage, and would be received by Her Majesty in private. She was instructed also to give the Queen the ring, which the page would deliver to her, as a proof of the identity of the said exalted personage. The note was signed by Richelieu.

'It is he, Madame, isn't it?' De Senlis had forgotten

how much she disliked Anne at that moment. Her mistress was undressed, her hair flowing down over her shoulders, and she stood with the heart-shaped ruby in her hand. The red eye of the stone and the bright glitter of the diamonds round it sparkled in her open palm.

'It is the King, isn't it?' De Senlis went on, gasping with excitement. After twenty years, when reconciliation seemed impossible, Louis was coming to visit his wife. And by secret passage, in the middle of the night. De Senlis felt as if she would burst with pride at being the chosen one to unlock the door, and go to bed with such a tremendous secret in her keeping.

Anne looked up at her, and flushed. 'Yes,' she said. 'It is the King. This is a ring I gave him.' She slipped it on her finger. 'Where is this door? I never knew about it.'

'There, Madame, by the figure of Juno in the tapestry. Look, I'll show you. My God,' she exclaimed suddenly, 'where is the key?'

'In your hand,' Anne said coldly. She was trembling now; the act of fate was suddenly real; the door which the waiting woman opened, squeaked and a dark passage showed beyond: at some time that night he would come through it and she would be alone with him.

'Madame, aren't you excited? After all this time, His Majesty comes!'

'De Senlis!'

'Yes, Madame?'

'You realise that the King wants this to be kept secret? You know that you mustn't whisper one word of this to anyone, or he will have you sent to the Bastille? Do you understand? One word, and you know His Majesty these days. I shan't be able to protect you, and if you disobey me, I won't even try.'

'Not a murmur,' de Senlis promised. She had become quite pale with fear. Of course the King wanted to keep the business secret. What would de Hautfort think if she knew he were in the Queen's bed again? Suppose it failed, suppose the Queen didn't please him after all these years – there were a dozen reasons why she shouldn't speak a word of what she knew. The anger of Cardinal Richelieu with those who annoyed the King, was the most cogent of them all.

'Not a word Madame. Shall I blow out your candles, or shall I leave one burning?'

'Leave one. And draw the bedcurtains. You may go now.' Anne climbed into the bed; the curtains were pulled close, and she blew out her little taper, so that she was lying in total darkness. There was no way of knowing how much time had passed when she heard the creak of the door in the wall opening. It might have been a few minutes or an hour after de Senlis had left her. She lay with her eyes shut, listening to the sound of someone moving across the floor. She felt the bedcurtains being drawn aside, and opened her eyes suddenly to find a candle held above her, revealing for a brief moment a pale bearded face with luminous grey eyes. Then the candle flame was blown out.

10

The sound of a harpsichord drifted through the sunny rooms of the Queen's apartments at the Louvre, the notes as delicate and clear as fountain water. The musician was one of the ladies-in-waiting, Madame de Mortemart; the King himself had commanded her to play for him, and the Queen and her ladies had taken their places in the main salon for the concert, while Louis retired into the window seat of an ante-chamber with Mademoiselle de Hautfort. From there he could look into the salon, seeing and also being seen, as etiquette required. The music was just a pleasant background, so he could talk to his confidante in peace. Marie de Hautfort was less shy with him now; she no longer blushed and murmured trivialities when they were together. She spoke quite boldly of controversial subjects like the continuing war with Spain, and even tried to praise the Queen to him, which irritated Louis so much that he responded by sulking for days on end. But he sulked in Anne's apartments, forbidding his wife and her ladies to enjoy themselves because he was miserable and out of sorts with de Hautfort. It enraged him to find that the object of his timid phantasies appeared to be loyal to her mistress, and it enraged him still more that Anne herself accepted his devotion to de Hautfort with amiable indiffcrence. He could see her at that moment, sitting in the middle of the circle of women, listening to the music with an expression of serenity on her face that made her even more beautiful these days. She seemed happy, and Louis couldn't understand it.

She was calm, and this calmness permeated everything she did; it was as if she had come to terms with her life, and even with the Cardinal. Months had passed since he had received her letter, humbly asking his pardon for writing letters and disobeying his commands, and he had clung to the hope that in spite of everything, she hadn't truly reformed. But nothing happened. Anne had cut herself off completely from the political intriguing which had occupied her for the last twenty years; she received him with the same icy politeness, but with indifference instead of resentment. It was as if he had ceased to matter to her, and nothing mattered less than his clumsy pursuit of her lady-in-waiting. Anne smiled on the girl, treated her with friendliness and generosity, and as a consequence, had won her gratitude and respect.

He leaned back, considering his wife and the change which had taken place in her in the last few months. He didn't like it, whatever the reason. He had a sixth sense for happiness in other people because he was so miserable himself, and he knew beyond doubt that Anne was content in a way that she had never been before. He turned to the beautiful blonde girl beside him, and touched her sleeve.

'You're not paying me attention, Mademoiselle. Your thoughts are far away today!'

'I beg your pardon, Sire. I was listening to the music.'

Louis scowled. He knew by the way she answered that she was going to be difficult. They wouldn't have a pleasant tête-à-tête after all, allowing him to go away and dream that all might have been different if he had married her, instead of that arrogant, cold-hearted Spaniard. Women were difficult and cruel; they could never be trusted; he glanced at her angrily, already resenting her for being what she was. Women were hateful. There was no one in the world that he could love, or who loved him.

'You didn't come hunting this morning,' he said. 'I was disappointed.'

'Her Majesty needed me, Sire.'

'When I want to see you, the Queen must let you go,' he said. 'She's no right to thwart me. I shall tell her so!'

Mademoiselle de Hautfort flushed; she answered him so sharply that he winced.

'I must beg you not to, Sire. I serve the Queen, and I wouldn't neglect my duty to her for anything in the world. I couldn't bear her to be hurt or humiliated on my account!'

'You're very foolish,' Louis said. His temper was rising fast. The day was ruined; his dream was proving herself a shrew who didn't understand him. 'You're loyal to someone who doesn't know the meaning of loyalty. Or gratitude! Where are the others who've taken her part against me? Exiled, dead, imprisoned – all of them! You should know whom to trust, Mademoiselle; believe me, it isn't the Queen.'

'I beg your Majesty's pardon,' de Hautfort said coldly. 'But I must disagree.'

239

'Then I must leave you,' Louis snapped. He got up, and immediately the harpsichord recital stopped and everyone in the main salon was on their feet. Anne came towards him as he walked to the door.

'Are you leaving so soon?' He looked into the clear blue eyes and the revulsion in them made him cringe. She had always made him feel a worm in the dust, just by looking at him.

'The atmosphere stifles me,' he said angrily. 'I need fresh air.' She always made him stammer too, so he said as little to her as possible.

'Good day, Madame.'

She curtsied, he pretended to kiss her hand, and then the doors closed after him. Anne paused for a moment and then went to where Mademoiselle de Hautfort stood, her cheeks blazing.

'Not another quarrel?'

'Yes, Madame. I'm afraid he's very angry with me.'

'What happened? My poor de Hautfort, you must try to be more patient with him. You know he dotes on you.'

'And I dote on *you*, Madame,' the girl said passionately. 'I wouldn't let anyone speak against you! Not even the King!' De Hautfort was a girl of strong character and definite principles; she was also perceptive and intelligent, and she had soon discovered the pettish, vindictive nature of the King. She was no longer in awe of him; she bore his attentions because she dared not refuse them outright, but she also enjoyed frustrating him.

'You mustn't take any notice,' Anne said gently. 'Let him say what he pleases about me, so long as you don't believe him. He's the King, my child, and you mustn't anger him too much, or he'll make you suffer. For my sake, be kind to him, and keep the peace.'

Mademoiselle de Hautfort suddenly sank down on her knees in front of Anne. She took the Queen's hand and kissed it.

'Madame, you're an angel of goodness! May God bless you!'

'He has,' Anne said, and lifted the girl to her feet. 'He has, in many ways.'

She saw Madame de Senlis watching her. The woman was so bemused by what had just happened that her mouth was still a little open. She had brought Anne the ruby ring again that afternoon. She had never spoken a word about the visits, which took place almost every night, preceded by the same strange rigmarole as the first time. The ring was delivered to her; she gave it to the Queen who wore it. In the morning it had gone. The door into Anne's bedroom was permanently unlocked. The Cardinal had sent for her after the first visit, and shown himself so stern that de Senlis left him trembling with terror. One word of the secret passage, one whisper that all was now well between their Majesties . . . The Cardinal had shown her an order to the Governor of the Bastille with her name on it, and the unhappy woman nearly fainted. She left him vowing with tears that she would be more silent than the dead.

'Go on, de Mortemart, please finish your playing. We were enjoying it.'

Anne sat down again and listened with her eyes closed. He was coming that night; she touched the ruby ring on her finger, turning it round and round. She felt the lethargy creeping over her at the thought of that door opening and the first caress he would give her in the darkness. They had never spoken; he possessed her in silence and she submitted in silence. But after twenty-six years of marriage, Anne had learnt the secret of physical love for the first time.

He had said he loved her before they became lovers, but he had never asked her if she loved him. Nor could Anne have answered him. But she could watch Louis paying his pathetic court to the beautiful Marie de Hautfort, and even pity him, because she knew now what a man could be like, and what he was capable of giving to a woman.

* * *

'She has made you happy, Armand. But that can only increase your sin,' Father Joseph said. 'And now she is sinning too. Have you no fear of hell?'

'Hell is tomorrow, Father,' Richelieu answered him. 'Today I have a foretaste of heaven. That's enough for the moment. Is it such a sin to love? Have you never felt the temptations of the heart?'

'My heart has always belonged to God,' the monk said quietly. 'Yours, and your soul with it, are given to the things of this world. And now to the Queen. Does she love you, my friend? Apart from the pleasure she has in you, does she feel anything for you beyond that?'

The Cardinal hesitated for a moment. It was a question he refused to ask himself.

'I didn't ask for love,' he said. 'No one can make love part of the terms in a bargain like ours. I asked for what I've been given. I'm content with that. If *I* love *her*, then that is something else. And I do, Father.

I haven't many weaknesses,' he added, and he smiled. 'You must allow me that one.'

'And if there is a child?' the monk asked. 'What will you do then? What will become of both of you?'

'There must be a child,' Richelieu answered. 'And it must be a son. I have been King of France in all but name for many years. It's only fitting that my son should succeed me. I shock you, Father – I'm sorry. It's late, and I must go, my friend. Pray for my soul's salvation; I'm not yet ready to repent!'

Father Joseph bowed and took his leave. He moved slowly with the caution of a man who is constantly in pain. He had never seen Richelieu in such a human light before; he could truthfully say that until the last few months he had never heard the great Minister laugh aloud. Now, because he was committing sacrilege and adultery, his heart was light and his energies revitalised. He worked eighteen hours a day, and his objective was to bring about peace with Spain, whose military invasion had been a failure. He was complete master of France and of the King; his enemies were scattered, and the astonished Court beheld the most bitter and implacable of them, the Queen herself, submissive and polite to the Minister. Gaston sulked as usual, but there was nobody left to take him seriously. He was placated with enormous sums of money which he squandered on women and gambling; the suggestion that he might wish to resume his life in Brussels with his mother, was enough to quell his feeble outbursts. Richelieu had triumphed over them all; the strangest conquest was the one he had confessed to the Capuchin, his liaison with Anne of Austria. He had revealed, rather than confessed; there was no repentance, no desire for absolution.

Father Joseph knew too much about the vagaries of human nature to be surprised by anything. He accepted the extraordinary love affair, the nights they spent together when their bodies communed in an unlawful passion and yet neither spoke a word. They were too proud to submit to each other in the real sense. Communication between them was safe so long as it was purely physical; it allowed the woman to keep her dignity and even to delude herself that she was not responsible, and the man to enjoy his triumph in the way that appealed to him most. Love. The monk made his slow way down the long corridors of the Palais Cardinal; was this love, this relationship? What did it truly mean to the Queen, whose heart might well be as cold as ice while her senses burned – love had meant many things to Richelieu himself, not least the profanation of his priestly vows. Richelieu had laughed, calling that love his weakness. Now there was a second, more dangerous than any mortal passion. The pride which wanted to place his bastard son upon the throne of France.

At eleven o'clock on the last day of November 1637, Anne sent her ladies-in-waiting out of her bedroom, refusing to let Madame de Senécée help her into bed and pull the heavy curtains. She wished to pray, Anne said, and she was not to be disturbed again that night. When she was alone, she did fall on her knees before the little shrine of the Madonna and child which had travelled with her when she left Spain. But prayer wouldn't come; it was impossible to gaze up at the serene, chaste image of the Mother of God, and ask for help in her condition. In despair Anne got up from her knees, and began to pace the bedroom. The ruby ring gleamed on her finger; he was coming again that night, the shadowy lover whose face she had seen only once, the first night of her seduction. They met constantly in public, both hiding behind the strictest formality, and in all these months no word of intimacy had ever passed between them. Now they must come face to face; they could no longer hide from each other in the darkness. At midnight the tapestry door in the wall began to open; Anne swung round, facing it.

He came into the lighted room, and hesitated, one hand on the edge of the door; he wore a long robe of dark green silk, and his head was bare. He saw her standing there, still dressed in her robe de nuit, the frothing lace of her nightdress spilled out of the neck and loose sleeves. Her red hair hung down her back, and she was pale from weeping.

Richelieu came up to her, and gently took her hand.

'How very beautiful you look, Madame,' he said. 'This is a delight that I have missed so far. You must always receive me like this.' He turned her hand over and kissed the palm.

'We are ruined, Richelieu,' Anne spoke in a whisper. 'Destroyed. Soon the whole world will see us in the light.'

'Be calm,' his soft voice said. Both hands were holding hers, caressing it. 'What's happened? Tell me.'

Anne shivered and drew back from him. 'I am pregnant. You understand what this means? I am ruined, disgraced! The King hasn't touched me for fifteen years – I shall bear a bastard before the world!'

'You will bear my son, Madame,' Richelieu said. 'And yours; you have fulfilled all my hopes. You've made me very happy.'

'You must be mad,' Anne cried out. 'I've fulfilled your hopes! What hopes? To have me divorced, imprisoned, executed for adultery – my God, was this your purpose, your revenge on me?'

She covered her face with both hands and began to weep hysterically. He moved to her very quickly; for a slightly-built man he was very strong. He placed his hands on her shoulders, forcing her to look at him.

'Madame,' he said. 'Our child is a blessing, not a disaster. You must trust me now more than ever.'

He looked into her eyes and smiled; there was no mockery, no challenge in that smile. Only a deep tenderness.

'You're more helpless now than you were six months ago,' he said. 'I find that it becomes you. Think clearly, and you won't be afraid. France needs an heir. And you're going to give her one. Your child will rule this country if it's a son, and I feel in my heart that it is. An end to civil war, an end to the prospect of Gaston d'Orleans wearing the crown of St Louis. You will be truly Queen of France, mother of the Dauphin. Come,' he said gently, 'where's your courage? You've never shown a faint heart before.'

'But the King,' Anne implored. 'The King will know it isn't his – he'll never acknowledge it.'

'He'll have to, if we manœuvre him properly. And we will, of course we will. He'll never know whether it's his or not, and if he doubts, he'll never dare to say so! How far are you advanced?'

'Not far,' Anne said. She had begun by resisting him, now she leant against his breast and let him hold her. He was so confident, so much at ease. And he never failed; he could do anything.

'I didn't dare delay telling you. Besides, I'm sure; it's almost a month now. There are other signs too.'

Her breasts had enlarged slightly, and the first morning nausea had begun. It was so mild that she was able to conceal it. In her first pregnancy of many years ago, she had been prostrate with sickness after the first few weeks.

'What can I do?' she said.

Richelieu let go of her, kissed both her hands, and began to walk up and down the room, his reflection mirrored in the glass on the wall and the mirror on her toilet table; he seemed to be everywhere as he moved.

'You will have to seduce the King,' he said at last. 'You will have to persuade him to stay with you. Once is all you need, but it must be very soon.'

'He won't do it,' Anne said. 'He hates me; besides you don't know what he's like. Nothing will happen – almost nothing happened before . . .'

'Enough can happen to compromise him,' Richelieu said. 'One night spent under your roof, an hour or two in this room alone with you, and you will have your proof for the world.'

'I can't do it,' Anne said. 'I can't bear him; he makes me sick!'

'Everything will make you sick for a while, Madame,' Richelieu mocked gently. 'You must overcome it. You're a most beautiful woman; you could seduce a saint if you chose. Be charming to him. Be warm. I'll produce the King for you, and you must do the rest. This isn't the time for scruples. And it's not the time for anxiety either, or you might lose our little Prince. Have you been crying? Yes, I can see that you have. Come here. No more tears, Madame. No more terrors. Trust me. Together we won't fail. This is just the beginning of our triumph.'

'A bastard,' Anne whispered. 'A bastard Prince.'

'My son and yours, Madame,' he answered her, 'will be the greatest King that France has ever known.'

*   *   *

One mid-December afternoon, the King decided to leave the Louvre and spend the night at his hunting lodge at St Maur. He was suffering from an acute attack of depression and boredom, aggravated by a deep sense of spiritual unease. He had a new confessor, appointed by Richelieu, and Father Sirmond lectured the unhappy penitent at every opportunity on the sinful state of his marriage to the Queen.

Louis listened, argued, and took refuge in obstinacy, but the feeling of guilt his confessor aroused in him began to root into his mind. It was useless to tell the priest that he disliked her, that she had betrayed him with others, that he found her cold, and the whole physical aspect of marriage repelled him. The Father agreed with everything he said, but pointed out with unanswerable logic that Kings married for duty, not for inclination, and that if he died, he would leave his country at the mercy of Gaston d'Orleans and the most irresponsible elements at Court. France would be devoured by Spain, the dynasty of Bourbon would perish, and it would all be his fault because he wouldn't give his Consort a child. There was no answer to this, and Louis knew it. He left his confessor more miserable and sullen than ever, and now the Cardinal added his advice in the same vein. Be reconciled with Anne. She had proved herself obedient at last; receive her and do your duty to France.

The very thought of it drove Louis from his Palace that December; so great was his spiritual conflict that he stopped at the Convent at the Faubourg St Antoine, to pray and refresh himself by visiting a former lady-in-waiting of his wife's who had renounced the world and become the saintly Sister Angélique. Her words to him were the same as the Cardinal's and his confessor's; be reconciled with your Queen. It was like a monstrous conspiracy to make him do something so abhorrent that he couldn't think of it without lapsing into melancholia. What tortured him was his self-knowledge, he knew in his heart what those pious advisers did not. He hated Anne because he didn't want to go to bed with any woman. He wanted to flirt with de Hautfort and be safe. He left the Convent more gloomy than when he went in, and as if to match his mood, the skies opened in a torrential rain storm, a wild wind blew up, and the Royal party found themselves unable to go on to St Maur. As they sheltered under a group of trees, Guitaut, the Captain of his Guard, dismounted, and approached the King.

'The storm is getting worse, Sire. We dare not risk going any further into open country.'

Louis looked down at him and scowled. He was already soaked through, and he had a morbid fear of catching cold.

'We can go to Versailles; everyone has left my apartments at the Louvre. Nothing will be prepared for me. We'll go on to Versailles and sleep there!'

Guitaut shook his head. 'Look at those clouds, Sire, coming up from the east. It will be dark in twenty minutes, and we'll be in the middle of a thunderstorm. Anything could happen on the road. Your own apartments may not be ready at the Louvre, Sire, but so long as Her Majesty is there, you won't lack food or a warm welcome!'

It was a chance and being a bold man, the Captain had taken it. If he succeeded, Richelieu had assured him his future would be made. He was one of many in contact with the King, who had been told to take an opportunity when it arose. And this storm was God sent. They couldn't hope to go on.

'I want to go to Versailles,' Louis shouted angrily. 'I don't want to turn back.'

'You risk your life, Sire,' Guitaut protested. A fierce squall of wind lifted Louis' hat off his head and sent it rolling through the muddied pools of rain water in the road.

'Lightning will make the horses bolt – thunder accompanies it – your mare is terrified by storms! I must insist, Sire, that we turn back to Paris!'

Suddenly it was too much for Louis; he felt tired out, harassed on all sides, cornered by nature itself into the one situation he most wished to avoid. The will to resist went out of him. He took his wet hat from Guitaut, shook the dirty water out of it and pulled it on his head.

'To the Louvre, gentlemen,' he said, and turned his horse back the way they had come.

*   *   *

'What happened?' The voice in the darkness whispered to Anne. 'He hasn't said a word to me, or to his confessor.'

'I got Guitaut's message in time,' she answered. 'Everything was ready for him. He had his favourite supper, de Hautfort did as I told her, and charmed him into a good mood; we were all very gay and made him welcome. There was nowhere for him to sleep but here.'

She closed her eyes and shivered for a moment. It had been the most difficult ordeal of her life, that long tense evening with her husband, when the onus of winning him was hers alone, and every instinct screamed in protest at what she was going to do.

'Will he acknowledge the child?'

'I think so. Please don't ask me any more about it.'

'I do congratulate you, Madame. You're not to think about it any more. It need never happen again; just once was all we needed.'

'I was so afraid,' Anne whispered. 'So afraid for this child. Bastards born to a Queen can be strangled at birth, can't they?'

'I believe so,' the voice said gently. 'If the mother doesn't want them. It's not part of French law to murder an innocent baby. You do want the child, don't you?'

'Yes,' she said. 'Oh, yes, I do want it now! I was frightened at first. I prayed to miscarry; I couldn't think what would happen. Now if I lost it I should die. I feel sure it's a boy.'

'So do I. And it will be a great King. But you know what this means now, Madame? You must take back your ruby ring tonight. I shan't come again till the child is born.'

She didn't answer him at once. She didn't love him, no, no, she protested, that was unthinkable; then why was she crying suddenly, and what caused the feeling of pain, as if she had been struck a blow above the heart – 'Why not?' she heard her own voice ask him, thick with tears. 'Why can't you come – I need you now!'

'That pleases me,' he said gently. 'That pleases me very much. But it's too dangerous. De Senlis may begin dropping hints; why should the King visit you in secret when he has done so publicly? Be brave, Madame. Be patient and trust me. Think of your child and the joy that's ahead of you. You won't need me after he is born, believe me. And don't weep, I beg you. We have some time together still. Don't squander it in tears.'

11

On Sunday, 5 September, 1638, Anne woke from a
deep sleep in the early hours of the morning. She had
become so tired in the last few weeks of her pregnancy
that she moved through the endless ritual of Court life
in a haze of weariness. The King and the Court had
moved with her to Saint Germain-en-Laye, where the
child was to be born. Everything was ready; the infant
had its household appointed, its nurseries prepared,
and Anne herself was surrounded by courtiers who
couldn't abase themselves enough before the mother
of the future Dauphin. It was sure to be a boy. The
fortune tellers all over France were doing a great trade
in predictions of the birth; nobody even mentioned
a Princess. Anne sometimes wondered wistfully if
the unborn were really a daughter, and determined
that she would love it all the more if it should be.
Maternity had changed her; her beauty softened and
her spirit mellowed. And when she was lonely or ill,
she had the comfort of the letters which were brought
to her in secret, and she read them greedily. They
were love letters, written by someone who had never
expressed himself in terms of intimacy, but she knew
what the formal phrases meant, and smiled at the
innate caution of the man. He had read too many

letters written by her and to her in the past, to trust himself entirely to someone so unlucky in their private correspondence. He assured her of his devotion and respect, and remembering how they had parted, she knew what this meant and was comforted.

Now, on the dark September morning, she felt the first pains of labour. For three hours she forbade the midwife Madame Peronne and her Almoner the Bishop of Lisieux to tell anyone what was happening. She heard Mass quietly in her own bedroom, and then by five o'clock the labour entered a stronger phase, and the King had to be informed. As the dawn broke, Anne lay in the special bed with foot rest and rails at the head, which had been used by Marie de Medici at her children's births, the hangings drawn back so that she might be seen at all times, while her bedroom filled with people. Chairs covered in cloth of gold were ranged against the walls for the eight most important ladies in France and her principal attendants; they took their places and sat down to wait and watch. Every corner of standing space was filled with priests and nobles who had the privilege of attending the birth, and when Anne opened her eyes between the pains, the room was a drifting sea of faces, all craning towards her, staring, talking, sucking in the air which she was gasping to breathe. It was stiflingly hot; there was a continuous din of noise, coming from the ante-chambers outside her rooms, apart from the loud excited chattering all round her. She became immersed in pain, as if she were drowning; the heat and disturbance began to slide away, leaving her isolated with the intolerable suffering which seemed as if it couldn't get worse and yet increased with every moment. The

King had not come near her; this was noted by Madame de Senlis, who thought it very odd, and by Mademoiselle de Hautfort, who was among the crowd standing outside the bedchamber.

It was nine o'clock when the cry went up.

'Send for the surgeons! Quickly, the Queen is in danger!'

And then Louis came at last. Somehow the crowd made room for him, pressing back upon each other so that he could approach the bed where his wife lay in such extremes of agony that he turned away from her immediately, his sallow skin blanching to a sickly yellow.

He didn't want to see her suffering, or to stay and hear her cries. She had betrayed him and he knew it, as only he could know, and now as the birth of her child approached, he couldn't hide it from himself. He had acknowledged the pregnancy, accepted the congratulations of the world, and pretended to himself that what had happened between them that night on his return to Paris, had resulted in this. But in his heart he had always doubted, and now, standing in her bedroom, watching the final convulsions of childbirth, he knew that whatever the child was, it wouldn't be his. He turned aside and went out of the room.

In the large ante-chamber, the crowds were hushed; Louis moved among them, his eyes roving the faces, looking for someone to talk to at this moment. Marie de Hautfort was by a window; he moved towards her, and when she saw him she burst into a flood of tears. The Bishop of Meaux had begun reciting the Divine Office and the crowd in the salon were making the responses with him. Louis held out his hand to the girl who was on her knees, the tears streaming down her face.

'Get up, and don't cry. I hate to see you cry.'

She shook her head at him, and her proud temper flared.

'Your wife is dying, Sire! I have tears for her, if you have not!'

'If she dies,' Louis said suddenly, 'I shall marry you, Marie. So don't weep for her now, will you?'

Marie de Hautfort got up, she was trembling with emotion, and she completely forgot that the dour man in front of her was the King of France and what he had offered was to make her his Queen.

'You should be ashamed,' she gasped at him. 'May God forgive you for saying such a thing! Go away, Sire; I never want to speak to you again!'

He paused for a moment, his sad eyes fixed on her flushed face. She was loyal, and she was incorrupt. He truly admired her for both qualities. She would make him happy, as far as any woman could. She would protect him and even mother him a little if he married her. He mustn't let her think him heartless. If Anne was going to die, he must be on good terms with Marie. He came close to her and bent down a little.

'You think me very cruel, I know. But I'm not. She has betrayed me yet again, Marie. This child is the ultimate betrayal. Now you may pray for her if you wish.'

He made her a little bow, and turned away. Marie de Hautfort stood staring after him, her colour slowly deepening, one hand pressed hard against her breast.

The child was a betrayal. He couldn't have meant that. It was impossible. Anne was virtuous, kindly, pious – he couldn't have said that. She must have misheard him, misunderstood. 'If she dies I shall marry you.' He had said that too. She sank down on her knees again, not to pray but because she was overcome by sudden weakness, and now by an increasing doubt. He hadn't gone near the Queen till he was forced to do so; he had talked of her death and proposed to her in the same sentence. And he had said quite clearly that this child was not his. If he believed this, if it were really true, then this accounted for it all. She covered her face with her hands and stayed very still. It was too much to accept. She needed time to think, and the time was not now.

Nature had called up the last reserves of Anne's strength so that she might give the new life; by good fortune Peronne the midwife had called the surgeons in time, and this had saved the life of the child, and rescued the Queen at the last moment.

She was semi-conscious, aroused from the torpor by the piercing shrieks which she dimly connected with her own intakes of breath, and then the birth itself took place. There was a moment of clarity when all her senses were restored, when she could see clearly and hear distinctly, and her emotions welled into a flood of relief and exultation, as she heard the first faint cry. And then the midwife was leaning over her, tears shining on her cheeks.

'A Dauphin! God be praised, it's a Dauphin!'

Anne smiled; it was a great effort to do so, but she managed it.

A son. She had given birth to a son. Richelieu was directing the campaign in Picardy.

'What a pity,' she whispered, 'he wasn't here to see . . .'

'His Majesty's on his way, Madame,' the midwife said. But Anne didn't hear her. She had fainted.

*　　*　　*

The cannon of the Bastille and the Arsenal told the people of Paris that France had an heir; the thunder of the guns was joined by the pealing bells of Notre Dame and Sainte Chapelle; fireworks exploded in the sky, turning the night to day, illuminations made the capital a fairy city, and for three days food and drink was given away outside the Hotel de Ville. The celebrations continued all over the country, many of the provincial towns outdid Paris itself in their extravagance, and the great religious houses distributed alms and held services of Thanksgiving. And on 29 September, the Cardinal de Richelieu arrived at Saint Germain-en-Laye to see the Queen and do homage to the new Dauphin. Anne had been up for almost a week; she had recovered very quickly from the birth, and accompanied by the rigid, silent King, had offered thanks in public for her son and shown him to the foreign Ambassadors. She sat under her canopy of State, dressed in gold-embroidered green velvet, her Peruvian emeralds blazing round her neck and in her fiery hair. The little Dauphin slept in the arms of his gouvernante the Marquise de Lansac, who stood on the Queen's right hand. All her ladies, the Bishops of Lisieux and Maux were with her, and it was this setting which she prepared for Richelieu when he came to see his son. He walked towards her in a solemn little procession, led by the King, who couldn't bring himself to look Anne in the face, and as the Cardinal approached her, Anne got up and took the baby from de Lansac. Holding him in her arms she stepped down and came to meet the Cardinal. For a brief second their eyes met, and there passed from him such a glance of pride and passionate joy, that she flushed deeply and the tears came into her eyes. Gently Richelieu put out his finger and touched the tiny clenched fist of the baby; the fingers opened and closed round his. The eyes were already dark brown and very large; they opened and seemed to look at him. After a moment Richelieu spoke to Anne.

'Madame,' he said. 'A most beautiful Prince. Could I ask a great favour?'

'Of course.' Her voice shook a little, and she saw Louis glance up at her.

'May I hold the Dauphin in my arms?' Richelieu asked.

She put the child into them herself, and for a moment Richelieu cradled him, and his lips touched the top of the very dark head.

'May God bless him,' he said solemnly. 'And grant him long life and glory.'

He gave him back to Anne, who continued to hold him, in spite of the uneasy movements of the Marquise de Lansac who felt that mothers shouldn't show too much affection for their children. She couldn't understand how the Queen, normally so dignified and strict about protocol, insisted on nursing and playing with her little son like any peasant woman.

Richelieu turned to the King. 'Sire, how can I congratulate you? Words won't come to me at this moment – God has blessed you and France in this beautiful child. And Her Majesty too.'

The glowing grey eyes blazed at her again, too

quickly to be seen by others. The Marquise de Lansac said afterwards that the Cardinal seemed quite overcome by the little Prince. It was a touching and unsuspected side to his nature, this tenderness for children.

Before the end of the year Anne and her household returned to the Louvre. In the weeks since her son's birth she had been too pre-occupied and happy to notice what was happening in her immediate circle. She received in audience every day, went off to Mass with the King, dined in public with him, and insisted, again to the horror of Madame de Lansac, on taking her little son out in her coach in the afternoons.

It was Richelieu's suggestion that she should return to Paris; he paid her daily visits, always in the presence of a dozen other persons, and endeared himself further to the Marquise de Lansac by his interest in the baby Dauphin. He sought excuses to visit the Queen when he knew that the baby would be in her apartments, and often nursed him for a few moments. And during these visits, while he made conversation with Anne in a voice loud enough to satisfy her ladies, he whispered his advice that she should go to Paris.

'Why?' Anne murmured quickly. 'I have the baby, I'm perfectly happy here.'

'Gaston is leaving St Germain.' Richelieu said it with a smile as if it were the most ordinary observation. 'He's saying the King isn't the Father – ah, Madame,' his tone became audible again, 'Paris is preparing a great welcome for you. A Procession to Notre Dame, many excitements. All the world waits to see the Dauphin!' He nodded encouragingly to Madame de Senlis, who curtsied. '*She* must be dismissed. She's been whispering; all your women must be replaced. I'll get the King to do it. You must agree when the order comes.'

'My God,' Anne said. 'If Gaston is saying that . . . Oh, get rid of whom you please, do anything. But don't let anyone try to harm the boy!'

'They may talk,' Richelieu got up and bowed very low over her hand. 'But nothing can be proved. Not now or ever. You and the little Prince are safe. Watch Marie de Hautfort. There's a nuance there which I don't like. Just watch her a little.'

When he had left her, Anne went into her little oratory, and for the first time since the baby's birth, she fell on her knees and burst into a fit of bitter crying. She had never known what love meant until now, and the discovery was the most important one of her life. She had loved the Duke of Buckingham – but was that really love, that mixture of immature emotions, compounded of romance, vanity and loneliness? What did she feel for the man who had just left her – desire, dependence, gratitude? What had she ever felt for anyone compared to the passion which overcame her when she held her son in her arms? This was love, this fierce maternal burning, this tenderness so strong that it was like a bruise that ached. For this kind of love she would do anything, commit any crime, sacrifice anyone.

And she knew that she and Richelieu shared it. The baby sleeping in his splendid golden cradle, pillowed on linen blessed by the Pope as a special gift, this child was the greatest bond that any man or woman could enjoy. She thought of Gaston with loathing. A vain and cowardly wastrel, indulging in a fit of spiteful pique because he was no longer the heir to the throne. But even so he had touched on the truth, and the truth was something which must be hidden at all costs. Let him leave the Court, she thought angrily, let him pit his feeble wits against the Cardinal once again, and see how he would deal with him, now that France had a Dauphin! Slowly, as she regained her self-control, Anne grew calm again. Everything had changed because of her son; Gaston might flounce out of St Germain but there was nothing more he could do. His mother Marie de Medici had registered her protest before the world by ignoring her grandson's birth, and for this Anne felt unable to forgive her. They would all like to cheat her son of his birthright, because he had snatched the prospect of power from them; even had he really been Louis' child, Gaston and his mother would have tried to undermine him anyway. Two years ago she would have protested against the dismissal of her ladies as an insult and a privation; now, because they had begun to talk behind her back, she couldn't wait to see them go. And what had Richelieu said? Watch de Hautfort. Only a fool ignored his advice; she would watch the girl every moment, especially when the King was with her. And he was right about leaving St Germain. She couldn't afford to hide in seclusion, lavishing love on her baby and forgetting that he must be presented with all the pomp and splendour of his titles to the world. She would return to Paris as soon as her apartments in the Louvre were ready, and she would walk in the procession to Notre Dame, with the King beside her, publicly acknowledging his son. Anne remembered at last where she was and said a prayer. It was the one she said every day, to the great St Louis, King of France, to protect the child who had been given his name and would be the fourteenth of his line. Then she went into her cabinet, and immediately the assembled women rose to their feet and curtsied. She paused a moment, looking at them all in turn, holding the glance of Marie de Hautfort longer than the rest. There was a coldness in the girl's eyes which had never been there before. Now that she thought of it, Anne realised that the warmth and gentleness which had characterised de Hautfort's attitude towards her and her embarrassment with the King had changed completely. Richelieu was right. As always. There was the germ of something dangerous here. Ambition perhaps, jealousy. The maid of honour had become an enemy.

'Ladies,' Anne said. 'We will be returning to Paris by the end of the month. Madame de Lansac, you will see that the Dauphin is ready to travel with us. We've been in retirement from the world too long.'

The New Year opened with great pageantry in the capital; the Queen was no longer the prisoner of the Louvre, as she had often described herself in letters to her brother in Spain. She was present at every Court function, her jewels and gowns more opulent than ever, her voluptuous beauty glowing with the new dimension of her triumphant motherhood. She was so altered that the English Ambassador filled pages of his official despatches with descriptions of how meekly she had accepted the changes in her household, dictated by some irritable whim of the King's, allowing all her old intimates to be replaced and sent to their estates without a word of protest. Strangest of all, the King was as cold to her as he had ever been, in spite of the Dauphin's birth, and her relations with the Cardinal Minister seemed to have progressed from a polite state of peace to positive amity. They were often seen smiling and talking together, apparently on the best of terms. This, the Ambassador added, only gave credence to the disgusting rumours which were circulating in Paris, and indeed through many European cities. Of course they were untrue, he insisted, while he repeated them in detail. The little Prince could not possibly be the son of Richelieu; he was black eyed and dark haired like the King, albeit he was lively and very advanced even before his first birthday. He showed remarkable high spirits, quite different to his Royal father's gloomy temperament which seemed to grow worse instead of better. M. d'Orleans had confined himself to grumbling and reading every scandal sheet he could find on the subject of his sister-in-law and her miraculous fecundity after so many years of barrenness.

And the King consoled himself with his extraordinary pursuit of his wife's lady-in-waiting Marie de Hautfort, a pursuit, the English envoy added tartly, that never reached any conclusion. This was the only member of Anne's household who had kept her place, because, it was said that the King insisted on it, and she had not improved in manner in the past twelve months. Formerly gentle and innocent, she now displayed an arrogant and even bitter character to those at Court, alternately driving the King to despair by her moods, or bringing him to her feet with such a display of coquetry that it would have compromised her utterly with any other suitor. And she spoke wildly at times to her intimates, hinting that the King had so far forgotten all decency as to propose marriage when the Queen seemed likely to die in childbirth.

Most important of all, de Hautfort had become the implacable enemy of the Cardinal and a bitter critic of the Queen. A number of intrigues, originating in the Palais Cardinal, had failed to turn the King against her.

It was rumoured that unless the Cardinal removed her, Marie de Hautfort might yet succeed in driving a wedge between him and the King, and even effecting his dismissal. So the Ambassador reported and he did not exaggerate. Richelieu, working as hard as he had ever done, found himself plagued by the inexplicable hatred of the King's favourite, and he was also bereft of his closest friend and wisest counsellor. Father Joseph was dead. He had hung on to the fraying threads of life, driving his sick body in the Cardinal's service until the last strands snapped and he collapsed. His death was such a serious loss to Richelieu that he fell ill himself, and grieved alone until the demands of his office dragged him out of the Palais Cardinal, and he faced a hostile Court with its suspicious King, more isolated than he had ever been. He needed someone in whom he could confide, not in the role of confessor and friend which the monk had filled for nearly thirty years, but as a political collaborator. He wrote to Rome for help, explaining that no ordinary Church diplomat would do; he needed someone of exceptional intelligence, obedient disposition, and complete discretion. Some weeks later he received the Papal envoy, with a private recommendation from the Pope that this was the man he should attach to himself.

Giulio Mazarini was a young Italian of good family who had entered the service of the Church without taking Holy Orders. At thirty-two he was at the peak of his intellectual powers and the prime of his considerable good looks. He had negotiated with the great Cardinal Minister before, but years ago, and he had been overcome by awe of the Minister. Now he set out to impress and to please; he had been told the real purpose of his visit and already he envisaged himself at the right hand of the most powerful man in France. As he sat opposite Richelieu in the magnificent salon of the Palais Cardinal, he saw further still into the future. The Cardinal looked pale, and there was a transparent thinness about his gaunt face which made him seem much older than he was. The eyes were bright and piercing, but there were hollows under them and lines of pain round the mouth. He was a sick man, and the Italian had an acute sense for things unseen. The spirit didn't flag, the fantastic intelligence and the superhuman will would conquer nature for some time yet, but not for very long.

'I need a personal secretary,' Richelieu said suddenly. 'The Holy Father recommends you. I judge you to be a man of keen wits and political acumen. Would you accept the post with me?'

Mazarini didn't hesitate or pretend to be surprised.

'It would fulfil my dearest wish, Eminence. I want nothing more than to sit at your feet and learn from you.'

Richelieu got up, motioning the young man to stay in his chair. He moved round the room as he spoke.

'I'll teach you all you need to know about statecraft. I'll train you to follow one of the wisest and best men who ever served the Church – Father Joseph de Tremblay, my dear friend. Tell me, does power fascinate you?'

'Yes,' the Italian answered. 'Power first and human feelings second. One cannot hold on to one without understanding the other.'

'Good,' Richelieu said. 'Very good. I have a great deal of power, Nuncio Mazarini, and I need someone loyal and discreet to help me maintain it. In return I shall take you into my confidence. That will confer some of my power upon you. Will you serve France, as if you were a Frenchman? Don't answer hastily, because this is important. If you are to work with me, you must think of yourself as French. The first weakness towards Italy will find you out.'

Mazarini smiled; he had a charming smile, and a warm speaking voice.

'Italy is only a patchwork of provinces and states, Eminence. I wouldn't know which one I ought to be loyal to – I will adopt France, and call myself her son.'

'Begin by calling yourself Mazarin,' Richelieu said. 'It sounds better in French ears. I think you will suit me well. I shall ask the Holy Father for your services. Tomorrow, I shall present you to the King and Queen.'

The gardens of the Cardinal's country house at Reuil were in the full glory of their autumn colours; Richelieu had planned the sweep of lawns and trees with the same meticulous care and artistry that he brought to furnishing the Palais Cardinal. Ornamental fountains gave coolness in the hot summer days, and an avenue of beeches led to an exquisite Orangery, where Richelieu liked to entertain his guests.

September was still warm, though the magnificent trees were blazing red and copper, and when Anne accepted Richelieu's invitation, they dined in the Orangery and walked in the gardens afterwards.

The King was out hunting at St Maur; Anne and her ladiés had been splendidly entertained by the

Cardinal, and his niece, now married to the Duc d'Aiguillon, played hostess to the Queen. The Cardinal's Secretary, M. Mazarin, kept everyone amused. The Duchess now took her place at the head of Anne's ladies, while the Cardinal, bowing very low, offered his arm to the Queen.

'If we walk a little faster,' he said softly, 'we can talk freely. My niece will keep your women occupied.'

'I've been waiting to talk to you alone,' Anne said. 'Our opportunities are so few now; there are always people round us, and I don't trust de Hautfort an inch. She's becoming intolerable. When are you going to do something about it? You know I'm helpless – I daren't say a word to Louis! He's completely dominated by her.'

'I know,' Richelieu answered. 'And that's one reason I invited you here, Madame. I think I know how to break this liaison, but I wanted to discuss it with you first. She's terribly dangerous to us, this girl. I believe the King has told her something, hinted something about the Dauphin's birth. That's why she changed towards you. And of course why she abominates me. She suspects, and this has made her ambitious for herself. We've got to get rid of her; she's poisoning the King against me, and encouraging the kind of cabal that your dear Marie de Chevreuse assembled so effectively. But the alternative to her may shock you.'

'What is it,' Anne asked. 'Another of my maids of honour to play at amorous charades with Louis?'

'No,' Richelieu shook his head. 'Alas, there's no woman able to compete. But I have a young page in my service who I think will get Marie de Hautfort exiled to her estates within a month.'

Anne stopped abruptly. 'A page! A young man! Richelieu how could you . . .' He held her arm and forced her gently forward; the chattering and laughter of the crowd immediately behind them had drowned her horrified exclamation.

'I said you'd be shocked,' he reminded her. 'But you must consider the risk. If this woman goes on in the King's favour, she may persuade him to anything. The birth of the Dauphin has given him confidence in his own eyes; he's had to accept the parenthood and whatever his doubts in private, he's a man and a King in the eyes of the world. He's been able to forget what he really is because of Marie de Hautfort. This is her secret, Madame. He doesn't love her, or desire her in an ordinary way, and you know this as well as I. We all know where the King's taste really lies. That's why I say that Henri de Cinq-Mars is the only antidote to this woman, and to what she represents. A mortal threat to you and to your son. You know he asked her to marry him when you were in the middle of giving birth?'

'No,' Anne paled. 'No, I didn't know that.'

'Everyone else in Paris does,' Richelieu said. 'What a temptation for a woman, what a slur upon you, Madame, and the Dauphin! Of all the things the King has done to make you suffer, I find that last act impossible to forgive.'

'He hates me,' Anne said slowly. 'He has always hated me.'

'Then permit one who feels very differently towards you, to take what measures I think best,' Richelieu said gently. 'Accept Cinq-Mars. He's eighteen and quite brainless. He will do as I tell him, and we shall all have peace.'

'What else can I do?' she asked him. 'What could I ever do without your help?'

'You can be the most beautiful Queen in Europe and the most devoted mother of a splendid Prince. You could also decide whether to unlock a certain door again.'

'You said that was over,' Anne said after a moment.

'It is, if you decide so,' he walked onwards without looking at her now. 'I made a bargain with you, you fulfilled it. You're not obligated to me any longer. I only suggest, and very humbly, very humbly indeed, Madame. If the door doesn't open I shall accept it, and my feelings towards you won't be altered. Nothing could alter them in the past, and nothing in the future could do it now.'

'I don't know,' Anne said; she felt helpless suddenly, confronted with a relationship which she had preferred to forget and didn't need now that she had her son. But there was something in the man that touched her heart; he was tired and alone. She knew how he had suffered when Father Joseph died; the grief was in his face. She had needed him so often in the past two years and he had never failed her. She needed him still to protect her son against the charge of illegitimacy which could be levelled by a jealous and ambitious woman, with the connivance of the King. Louis was capable of any folly, any weakness; he had always been a tool in the hands of others, albeit a dangerous one, inclined to turn against his confidants. Only Richelieu had ever mastered him and kept that mastery. She looked at him as they walked to the end of the great avenue of beeches, the sun filtering down through the thick copper canopy of leaves, and felt a strange pang of tenderness. He turned and smiled at her.

'Forgive me,' he said. 'It wasn't a serious suggestion. I'm sure you've lost the key to that door.'

'No,' Anne said, and for a moment her fingers
tightened on his arm. 'I have it safely. And it won't
ever be used except to open it.'

They had reached the end of the long avenue, and
as they turned Richelieu lifted her hand and kissed
it. 'Madame,' he said. 'Your devoted servant.'

* * *

On 27 December, 1639, Marie de Hautfort left Paris,
exiled by the personal order of the King. She took
with her a pair of fine diamond ear-rings which Anne
had given her, and a sense of disillusionment with men
which was to last for the rest of her life. Virtuous and
determined, she had tried to fight the unspeakable
rival for Louis' affections from the moment he was
attached to the King's household. For some weeks
she had seen the King paying attention to M. de Cinq-
Mars without realising the significance. He seemed a
very handsome youth, genial, and interested in simple
things like hunting and bird snaring; the King liked
to hear him sing because he had a pleasant voice. But
only when he was appointed Master of the Horse,
an unprecedented honour for a boy of eighteen, did
the unhappy girl appreciate that this was more than
friendship. Cinq-Mars seemed very simple, very open
natured, but there was a mockery in his attitude to
her which roused de Hautfort's fiery temper and betrayed her into complaints against him to the King.

When she understood the true position, she re-
coiled in horror; only the support of friends like

Mademoiselle de Chemerault and of her grandmother Madame de La Flotte prevented her from leaving the Court at once. They argued that this creature was introduced by the Cardinal in order to seduce the King away from her and plunge him into infamy. It was her Christian duty to fight Cinq-Mars for the soul of Louis, and with more courage than insight, Marie de Hautfort tried to follow their advice. But it was useless. Louis had fallen a helpless victim to the charm and beauty of his new friend; all his slumbering tendencies awoke, his emotions became so involved with the splendid young man that he flared into jealous tantrums if he even spoke to women; he commanded Cinq-Mars to be with him every spare moment, whittling away at his wooden toys, hunting with him, snaring magpies, fishing the rivers. And with his new passion, Louis admitted to himself how tired he was of being hectored by de Hautfort, how bored he was with her virtue and her moods. Her blonde hair and bright blue eyes were insipid, even disgusting. Nothing compared for beauty with the splendid virility of the favourite.

The King came back from a visit to Amiens; Cinq-Mars complained that Marie de Hautfort had been unpleasant to him, and the next day Louis ordered her to leave the Court. Richelieu had removed Anne's rival. But he had replaced her by the last and most dangerous of his enemies, his protégé, the harmless-seeming Marquis de Cinq-Mars.

Anne's second son was born the following September. It was an easy birth, unlike the prolonged and dangerous delivery of the Dauphin, who was a healthy and active little boy of two. The new baby was a puny child, hastily christened Philip because he wasn't expected to survive, but he too gained strength as the weeks passed, watched over by Anne and Madame de Lansac who was resigned by now to having the Queen interfere.

Anne herself recovered so quickly that she was able to get up within hours of the birth, and as soon as the infant Prince was able to travel, she retired with both her children to Saint Germain where she now spent most of her time. Louis had been present at the birth; he had attended his wife with a curiously blank indifference, as if the bastard was of no consequence to him and her adultery of even less importance. She had carried Richelieu's second child with less anxiety than she had done the first, because there was no danger now of the King disclaiming it, or involving himself in a matrimonial upheaval.

He was the slave of his twenty-year-old favourite, and the favourite had plunged him into alternate heaven and hell with his caprices and his passions; Louis suffered agonies of jealousy because Cinq-Mars, like the half-forgotten de Luynes before him, still kept a taste for women, and the King spent days in black despair and violent sulks because the one he loved had visited the famous courtesan Marianne de Lorme and come back drunk and boasting of his prowess.

It didn't matter to Louis now what Anne did, or who crept into her bed. There was no longer any pretence left that he was a man like other men, or that he had anything to hide from himself. He was a man who found his manhood with men and his subjection by the vain and greedy young paramour was a pathetic parody of an ageing lover with a flighty mistress.

But if the Louvre was the centre of upheaval, emotional quarrels and passionate reconciliations, it was also the setting for a growing political struggle. Richelieu ruled France and Cinq-Mars ruled the King; hunting and making wooden toys soon bored the favourite, who desired influence over affairs of State as well as honours and riches at Court. He demanded a place on the Council and the infatuated Louis agreed. It would be nice to have Cinq-Mars beside him at the Council table; it would please him to teach the young man how to conduct the government of France, and at the same time it would irritate his Minister, whom he enjoyed tormenting now and then. Louis agreed, Cinq-Mars was delighted. Richelieu bowed low when the King told him of his wishes, and then afterwards sent for the favourite. He was tired, and his health had declined rapidly in the past year, yet he worked as hard as ever. At that moment his judgment failed him at the prospect of the spoiled Adonis who owed his entire fortune and position to Richelieu in the first place, demanding to sit in on the Councils of his benefactor. The Cardinal's head ached, and there was a persistent pain in his chest which kept him awake at night; he saw the boy of twenty in front of him, and lost his temper.

'Affairs of State are not for children! I brought you to the King's notice, my friend. I can just as easily persuade him to forget you!'

The Cardinal walked out of the room, and went to see Louis. The order for Cinq-Mars to attend the Council meetings was cancelled within the hour, and the young Marquis became Richelieu's declared enemy from that moment. News of the feud drifted through to Anne in her retreat at Saint Germain, but she refused to comment. Her small sons occupied her time and her thoughts. After the birth of Philip, she had received a package. It contained a magnificent canary coloured diamond set into a ring, and the key of the door to her bedroom in the Louvre. There was no message, but she understood that it meant an end of the Cardinal's visits. They had grown fewer in the last year, and often he spent the time talking, and then left her, respectfully kissing her hand. He was ill and he was prematurely ageing; the passion which had blazed between them had gently died away. Except for the two Princes in the nursery at Saint Germain, the relationship of the last three years might never have existed. Anne was satisfied by maternity; the turmoil of her past was like a dream, and she was secure in her position because the cleverness of Armand de Richelieu had made her so. She stayed in the country and was happy. He had counselled her in the latter part of the year to be patient, and to wait upon events. She was the mother of the future King of France; time was her best ally, and by this she knew he anticipated the King's death and her Regency in the name of her infant son. In December 1641 Anne was playing with her eldest child in the Dauphin's apartments at Saint Germain when a page announced that no less a person than the Marquis de Cinq-Mars was waiting to see her. Many courtiers made the short journey to Saint Germain from Paris to pay their respects, but a visit from the favourite was an extraordinary development.

Anne got up off the floor, and called Madame de Lansac.

'M. Le Grand is here!' This was the style by which Cinq-Mars was known to the King, and all except the Cardinal used it.

Madame de Lansac came hurrying forward, hand

outstretched to remove the Dauphin, who backed away and clung to his mother's velvet skirts.

'I'll take Monsieur le Dauphin away, Madame. Come, my little angel, little pet – come with me now!'

'No, wait,' Anne said quickly. 'Perhaps he's come to see the Dauphin. I'll see him here, in the nursery apartments. You go and greet him, de Lansac, and bring him to me. Louis, come here, and let me button up your coat. There's a great gentleman coming to see you. You must be nice to him, and give him your hand to kiss.'

The small boy looked up at her with large black eyes, brightened by the tears he had been going to shed at being parted from his mother. He was an extremely handsome child, already aware that he was different, even from his baby brother, and that certain standards of behaviour were expected of him. He adored his mother, and lavished affection upon her. He was more reserved with Madame de Lansac, whom he sensed was his inferior, even though he had to do what she told him. He came and put his arms round Anne's neck. She held him on her knee and kissed him.

'I want to stay, Maman. I want to stay with you.'

'And so you shall,' Anne said. She found it impossible to refuse the child anything. 'But you must be quiet and good, when the gentleman comes. Otherwise I shall call de Lansac and she'll take you out of the room.'

'I'll be good, Maman,' the child promised, burying his face in her shoulder. He loved the scent of his mother and the softness of her cheek. Already he knew that she was very beautiful, and he loved to play with the long silky red hair which curled over her shoulders.

That was how Henri de Cinq-Mars saw them when he was shown into the room. He paused, one hand on his left breast, and then swept the Queen and her son a very deep bow. The King was always complaining about his wife and muttering about her betrayals of him in the past, till Cinq-Mars was thoroughly bored by the whole subject. He found her very beautiful, even though old, because she was exactly forty, and she had always treated him with kindness. He didn't believe the stories of her hauteur and coldness which the King insisted upon telling him; he found her charming, dazzling to look at, and a woman occupied as women should be. With their children and a quiet domestic life. That was why he had come to her personally, against the advice of Louis' brother Gaston, of his dear friend de Thou, and of the mighty Duc de Bouillion, who had been such a turbulent rebel in the past. He trusted his own judgment, and above all he relied on his own charm. Anne would be easy to conquer. He came forward and kissed her hand, approving of the soft white skin and the slim fingers, enhanced by a quite magnificent yellow diamond. Then he made a deep bow and took the little hand of the three-year-old Dauphin of France.

'Madame! Monseigneur! Your humble servant.'

'This is an unexpected pleasure, Monsieur,' Anne said. 'You must forgive me for not receiving you in state, but as you see I spend most of my time in my sons' apartments. You may sit down, Monsieur de Cinq-Mars, and I shall do the same. Louis! Take your little cart and play over there, by the window. Now, Monsieur, I hope you will amuse me with stories of the great world. I live so quietly here.'

'Alas, Madame. The Louvre is a desert without you! We all pine in your absence.'

'But not the King, I trust,' Anne said coldly. To her surprise he laughed; it made his handsome, rather petulant face suddenly boyish and appealing. 'No, Madame, not His Majesty. Nor yet the Cardinal, of course. If the Cardinal were not so close to him, I think the King might come to see how dull it is for you out here. I feel quite sure of it.'

'You think the Cardinal is responsible for my obscurity?' she asked him gently. There was something deeper in this than a social call. She smiled at him, her pale face betraying nothing.

'I know he is,' Cinq-Mars said. 'He directs everything the King does, Madame. He is a tyrant, and the King himself admits this. Ah, when I look at that beautiful child, our Dauphin, my heart bleeds to think of him suffering under the rule of that odious man, with yourself deprived of all rights and power.' He sat back watching her to see what effect he was having.

'I don't understand you,' Anne said. 'I don't understand a word of what you say, Monsieur. I have no power, nor do I want any. How can I be deprived of what I haven't got? How can my son suffer anything while the King lives?'

'But if he dies, Madame! What then? Who will be Regent of France, who will protect the little Dauphin then?'

Anne rose quickly. 'You are not to discuss the King's death with me, Monsieur. That's treason. I forbid it.'

This was not what he'd expected. Gaston d'Orleans had said she was the Cardinal's deadly enemy, that she had twenty-five years of misery and persecution to avenge. She wasn't behaving as he expected, and he lost his head in his efforts to embroil her.

'Madame, listen to me. You must listen! I am in constant touch with the Duc d'Orleans . . .'

'Who is at Blois, under the King's displeasure,' Anne interrupted him. 'You're being very foolish, Monsieur, I can tell you that! Nobody trusts Gaston.'

'I trust him, Madame,' Cinq-Mars insisted. 'And so does the Duc de Bouillion and M. de Thou, and my friend Fontrailles, to name only a few! Do you know what the Cardinal intends if anything happens to the King? To make himself Regent of France! To dispossess Orleans and you of your rights to govern France for the Dauphin. To imprison me, to continue the Protestant alliance against Spain, your country, Madame! That's his plan!'

Anne faced him calmly. Her son played obediently in the corner; he had put his wooden cart down and was watching the scene between his mother and the strange young man in his gorgeous clothes who was raising his voice in that excited way.

'May I ask what *your* plan is?' she said. 'Obviously you have one, Monsieur, and for your own good, I think you should confide it to me.'

'Ah, Madame,' Cinq-Mars exclaimed, 'I knew you would listen to me. Look at your son, and listen well to everything I say. His future is at stake; the King is in bad health again; the Cardinal dominates him and tyrannises over the Court, over you too, Madame – I know how he's persecuted you in the past, how he's made you suffer! Now is your chance to revenge yourself and protect the Dauphin at the same time. You should be co-Regent with Orleans!'

'How do you propose to achieve this?'

'By killing the Cardinal,' Cinq-Mars cried out. 'By assassinating the monster, the tyrant and freeing us all!'

'You seriously mean that the Duc d'Orleans is a party to this? And de Bouillion?' Anne asked him.

'And that's not all,' Cinq-Mars lowered his excited tones. 'The King approves of it, Madame! The King himself longs to be free of the creature. Now what do you say!'

Anne looked at him and slowly shook her head. 'My poor friend,' she said, 'the King couldn't possibly do without Richelieu. He likes to pretend so, and that's all he's doing with you. Pretending. Daydreaming. He'll betray you to the Cardinal at the last moment. For your own sake I implore you to forget the whole plan and never speak of it again. As for myself, I won't listen to another word.'

'Madame,' he said urgently, 'you're thinking in terms of the past. I know others have tried to turn the King against Richelieu, but who have they been? His mother? Orleans? That stupid de Hautfort creature who went on lecturing him like a governess? But not *me*, Madame. I'm the one the King can't do without, believe me. It sounds like vanity but it's the truth. If I abandoned him, Louis would die. And I tell you he's ready to give up the Cardinal, simply because I've persuaded him.'

'You say that the King agrees to Richelieu's murder,' Anne said. He was so young, this man, and so sure of himself. If he were right, and Louis had fallen so low, then Richelieu was in mortal danger. 'You really believe this?'

'I *know* it,' Cinq-Mars retorted. 'Don't think me

very foolish, Madame, just because I'm young. Do you suppose I haven't made a very careful study of the King? Do you think I haven't made it my concern to know every mood of his, every twist and turn of his character? I can read him like a book, and that's why I can dominate him. He loves me, Madame. Forgive the expression, I mean only in the way of a man for his son, or an elder brother, you understand.'

'I understand only too well,' Anne cut him short. 'He loves you. Very well. So he's agreed to let you murder his Minister. Then why come to me?'

'Because he may not live for long,' the Marquis said impatiently. 'And we need you, Madame, to support us. We need Spain. An internal Court intrigue is not enough to guarantee getting rid of Richelieu and undoing his work!'

'Have you approached Spain?' She turned because her son had come to her knee and was pulling at her sleeve.

'I want to sit with you, Maman.'

'Not now, Louis. Go to Madame de Lansac. I will find you in a few minutes. Go now. At once, little one.'

He pouted, scowling at Cinq-Mars who he supposed must be the reason why his mother didn't want him, and then ran out of the room. His shrill cry echoed back to them down the corridor. 'De Lansac! De Lansac – where are you?'

'Yes,' Cinq-Mars said. 'Our emissary is there now. Negotiating a treaty, on our behalf with your brother the King.'

'And the terms?' she said. She had sat down again and now she folded her blue velvet skirts in careful pleats over one knee; it concealed the way her hands were trembling. Spain was still nominally at war with France. Her chief Minister D'Olivarez would agree to anything which promised an advantageous peace and the death of her greatest enemy. This was no idle Court intrigue but a political manœuvre of the first importance. Not even in Anne's wildest acts of treason and rebellion against her husband and against Richelieu, had she dared do more than write and make suggestions.

This boy, all fluffed out in lace and silks, was talking of a Treaty. And a separate Treaty, negotiated with a nation with whom France was still at war.

'Tell me,' she went on, 'what are the terms you offer Spain? I imagine the King doesn't know about this?'

'No, no, of course not,' Cinq-Mars said. 'It's a precaution in the event of his death. Our terms are the death of Richelieu and the establishment of you and Orleans as joint Regent for the Dauphin. And the end of the war.'

'What will you hope to gain from this – for yourself?'

'A continuance of my position, Madame. The King himself wants me to join his Council; the Cardinal wouldn't agree to it. If we get rid of Richelieu, the King will be happy and free to do as he pleases. If we get rid of Richelieu and the King dies, Orleans has promised me a place in the Council of the Regency, and I know you would be grateful, for securing a part Regency for you. That's all I want. To rid myself of an enemy and continue to serve France.'

Anne said nothing for some moments.

Then she turned to him and held out her hand. He knelt and kissed it.

'When I have proof that Spain has come to terms

with you, Monsieur; then you shall have my answer. But unless I see that treaty, signed by my brother the King, I will not join you.

'You shall see it,' Cinq-Mars exclaimed. 'You shall have it in your hands before the end of February, Madame. I swear it.'

'Go now,' Anne said quietly. 'And keep good council. Impress discretion on the Duc d'Orleans. And believe me, he's not to be trusted with too many secrets. His heart is far from bold.'

'But mine is like a lion's,' Cinq-Mars declared. 'Have no doubts, Madame, I shall conduct the whole affair, and bring it to success. Farewell! Your very humble servant!'

She watched him back to the door, make her another flourishing bow and then disappear. The large sunlit room was very still; she moved over to the window and stood for some time looking out over the gardens, their trees and shrubs stripped clean by the fierce winds of the preceding month; in spite of the sunshine, frost glittered like spilled diamond dust upon the paths. By the end of February, he had said. He would show her the treaty in a little more than two months. Now she had to decide what to do, and she was suddenly in an agony of doubt. Richelieu's life was in danger and the King himself was among those planning the assassination. She had mocked Cinq-Mars, basing her doubts on Louis' relationships in the past. But as she thought of it, calmly now, she suddenly knew that he was telling her the truth. There had never been anyone in Louis' life like Henri de Cinq-Mars; his influence was absolute over the King. Even living in seclusion at Saint Germain, Anne had heard stories of the tempestuous scenes, with Louis prostrated after a quarrel, begging Richelieu himself to mediate between him and the capricious favourite. She had heard the story of the Council meeting, and she could imagine Richelieu's contemptuous dismissal of the boudoir beau's political ambitions. He had thwarted Louis and his confidant, but perhaps he had done so just too often. Perhaps Louis was really chafing under the rule he had borne for nearly twenty years, and his infatuation had blinded him into casting the Minister aside at last. But not by dismissing him; that was beyond his capacity. He feared Richelieu too much to face him and say, Go, I have no more need of you. Or even to serve him as they had both served others, seizing him by means of the lettre de cachet and burying him in a fortress. Louis couldn't bring himself to leave the Cardinal alive, dismissals could be ignored, even as a prisoner he might yet escape and wreak a fearful vengeance on his faithless Master. She could imagine the indecision and fear of her husband. Cinq-Mars was right. If Louis intended to be rid of Richelieu then he would prefer to have him murdered. He had done it once before, when he watched the body of his mother's favourite Concini dragged from the Louvre by its heels. He would agree to Richelieu's death.

And if this was true, as she believed it, then nothing could save the Cardinal. She might warn him, but with the King as his chief enemy he had no hope. Unless he could show Louis positive proof of how far this conspiracy had really gone. And the Treaty with Spain would provide that proof, if only she could get it for him.

12

'You must rest, Eminence,' Mazarin said gently. He placed one hand on Richelieu's shoulder and prevented him from trying to sit up. The bedroom in the house at Tarascon, where Richelieu had been taken ill, was in reality a little salon, dark panelled and gloomy, on the ground floor. The Cardinal was too sick and weak to go upstairs, and his side was severely ulcerated so that it caused him agony to be lifted. Therefore the bed had been moved down and the little room transformed into a sick room. Mazarin sat beside him, reading State documents to him, taking letters at his dictation.

Richelieu refused access to anyone but the Italian; he had come to depend upon him and to trust him; he admired his diplomatic skill and he was in pitiful need of a friend. The King had broken free of him at last. This, more than his illness and the pain of his ulcerated side, had caused the great Cardinal to collapse until he was expected to die.

'How can I rest? Everything is being pulled around my ears by that ungrateful cur Cinq-Mars! I made him what he is, Mazarin, and before I know it, he's turned against me. And turned the King against me too. Louis knows I'm ill here, and he hasn't sent me one word! In the last few weeks he hardly speaks to me.'

'He's completely under Cinq-Mars' influence,' Mazarin said. 'You mustn't blame him, Eminence; he's lost all sense of justice.'

'No,' Richelieu corrected him. 'My dear friend, you don't understand the perfidy of human nature. I've made him a King in spite of himself. I've raised France to a great position in the world, and bathed him in her glory; I've defeated his enemies because they were the enemies of the Crown, and only the Crown can keep France strong. There was a time not long ago, when the Kings of France were little better than the hostages of the Huguenots and the nobility. Now the sovereign is supreme. That miserable man is a great monarch now, because of me. And do you know – that's why he hates me?

'He's resented everything, because I was strong and he was weak. At last he feels he can do without me. I shall be murdered, Mazarin; I know that's the plan. They're only waiting now to see if I die here at Tarascon before they act. And the King is first among the plotters. There's nothing I can do.'

'You surprise me,' Mazarin said softly. 'I truly believe you expected gratitude! We Italians have a proverb: God put me at the mercy of my foes rather than my debtors. The King hates you because you've served him well. It is inevitable. Be reconciled, and don't let it tear at your heart. You're not lost, Eminence, because of a weak King and a treacherous boy! Recover your strength and then fight back!'

Richelieu turned his head away.

'I haven't the will any more,' he said. 'All my life I've struggled for power. I've had no friends, save Father Joseph and yourself, and only loved one woman to the damnation of my soul. Now even she has abandoned me. I shall die as I've lived, Mazarin – alone and without a living soul to care for me.

'Who is this woman?' the Italian asked him gently.

'A woman whose name you'll never know,' the Cardinal said wearily. 'I've had word from de Chavigny that she is part of the conspiracy. I think that is what is killing me, my friend.'

Richelieu had heard of Cinq-Mars' visit to Anne at Saint Germain; he had received no word from her, no warning. And he had waited for word, for proof that she would not turn against him at the end. He had never asked for her love, but he had hoped for it, for twenty years. It was Anne's betrayal that had robbed him of the will to get better and to defend himself.

'I tell you, Mazarin,' Richelieu said suddenly, 'if it weren't for my country, I'd welcome death. Life has no more to offer me now.'

*　　*　　*

For the last hour Anne had been shut up in her private salon at St Germain. It was nearly four in the afternoon, and already the light was fading. It would soon be too dark for a messenger to ride any distance. She finished the letter she had been writing, and then sanded it. She sealed it with a plain seal, and folding a thick sheaf of papers, enclosed both in a single packet, sealing and double sealing it. The Spanish Chargé d'Affaires in Paris had presented himself that day among a little group of courtiers, and when he asked for a private audience, Anne knew that Cinq-Mars had kept his promise. It was a great personal risk for her to admit him; the King had forbidden her ever to see or communicate in private with a member of the Spanish Embassy. He had paid a short visit to Saint Germain after Cinq-Mars, and been furious because the little Dauphin burst into tears when he picked him up. He had thrust the child away from him and left the Palace. Three days later Anne received a letter threatening to take both her sons away from her, since she was not bringing them up with a proper respect for him. Anne had no pride where her children were concerned. She wrote him a long and pitiful letter, begging him not to separate her from her sons. He had not replied. If she were accused of receiving the Spaniard against his orders, Louis would punish her by seizing the Dauphin and the little Philip d'Anjou. And now that Richelieu was abandoned and out of favour, there was nothing he could do to intervene. In the weeks following her interview with Cinq-Mars, Anne had stayed quietly in the country, but even her little Court was like a beehive with rumours buzzing back and forth of the great Cardinal Minister's disgrace and fall from favour. The King hardly spoke to him; he went travelling everywhere accompanied by Cinq-Mars and his circle of friends, and the Cardinal was forced to follow, only to be snubbed and ignored by the King and abused by the favourite.

Now he was lying ill at Tarascon, while Louis amused himself at the siege of Perpignan, and the conspirators waited for their enemy to die.

Anne had not written to Richelieu. She had stayed completely neutral as far as anyone could see, but it was generally believed that she was encouraging his enemies as she had done in the past.

At two that afternoon the Chargé d'Affaires was

shown into her apartments, where she retired with him to a window seat, watched by Madame de Lansac. The Dauphin's official governess tried very hard to listen, but all she could catch was the murmur of voices, and when the Queen turned her back, the Spaniard did the same; the Marquise was sure she heard something rustle, like paper, but she could see nothing. The interview lasted only half an hour; the Queen dismissed the Chargé d'Affaires, remarking that she had forbidden him to come again without the King's permission, and then retired into her private salon, saying she was not to be disturbed.

Now she had finished her letter to Richelieu.

'I have known there was a conspiracy against you for some time. I also know that the King is a member of it. But he is not aware of the existence of the enclosed Treaty with Spain, drawn up and signed by Cinq-Mars' emissary on his behalf. I believe that this is treason, and therefore I send it to you to use as you think best. You know your chief enemy; beware also of M. de Thou and the Duc de Bouillion. This comes from the hand of one who cares for your welfare above all things.' She had signed only her initial, 'A'.

The letter was enclosed with the copy of the Spanish Treaty which the Chargé d'Affaires had just handed over to her. Anne rang the handbell on her writing table. A page opened the door and bowed low.

'Your Majesty commands?'

'Bring me a courier at once. Conduct him here.'

When the man stood before her Anne held out the package. His name was Délon, and he had been in her service for ten years.

'Take this package to Tarascon and deliver it to

Cardinal Richelieu personally. To no one else, only to the Cardinal, you understand?'

'Yes, your Majesty. Only to the Cardinal.'

'Here are twenty pistoles for you. Take the best horse in the stables and get to Tarascon as quickly as you can!'

*   *   *

The King of France knelt before a crucifix hanging in the alcove beside his bed. In the background, the Cardinal Richelieu's emissary, M. de Chavigny, waited in silence with his head bent as if he too were praying. He heard the sound of sobbing and glanced up long enough to see the kneeling King convulsed by violent weeping. The letter Richelieu had written to him lay on top of the copy of the Spanish Treaty on the King's night table. Louis had read and re-read that long document, sometimes mouthing parts of the text aloud. Sedan, the great independent stronghold held by the Duc de Bouillion, should be garrisoned by Spanish troops. 12,000 foot and 5,000 Spanish horse placed at the disposal of M. de Cinq-Mars and the Duc de Bouillion. Sedan to be a place of refuge for the Queen and the Dauphin, should the need arise. The Cardinal de Richelieu to be murdered as a preliminary to any of these moves. The Regency of France to devolve on the Duc d'Orleans and Queen Anne at his death.

Chavigny had gone over the Treaty with him, clause by clause, developing the points in Richelieu's letter. The Cardinal was a very sick man, saddened by his disfavour with the King. At the risk of increasing his disgrace, he exposed the treachery of those whom the

King trusted in preference to his old servant. Cinq-Mars had negotiated with the King's enemies, agreed to deliver the great fortress of Sedan into Spanish hands, and presumed in the most heartless way upon the King's early death. The repeated treason of the King's brother Orleans needed no emphasis.

For some time Louis had sat as if he were stunned by a physical blow, his fingers nervously tracing the writing on the papers in front of him; his dark eyes filling with tears. Cinq-Mars had betrayed him. Cinq-Mars whom he had loved and trusted, had flouted his authority by treating with his deadly enemy Spain, behind his back. The boy on whom his lonely heart had lavished love and favour, foresaw his death without a qualm, and made his plans to profit by it.

'I don't believe it,' Louis had said at last. 'I won't believe it!'

'Alas, Sire,' Chavigny spread his hands wide. 'There can't be any doubt. That Treaty is an authentic copy, bearing the Spanish Royal seal. It's signed by M. Fontrailles on behalf of M. le Grand. You have been betrayed by them all. I promise you, it all but broke the Cardinal's heart to send you this. But you're in danger, Sire. You had to know the truth.'

'What danger?' Louis muttered. 'What danger threatens anyone but Richelieu . . .?'

'Your death is mentioned several times,' Chavigny pointed out. 'The Regency is agreed between these traitors and Spain while you are still alive. After the murder of your Minister, who would these scoundrels kill next? Your danger, Sire, has never been greater than at the hands of those you loved and trusted.'

'The Queen is mentioned,' Louis had said suddenly. 'The Queen is one of them!'

'The Queen sent this Treaty to His Eminence,' Chavigny said. 'Without her loyalty to you, it would never have been discovered.'

'I am accursed,' Louis said out loud. 'God pity me, in all the world there's no one I can trust!' And he fell on his knees to weep and pray for strength to face the truth.

When he got up, his face was sallow and blotched, and Chavigny thought in astonishment that the unhappy King had become old in the space of that interview.

'Where is Richelieu?'

'At Tarascon, Sire, where he's been lying ill for some weeks.'

'I need him. Or Mazarin. I need someone to help me protect myself. You know Cinq-Mars is with me now? What can I do, Chavigny – what can I say to him?'

'Say nothing, Sire. Just send for the Captain of your Guard and order his arrest. And have the Duc de Bouillion taken, and the others named in the Cardinal's letter. You dare not delay.'

'I can't do it,' Louis mumbled. 'I love him. I can't have him arrested . . .'

'He betrayed you,' Chavigny said. 'He took all you had to give – your affection, your royal favour, wealth, honours, all! And he treated with Spain and made plans on behalf of your brother. Do you know where he is, at this moment? At this very moment while you shed tears and are tempted to be merciful?'

'No,' Louis said, shaking his head. 'No, I don't know where he is, except asleep in bed.'

'In bed, Sire, but not asleep. He has a mistress

in the town, a gunsmith's daughter. He's with her now.'

Chavigny saw the King flush a dull red.

'Send for Charost,' he said. 'And call the Guard. They're to go to this whore's lodging and arrest Cinq-Mars.'

At dawn on the following day a courier left for Tarascon bearing the hurriedly written report of Chavigny to Cardinal Richelieu. It was all over, the letter said. Cinq-Mars had been arrested and the orders were out for de Thou and de Bouillion. The King asked that his Minister should return to him as soon as possible, or else send Cardinal Mazarin. The conspiracy was over. The Cardinal had triumphed.

In his gloomy bedroom, Richelieu lay propped up on pillows, Mazarin at his side. He sipped wine from a silver cup and there was a faint colour in his face.

'I told you,' the Italian said, 'that you would win.'

'I won, yes. And I am happy, Mazarin. This is my last victory, and my most important.' He turned and smiled, and some of the pale fire gleamed in his hooded eyes.

'I am still in power, and I am not abandoned as I thought.'

'Whoever sent that Treaty saved you,' Mazarin said.

'Yes,' Richelieu said. 'That is the most important thing about my triumph. I shall not die unloved; I feared that more than anything. Go to the King for me; he trusts you, you know how to soothe him. I shall get better now, my friend. For a little while; just long enough and strong enough to see

Cinq-Mars and his friends go to the scaffold, and to make sure that those I love are left secure. I shall sleep, Mazarin. I'm very tired.'

* * *

The Marquis de Cinq-Mars and M. de Thou were tried in August of that year, and sentence of death was pronounced upon them. Fontrailles escaped from France disguised as a Capuchin friar, and took refuge in Brussels. The Duc de Bouillion was captured, but pardoned on condition that his Duchess surrendered the great fortress of Sedan to the King. Her threat to deliver it to the Spaniards or the Dutch had influenced the Cardinal and the King to mercy, where none was shown to Cinq-Mars. Gaston was banished from Court and disinherited from the line of succession. He had betrayed the conspirators as eagerly as he had encouraged them. Louis was very ill that summer; he could eat very little and hardly slept at all. He was prostrate with fits of depression which were so intense that he sat for hours without speaking or moving, and as the time for his favourite's execution drew near, his health declined even more rapidly. Another cause of grief to him, albeit overshadowed by the frightful doom of that other loss, was the death of his mother Marie de Medici.

She had come to rest at last in Cologne, where her much depleted household bickered and idled the days away, and the Queen Mother grew enormous with dropsy and ran into debts which she could not pay.

She sank so low that she wrote to Richelieu, whose head she had publicly promised to cut off if she returned to power, begging him to intercede with her son and let her end her life in France.

His answer had been a courteous but firm refusal, and Marie's outbursts of temper gradually declined into a state of irritable depression aggravated by the misery of her disease. On 3 July 1642 she lay in bed in the small house in Cologne, surrounded by those of her ladies and gentlemen who had remained faithful, in a room bare of furniture because it had been chopped up and used for firewood during the freezing winter. The Queen Mother of France was too poor to buy fuel in the last nine months of her life. Only the Church remembered her, and gave her the dignity in her dying which had been denied her in her years of exile. The Papal Nuncio and the Archbishop of Cologne attended her and gave her the Last Sacraments. The Nuncio bent over her. 'Madame, do you forgive your enemies, as you yourself hope to be forgiven?'

Marie nodded her head, and whispered, 'I forgive them all. May God be likewise merciful to me.'

Forgiveness was not easy for her, even at that solemn moment; but with an effort she was able to bequeath her diamond betrothal ring to her daughter-in-law Anne, whose children she had never acknowledged. She was sure they were bastards, and said as much, but now it didn't matter. It didn't matter that her darling Gaston would never be King of France because he too had abandoned her, more shamefully than anyone, and he was another she had to forgive.

'And the Cardinal Richelieu,' the Nuncio said gently. 'Can you forgive him, Madame, for all your grief?' The sunken eyes blazed up at him, and the swollen hands clenched on the sheets.

'As you hope to be forgiven,' the priest prompted. 'Try, Madame. For your soul's sake.' There was a sigh and the old Queen's head turned away from him. 'I forgive him too. And my son Louis.'

An hour later she died.

*   *   *

By the middle of October Richelieu had made the journey back to his house at Reuil. It was a triumphant progress, beginning at Lyons, where Cinq-Mars and de Thou were publicly executed during the Cardinal's residence in the town, and since the Minister was suffering from multiple ulcers on the body, most of the journey was made by river, as he couldn't endure the jolting of a carriage or even a horse-drawn litter. Where the procession had to cross land, Richelieu was carried in a magnificent litter on the shoulders of twelve men. When he stopped at a house to rest, the walls were pulled down to give entrance to his bed; there were deputations of the municipal authorities awaiting him at every town. Cannons were fired in salute and bells were pealed. The Royal armies had been victorious at Perpignan, and for the first time in centuries, the family of de Bouillion ceased to be sovereign princes over the great fortress of Sedan. The Duchess had handed it over to Cardinal Mazarin and a Royal garrison, in return for a free pardon for the Duke. Victory and stability of government were the Cardinal Minister's last achievements for his country, and as he made his painful progress back to Reuil, it was the journey of a King coming home to die.

And at Reuil Anne came to visit him with the Dauphin. His niece Madame d'Aiguillon, whom Anne had never liked, brought the Queen and the little Prince to the ground floor salon where the Cardinal lay night and day on a couch, receiving visitors and conducting the business of the government. Officials, Ambassadors, petitioners of every kind, crowded to the dying Cardinal at Reuil, as if it was impossible that such a man could die, or surrender his power.

At the door the Queen turned to Madame d'Aiguillon. Whether she liked his niece or not, there was no doubt about her feelings for her uncle. Even as she looked at Richelieu, her eyes filled with tears.

'You may leave us, Madame,' Anne said. 'And return in fifteen minutes. I don't want to tire His Eminence.'

Then taking her son by the hand, she walked towards him. It was many months since they had met, and Anne was unprepared for the change in him. He lay on his couch covered by a magnificent sable rug, propped up on pillows, his hair snow white under the little scarlet cap. He was an old man, wasted by sickness and marked by weeks of excruciating pain. Only the eyes were as she remembered them; they blazed with life in the pale face, and as she came close to him he smiled. He held out his hand to her; the big Episcopal amethyst slipped round his finger, and the hand she caught in hers was cold and skeletal.

'Forgive me, Madame,' he said. 'I can't get up to greet you or the Dauphin. I can't move without help.'

Anne's eyes had filled with tears.

'I knew you were ill,' she whispered, 'but I had no idea how you'd suffered. Don't move, I know it hurts you.'

He inched his body upward, wincing as he did so. 'I can't see you properly, or the Dauphin, ah, that's

297

better. He's very beautiful – see how he meets my eye!
Like a true Prince. Sit down beside me, Madame. I
have so much to say to you and very little time.'

Anne sat in the chair near his couch, and told her
son to fetch a stool for himself. The little boy did so;
he was rather over-awed by the strange old man who
kept staring at him and smiling. He crouched at his
mother's feet and listened, watching them both.

'How is the little Philip?'

'Very well,' Anne answered. She brushed away
the tears which she was helpless to keep back, and
even tried to smile to please the dying man. 'Quite
different to Louis; much naughtier.'

'Ah,' Richelieu murmured. 'He'll make a good Duc
d'Orleans then, when his time comes. But this boy will
be a great King; it's in his eyes. How much does he
understand?'

'More than one thinks,' his mother said quietly.
'My son, go and look out of the window – see if
you can see His Eminence's great moving bed you
heard about. He knows everything. The King detests
him for it.'

'The King is a lonely man,' Richelieu said. 'He has
never recovered from losing Cinq-Mars.'

'It's broken his heart,' Anne said. 'I've only seen
him twice since the execution and I hardly recognised
him. Did Cinq-Mars have to die, Richelieu?'

'Yes,' the Cardinal said. 'I couldn't leave you and
the Dauphin in the hands of such a man. I had hoped
to outlive the King, but this won't be.'

'You mustn't say that,' she protested. 'You'll get
well, Richelieu. There's nothing to trouble you now.
What would we do without you?'

'What would I have done without you?' he asked

her. 'I was lost, Madame. For the first time in my life I was truly helpless; struck down by illness, abandoned by everybody. For a time I believed you too had forgotten me. Now I shall go to my grave a happy man because you showed you had a little care for what became of me.'

'I care very much,' Anne said. She had begun to weep openly.

'I know that,' the Cardinal said gently. 'And I'm very grateful. Please don't cry, Madame. I could never bear your tears, you know that. Let me see you smiling, as beautiful as always. So many people come to see me here, none of them matter to me now. They won't believe my end is coming, and I've never admitted it to anyone but you. And Mazarin, whom I trust. I'm dying, Madame, but so is the King. I killed him when I revealed Cinq-Mars' treachery as surely as if I'd fired a pistol at his heart. He won't survive me long, and that's one reason why I won't permit myself to die just yet. I want you and the Dauphin to be safe. I promised to make you Regent, didn't I?'

'It doesn't matter,' Anne said desperately. 'Nothing matters, except losing you.'

'It matters very much,' he said. 'And I've been thinking how to do it, even from the grave. You'll need a friend, Madame. I think I have the man at hand. You like Mazarin, don't you?'

'Yes, yes he's very charming,' Anne said. 'But I've seen little of him, I can't really judge.'

'I've seen a great deal,' the Cardinal corrected her. 'He's young, and he's ambitious, but he has more heart than I had.' He smiled at her, and for a moment touched her hand. 'If you were so potent with me, Madame, you'll win him in a week or two. I want you to put yourself in his hands. He knows what I desire, and he also knows how to manage the King. He'll be First Minister after my death. Ally with him. I've already charged him to look after you and the Dauphin and to safeguard your rights. You can trust him.'

He leant back and closed his eyes; the effort seemed to have exhausted him. Anne saw him wince with pain.

'Let me get your niece,' she begged. 'You're suffering, let me get something for you . . .'

'No,' Richelieu said. 'No, I want nothing. Give me your hand. Mazarin is not a priest, but you are not to fall in love with him. It'll put you at a disadvantage. This isn't just jealousy, Madame; it's good advice. Call the Dauphin to me; I want to look at him once more.'

The little boy came away from the window, and at his mother's command, came to the side of the couch and gazed at Richelieu with his large unblinking black eyes.

'Farewell my Prince. Give me your hand that I may kiss it. So. And yours Madame,' Richelieu said softly. 'You liked my ring, I see.'

'I'll wear it always,' Anne turned away from him trying to hide her tears. The Dauphin watched his mother in astonishment. He had never seen her cry before.

'Don't weep, I beg you,' Richelieu said. 'I shall die happy. My work is nearly finished. France is a worthy kingdom for our Prince to inherit. Remember, I give you Mazarin to care for you. And what you have always had – the love of my heart. Farewell.'

*   *   *

On 14 May 1643, five months after the death of his great Minister Armand de Richelieu, the King of France died in the Louvre, attended by the Court, his wife and the two little Princes. He died in the manner expected of a Christian King forgiving his enemies, including the woman he had married who showed herself very human in his last few hours. He forgave her, but he would have preferred to die without her watching him. But protocol shaped the death of a King as well as the way in which he had lived. At one point he shed tears, but they were for Cinq-Mars, the last love he had ever known, whose treason now seemed such a little thing for which to take that gay, beguiling life.

The King died as a good Christian should, supported by the Church, comforted by his new Minister Cardinal Mazarin, whom he had grown to like since Richelieu's death, surrounded by weeping officials and nobility. It might have deluded a vain man into believing himself popular, but Louis died as he had lived, pessimistic and alone. The same evening, Anne was in her private apartments in the Louvre. She felt drained of all feeling, exhausted physically by hours of sleepless watching in the King's room, and the futility of the dead man's whole life had made her cry for him. Everything was changing. Richelieu had died in December 1642, and in a way that moved even his enemies, he combined courage and humility with steadfast self-control. He had asked forgiveness for all his faults, accepted his agony, and submitted himself to the ultimate judgment of God.

Now the King was dead too, and the little four-year-old boy asleep in his nursery, was the new King of France, Louis XIV. And Anne was Regent. The dream of her youth had come true at last; she was free and she was in power, albeit her husband had tried to limit it as much as possible. She should have been triumphant, exultant, but Anne felt nothing except a sense of loneliness and unreality. She had sent her ladies away and sank back exhausted in her chair, too tired and dispirited to think.

It was little more than two hours since the King's eyes had been closed and his doctors had pronounced him dead. She could still hear the cry echoing through the corridors and ante-chambers of the Louvre. 'The King is dead! Long live His Majesty Louis XIV!'

There was a movement close to her, and Anne started up; she had slept for a few moments. Her page stood beside her, and bowed.

'Your Majesty, Cardinal Mazarin is in the ante-room. He begs your Majesty to see him.'

Mazarin was the new Minister. One Cardinal had died, another had taken his place. But such a different one now wore the scarlet robes of power. 'Trust him,' Richelieu had said, 'He will look after you and the Dauphin.' Her son was a child, and she herself a woman who could always be out-manœuvred by men. She didn't want to see anyone at that moment, but the counsel of the great man who had loved her prevailed. 'Send in the Cardinal,' she said.

He came into the room very quietly, wearing his full ecclesiastical dress, and bowed very low to her. He moved very quietly and gracefully; his enemies said that he crept about like a cat. He already had enemies, because he had power.

'I beg your pardon for disturbing you, Madame. I only came to offer you my sympathy and say if there was any way I could be of service to you – you must be very tired.'

'I am,' Anne said. 'I'm too weary to think, Monsieur Mazarin, even to feel. I appreciate your coming to me, but there's nothing you can do.'

She couldn't accustom herself to calling this good-looking young Italian by the title Eminence. It belonged to the man who had ruled France and who was now talked of even by those who hated him, as the great Cardinal. Mazarin bowed again and smiled. He had soft eyes, very dark brown and expressive; they conveyed his sympathy to the beautiful widow in her mourning dress and flattering veil, and they concealed from her his admiration.

'Take care of the Queen for me.' They were Richelieu's last words to him, and Mazarin had promised. They explained a great deal of the past and they promised much for the future.

'You must console yourself, Madame,' he said gently. 'His Majesty has gone to a Heavenly reward. France has a new King and a new future. You are part of that future.'

'I feel as if there were nothing left for me,' she said. 'I feel too weak to carry the burden for my son. I almost wish my life were over!'

The Italian came to her, and lifted her hand to his lips. Richelieu's beautiful yellow diamond blazed on her finger.

'The *past* is over, Madame,' Mazarin said. 'You are young and the mother of the King. What you feel now is very natural, but believe me, it will pass. I have a feeling that for you, your life is just beginning.'